INDIAN RIVER CO. MAIN LIBRARY

3 2901 0053 9658

Indian River County Main Library
1600 21st Street
Vero Beach, FL 32960

ONCE MORE INTO THE BREECH

SHERIFF BEN STILLMAN SERIES

ONCE MORE INTO THE BREECH

PETER BRANDVOLD

FIVE STAR

A part of Gale, Cengage Learning

GALE
CENGAGE Learning

Farmington Hills, Mich • San Francisco • New York • Waterville, Maine
Meriden, Conn • Mason, Ohio • Chicago

Copyright © 2015 by Peter Brandvold
Five Star™ Publishing, a part of Cengage Learning, Inc.

ALL RIGHTS RESERVED.
This novel is a work of fiction. Names, characters, places, and incidents are either the product of the author's imagination, or, if real, used fictitiously.

No part of this work covered by the copyright herein may be reproduced, transmitted, stored, or used in any form or by any means graphic, electronic, or mechanical, including but not limited to photocopying, recording, scanning, digitizing, taping, Web distribution, information networks, or information storage and retrieval systems, except as permitted under Section 107 or 108 of the 1976 United States Copyright Act, without the prior written permission of the publisher.

The publisher bears no responsibility for the quality of information provided through author or third-party Web sites and does not have any control over, nor assume any responsibility for, information contained in these sites. Providing these sites should not be construed as an endorsement or approval by the publisher of these organizations or of the positions they may take on various issues.

LIBRARY OF CONGRESS CATALOGING-IN-PUBLICATION DATA

Brandvold, Peter.
    Once more into the breech / Peter Brandvold. — First edition.
        pages ; cm. — (Sheriff Ben Stillman series)
    ISBN 978-1-4328-3040-3 (hardcover) — ISBN 1-4328-3040-6
(hardcover)
        1. Sheriffs—Fiction. I. Title.
PS3552.R3236O537 2015
813'.54—dc23   2014047828

First Edition. First Printing: May 2015
Find us on Facebook– https://www.facebook.com/FiveStarCengage
Visit our website– http://www.gale.cengage.com/fivestar/
Contact Five Star™ Publishing at FiveStar@cengage.com

3 2901 00593 9658

Printed in the United States of America
1 2 3 4 5 6 7 19 18 17 16 15

This one's for Joe Higgins,
my long-distance friend and supporter.

CHAPTER 1

"Fellas, don't pee down your legs just yet," said saddle tramp and general no-account, Gandy Miller, "but is that who I think it is out there?"

Miller was sitting at a table in a remote, beaten-down roadhouse in the Missouri River Breaks, within throwing distance of the river, in fact, and he was staring over his poker hand and through one of the two large, open windows in the front wall. Miller's two partners, Albert Queen and Jedediah "Two-Dog" Charles, who'd had his left ear chewed off recently by a Gros Ventre whore from Wolf Point, and who was drinking heavily to dull the throbbing pain, turned to follow Miller's gaze into the dusty yard fronting the roadhouse.

A tall man in a long, black wool coat that owned a coppery tinge over the shoulders had ridden up to the roadhouse on a fine grulla mare. He'd been trailing a blaze-faced dun outfitted with a packsaddle. He'd just swung gracefully down from the grulla's back and was leading the second mount up to a hitchrack.

Copper-colored dust swirled beyond the windows and the door propped open to let in some air. The dust was kicked up by the newly arrived horses and swirled a bit by the cool, late-September breeze. The dust obscured the tall hombre out there with the horses, but then it settled to reveal that he was an older gent, but sturdy, with a craggy but strong-looking, raw-boned face with curly gray sideburns that stood in sharp contrast to the almost Indian-red of his leathery face, which owned several pockmarks over the nubs of his chiseled cheekbones.

Deep, dark lines spoked around the corners of his eyes, which were almond shaped and a lucid frosty blue. A woman would have called the stranger handsome, but probably only a woman who liked her loving a little rough and didn't expect the hombre to snuggle much afterwards.

None of that distinguished the formidable-looking stranger as much as the fact that he was one-armed. It was the left arm he was missing. It had been replaced by a silver hook, which dropped down out of his coat sleeve.

"Well, I'll be damned," said Albert Queen, keeping his voice down. "I think it is."

"Who?" said Two-Dog Charles, canting his head from one side to the other and squinting his drink-bleary eyes. He placed a hand over the bloody bandage attached to what little remained of his left ear. "I don't recollect I seen him before."

"Battles," Miller said, squinting his own eyes but mainly against the stench of Two-Dog's sour breath. "Jacob Henry Battles. I followed his career in the illustrated newspapers. Long time ago. When I was a kid. Regulator. Gun fer hire. Sure as shit—that's who it is, all right. With them snakey-lookin' eyes and that hook. Lost his arm in a shootout with the federal lawmen who finally ran him down and put him away."

"No!" intoned Two-Dog, scoffing. "Battles been pushin' up rocks and cactus fer years!"

Both Miller and Queen shushed him with hard glares, keeping their heads low, as though they were afraid they were about to be shot between the eyes.

"Sure as hell is," insisted Miller. "I've seen his pictures. Went to jail for many years—territorial pen down in Deer Lodge. It was there behind them stone walls and strap-iron bars in which the plaintive wails of so many lost souls echoed throughout the long Montana nights that Jacob Henry Battles acquired the nickname, 'The Devil's Left-Hand Man.' "

Miller turned from the windows and door to see his two partners, both bearded and ugly, one drunker than the other, staring at him with their lower jaws hanging.

"What?" Miller said.

"You followed the stories purty close, didn't you, Gandy?" said Queen.

"Hell," said Two-Dog, "who woulda thought he could read?"

"Just cause you can't!" Miller cast his gaze outside again and absently caressed his holstered Colt with his right hand. "No, that's Battles, all right. I'd know him anywhere."

The stranger turned away from his grulla, whose saddle cinch he'd loosed so the horse could blow, and gave Miller a grin and a nod. Gandy ducked as though he'd been shot at, and said, *"Shit—he heard me!"*

The stranger slipped the grulla's bit from its teeth and, sliding his rifle from the saddle scabbard, strode toward the door.

"Here he comes!" exclaimed Two-Dog under his breath, pretending that his poker hand suddenly interested him again.

Red-faced with anxiety, Miller glanced meaningfully at his partners. "You boys thinkin' what I'm thinkin'?"

Boots pounded on the stoop and he jerked his head up and began fanning his cards out in his hand. "Well, lookee there— this hand's better'n the last one. You two fellas might just find your pockets inside out by the time we leave here."

"You're full o' corral dust," said Queen, also feigning interest in his cards, his eyes darting nervously toward the tall, black-clad stranger standing in the doorway. "The day you beat me at cards is the day I'm either a babblin' idiot or dead, or both!"

Miller dared a glance at the stranger, who stood sizing up the shadowy, sun-triped, low-ceilinged room before him. The man's face was expressionless, his eyes like gray-blue stones. Seeing him standing there—Jacob Henry Battles, the *Devil's Left-Hand Man himself!*—Miller felt that weird way a man feels when, on those rare occasions, he finds himself face to face with a primitive beast. A grizzly or a mountain lion, say.

A mythic figure of rarefied significance.

Seeing Battles was like seeing a ghost of the Old West come to life again. Miller felt gooseflesh rise across his shoulders and the short hairs prick along the back of his neck.

Battles obviously quickly saw that Miller, Queen, and Two-Dog Charles were the only customers in the place, and no imminent threat. He looked over at the bar comprised of cottonwood planks propped across three beer kegs, and then took three long, resolute strides to it. His high-heeled boots thumped and his spurs chimed.

Behind the bar stood the fat, middle-aged, half-breed barman in a greasy, blood-stained apron, his dark, beefy arms folded on his chest, a look of eternal boredom on his crude-featured face with drooping mustaches. Battles set his 1866-model, brass-framed Winchester repeating rifle atop the planks so that the barrel was aimed at the half-breed's bulging belly.

Miller wondered if the old regulator had purposely positioned his long gun in that fashion. But he pondered for only a second. Miller doubted that Jacob Henry Battles had done anything without cagey purpose since he was two years old. The old killer likely wanted to keep the barman more or less pinned down with his rifle behind the bar so he could focus the brunt of his attention on the three strangers pretending to play poker at the round table near the door.

Battles said, "You got any bottles with a label on 'em?"

The barman glanced down at the rifle barrel aimed at his belly from about a foot away. He shook his head slowly.

"Just barb wire, huh?" said Battles, doffing his flat-brimmed black hat with his hook and running his hand over the mostly bald crown of his head. "Well, after a long ride through the back of nowhere, I reckon barb wire will have to serve. Pour it up but strain off any gunpowder, will you?"

He chuckled to himself and then glanced over toward Miller, Queen, and Two-Dog, as though he were letting them in on the joke.

When the barman had filled a shot glass and slid it toward Battles, the old killer glanced down at the whiskey distastefully and then raised it to more closely inspect the light-amber liquid. Miller and his partners had not resumed their game. They were holding their cards in their hands as though they'd resumed it, but they hadn't. They were each too fascinated by the old gunman, an exotic relic of the Old West, to be able to concentrate on anything but Battles himself.

Miller was sweating. His heart was thudding heavily. He could sense that the same bodily sensations were being visited upon his two pards sitting ramrod straight in their chairs around him. Vaguely, he noticed that Two-Dog's alcohol stench was growing heavier, smellier, as the old busthead pushed out through his pores with his sweat.

As Battles inspected the whiskey, he said with an almost offhand air to the barman: "Little town called Clantick around here somewhere? I'm told it's on the Hi-Line. Nice little town."

"Clantick?" said the barman dully. "Yeah. The Hi-Line. Northwest about fifty miles. Other side o' the Two-Bears."

"You don't say." Battles threw back half of his shot. He swallowed and smacked his lips, closed his eyes, opened them. "You know—that's not too bad." His voice was a little raspy. "Make that yourself?"

Gandy Miller sat transfixed. He was pressing his right hand down hard against his holster. Sweat was oozing out of his palm and soaking into the leather, which he'd tooled himself during a long winter in a line shack around White Sulphur Springs. He

11

could feel the cold, hard curve of the Colt's hammer against the webbing between his thumb and index finger. He pressed his hand down harder, enjoying the pain of the hammer digging into his skin.

Sliding his little finger up from the side of the holster, Miller used it to free the keeper thong from over the hammer.

The barman lifted his mouth corners slightly at the old gunslinger's compliment as he stood with his bulging belly in front of Battles's repeater. Miller didn't know if the barman knew who was standing across the bar from him. Likely not. He doubted the half-breed could read the label on a whiskey bottle if he'd ever seen such a thing. And he probably wasn't old enough to have heard the stories of Jacob Henry Battles when they were fresh.

Still, as mushy headed as the barman was, Miller could tell that the half-breed could sense that he was in the presence of someone you didn't see every day. Maybe not greatness, exactly, but something far and away above the run-of-the-mill.

A legend in human form.

Battles was studying his whiskey again as he said in a slow, offhand way, as though he were just chewing up the time while flies buzzed over the blood-stained, whiskey-splashed counter before him, "I heard an old friend of mine lives up that way. Stillman." He looked at the bartender. "Ben Stillman. Heard he's livin' out his over-the-hill years with the star of a county sheriff on his shirt."

Battles looked at his whiskey again. "That right?"

He threw back the coffin varnish, closed his eyes and shook his head as he swallowed, and set the shot glass back down on the bar planks with the air of a man who'd just accomplished something of significance.

"Stillman? Yeah," was all the barman had to say to that. It was hard to know what he was thinking. He let his mud-brown eyes flick to the rifle on the counter in front of him, and then he quickly lifted his gaze to the old regulator again.

The marbles in Gandy Miller's head rolled to and fro.

Stillman.

Another one like Battles only on the right side of the law. But every bit the legend that Battles was. Stillman had been written up in the newspapers, too, a long time ago. His career as a deputy U.S. marshal had ended abruptly when a drunk whore had shot him in the back by mistake.

Miller had last read that Stillman had retired, faded away. What the hell was he doing up on the Hi-Line, in a little backwater like Clantick, for crying out loud? Wearing a sheriff's star . . .

"I heard Clantick was a nice place," Battles said, waving a hand for the barman to set him up again. "Peaceable little kingdom. That true?"

"I don't know," the barman said, splashing more of the light-amber liquid from the cloudy, unmarked bottle into Battles's glass. "Never been there. I hear it's hot up there in the summer, cold in the winter." He whistled softly. "She's up near Canada. On the Milk."

The Milk River, Miller thought. Yeah, he'd heard of Clantick. County seat though it probably wasn't much bigger than your average shotgun ranch. Just a water stop for the Great Northern Railroad still being laid along the Hi-Line and which would someday connect Chicago with Seattle. Or so it was said. Miller had never drifted through Clantick, but he'd heard that, county seat or not, it was nothing more than a jerkwater.

"Quiet up there, though, I bet," Battles said.

The barman didn't say anything to that.

Miller's heart was hammering like a locomotive fully stoked for a long uphill climb. As Battles nursed his drink, Miller glanced to Two-Dog on his left, who sat sideways to the bar.

13

Two-Dog slid his nervous, cagey eyes to Miller. His eyes were so intense that his brief stare nearly knocked Miller to the floor.

Miller tightened his grip on his holster and glanced at Queen, who sat with his back to the front of the room. Queen was staring at Battles. Miller couldn't see Queen straight-on, and Queen didn't turn to him, but Miller could tell that he was staring at Battles while shrewd, murderous thoughts—thoughts of killing a man with a high reputation—were storming through his mind like a Canadian clipper howling down over the Breaks in early December.

Queen's shoulders were so taut that Miller didn't think that anyone could have deterred his reputation-seeking partner if they'd run a wagon at him.

Miller was clenching his jaws. Sweat dribbled down his cheeks and into the little fringe of mustache he'd been trying to grow for some time. The tension was drawn so taut inside him that he thought he was going to scream if he or Queen or Two-Dog didn't make a move in the next few seconds.

He kept his eyes on Battles, standing facing the bar, leaning forward on his hook, holding the glass up close to his face though he didn't seem to be inspecting it anymore. He was staring at the barman. The half-breed stared back at him. The half-breed's brown face was bathed in fresh sweat that glistened in the sunlight angling through a window and open door outside of which Battles's two hay burners were drawing water from a stock trough.

Miller was thinking, *Oh god, oh god, oh god—we're gonna kill Jacob Henry Battles, the Devil's Left-Hand Man!*

As Miller started to do so himself, Two-Dog slid back his chair and stood and yelled in a surprisingly clear voice for all the skull pop he'd consumed, "Jacob Henry Battles, my name is Jedediah Andrew Charles, and this is your last day to live and breathe, sir, for I am sending you to *hell!*"

CHAPTER 2

Gandy Miller had just climbed to his feet and had gotten his Colt halfway out of its holster when he realized that, only about two seconds after it had started, it was over.

"It" being him and his two partners' intended bushwhack of Jacob Henry Battles, the Devil's Left-Hand Man.

Miller froze and looked down at his gun still only halfway out of its holster. He turned to his left to see Two-Dog Charles doing some kind of weird dance step toward the rear of the dingy, little roadhouse. Charles was screaming and firing both of his pistols into the floor.

Bam! Bam! Bam-Bam!

Meanwhile, to Gandy's right, Queen stood about three steps back from where he'd been standing only a second ago, when he, too, had leaped to his feet, drawing his guns. Queen took another, shorter, stumbling step backward, sort of rocking back on his spurs. He was looking down at the two ragged holes in the brown wool vest he wore over a pinstriped shirt.

He was holding only one of his Remington revolvers. The other was on the floor ahead and to his right. With his right hand, Queen was brushing at the hole on the right side of his vest, up near his shoulder, and as he did so, dark-red blood began to well up through the hole and run down his vest toward his gold watch chain.

At nearly the same time, the hole over the left side of Queen's vest began spurting blood several feet out in front of him. The arcing geysers hit the crude wooden floor with wet thuds. Queen dropped his other pistol and said in a voice dull with incomprehension, "The old bastard killed me."

The Remy clanked to the floor. Queen looked ahead of him, to where Jacob Henry Battles stood facing him with the butt of his smoking Yellowboy Winchester rifle pressed against his right hip.

Then Queen's eyes rolled back into his head. He dropped straight down to his knees and pitched forward so that his chin smashed against the seat of the chair in front of him with a loud bark. He rolled over and twisted around as he fell to the blood-splattered floorboards, neck bent, shivering as though deeply chilled.

Moving only his head, Miller shifted his gaze from Queen to Jacob Henry Battles. Battles was looking at him, Miller, through his own wafting powder smoke. Battles's lips beneath his thin gray mustache were quirking a grin, his eyes bright with what could only be the delight of the kill.

"No!" Miller screamed, thrusting his hands high in the air. "Please don't kill me!" He closed his eyes and turned his head to one side, unable to control the terror that came rushing out of him. "Please don't kill me! Please don't kill me, Mr. Battles! My gun's still in my holster. Oh, Christ!"

Miller stood trembling, hands reaching for the ceiling, wincing against the imminent crack of Battles's rifle and the crash of a bullet through Miller's brisket, blowing his shredded heart out a gaping hole in his back. He saw now that it was true about how a man facing death sees his whole life running like a galloping mustang before him. Miller saw it all now in a blur of streaming colors—every significant event from his first memory up to now, him standing here in some nameless roadhouse in the Missouri Breaks of Montana Territory, awaiting a bullet to be fired from the Yellowboy '66 Winchester of none other than

Jacob Henry Battles, the Devil's Left-Hand Man, himself.

Miller had never realized how afraid of dying he was, and he vaguely, fleetingly, reflected that it was a strange way for a young man to feel—especially one who, while he'd never been in a gunfight before and had so far in his twenty-three years only worked as a cowboy—and not a very good one, at that—had sort of aspired to the career of a gunslinger.

He heard a soft drumming sound. He opened his eyes and looked down to see urine dribbling down from inside the cuff of his right denim-clad leg to spatter off the top of his boot. The droplets shone in the light from the window as they ran down the side of his boot and traced the outline of its sole on the wooden floor.

Miller clenched himself. As the dribbling stopped, he looked at Battles staring at him from over the barrel of his Winchester, which he was still aiming straight out from his right hip. He held the gun with only his right hand. The hook hung straight down his left side. The half-breed barman stood to Battles's left, behind the bar, also raising his hands high above his head, his own wide eyes sharp with fear.

Flies were already buzzing around the two dead men on either side of Miller. The air was rife with the rotten egg odor of powder smoke as well as the coppery tinge of freshly spilled blood.

Battles no longer seemed to be smiling. He glanced down at the puddle on the floor around Miller's boot, and said, "Toss that hogleg out the door."

His voice was a low, resonate rumble.

Miller's heart lifted with the weightlessness of an angel's wing. He wasn't going to die! Eagerly, he lowered his right hand to the Colt thonged on his right thigh.

"Slow!" intoned Battles.

Miller winced and froze.

Moving very slowly, and using only his thumb and index finger—he didn't want to give the old regulator the slightest impression that he was placing his hand anywhere near the Colt's hammer or trigger—he slid the piece from the holster. He could hear the soft, slow snick of steel against leather. When the Colt's barrel cleared the leather, Miller flung it out a window and heard it plop in the dust several yards beyond the stoop. It startled the horses, which whickered and pulled at their reins.

Battles glanced at the barman. "Are you in Stillman's jurisdiction?"

The barman swallowed, let his arms begin to sag. "Yeah. Least, I think so. He rides through here, time to time."

Battles looked at Miller. "Kid, throw the carcasses of your friends there over their horses. Tie 'em good and tight to their saddles. You pick up any of their guns or your own out there in the dirt, you'll be joinin' 'em. Understand?"

Gandy, holding both hands shoulder-high, palms out, was almost grinning with relief. He was sure he'd grow ashamed in time of having pissed down his leg, but at the moment he was so happy to be alive that shame was the furthest thing from his mind.

He'd seen Jacob Henry Battles in full glory and lived to tell about it!

"Yessir, I sure do. You don't have to worry. I won't be goin' anywhere near them guns . . . uh . . . Mr. Battles."

"See that you don't."

Battles raised his rifle and depressed the cocked hammer with a click. He turned, giving his back to Miller, and set his rifle upon the counter once more. To the barman, he said, "That forty-rod grows on a fella. Set me up again and give me a water back."

As the barman followed the gunman's orders, casting occasional, wary looks at the dead men and the spattered room beyond the bar, Gandy looked down at Queen, who lay on his back, legs crossed at the ankles. Blood soaked his dead partner's shirt and vest.

Wrinkling his nose distastefully, Miller shoved the table and a chair out of the way as he moved up to Queen's head. He tried not to look at the dead man's eyes staring up at him glassily as he crouched down, slid his hands under Queen's arms, and began dragging the body out the door. Grunting and wincing with the effort, uncomfortable in his wet pants, he dragged Queen down off the stoop and laid him out by his horse, a brindle bay, who looked down at its dead rider skeptically, twitching its ears this way and that.

"Now, don't get fidgety on me," Miller told the horse as he hoisted Queen up onto his feet and leaned him against the side of the bay. Gandy was trying to maneuver his dead partner in such a way that he wouldn't get Queen's blood all over him. He bent down and grabbed Queen around his slack knees and then gave another, loud grunt as he heaved the dead man up and over his saddle.

He didn't get Queen up high enough, however, and when Miller released the body to try a different hold, the body slipped straight down the stirrup fender and piled up in the dirt.

The horse whinnied and sidestepped, not liking the procedure overmuch. Neither the bay nor any of the other horses tied to the two hitch racks fronting the roadhouse, including Battles's mounts, seemed to enjoy the sight of a dead man or the smell of fresh blood. Miller didn't blame them. He didn't like either smell, himself, but he was so damn glad not to have joined his partners in death that he thought he could accomplish the task without throwing up.

He'd known both Queen and Two-Dog only a few months, anyway. Queen, a known poker cheat, had gotten them fired from their last punching job. Two-Dog smelled like a grizzly den even when he wasn't drinking whiskey like water. Miller wouldn't miss either man though he would miss having someone to ride with.

He was a lonely sort.

When he'd finally managed to get Queen up and over his saddle, and had tied the man's ankles to his wrists beneath the bay's belly, so he wouldn't fall off while Battles was trailing him, Miller went in and dragged Two-Dog out. Two-Dog was lighter, so Miller didn't have as much trouble getting his second partner draped over his saddle. But he did end up with quite a bit more blood on him than he'd expected.

He tied the reins of Queen's mount to the tail of Two-Dog's. He tied the reins of Two-Dog's pinto to the tail of Battles's packhorse.

There was a rain barrel along the roadhouse's front wall, left of the stoop and near a low woodpile. Miller produced a rag from his saddlebags, soaked the cloth in the rainwater, and was scrubbing the front of his shirt and his vest, when Battles came out onto the stoop. The old regulator looked his horses over, and then he turned to Miller.

"You got them tied down tight?" he asked, indicating the two dead men lying belly down across their saddles. He pulled a long, black cheroot from the pocket of his coppery black coat, and stuck it in his mouth.

"Yes, sir, I do."

Battles scratched a match to life on the rail of the stoop, touching the flame to his cigar. When he'd gotten the cheroot drawing to his liking, he tossed the match into the dust, and thumped down the three porch steps. He tightened their latigo straps, slid his rifle into its scabbard, and stepped into the saddle.

Miller watched as he turned the grulla away from the hitchrack while holding the dun packhorse's lead rope in his right hand. Battles kept his cautious gaze on the young cowpuncher. He hadn't gotten to be as old as he was, fifty or older, by taking his eyes off of men who'd intended to bushwhack him. But there was humor in his eyes, too. Miller didn't feel insulted. He was too busy basking in the presence of Jacob Henry Battles.

"You headin' to Clantick?" Miller asked him.

Battles stopped the grulla, frowned at the kid skeptically.

Miller hesitated. He knew he was treading in dangerous water, but he couldn't help himself. "You goin' up there to . . . uh . . . see Stillman?"

Battles continued to study him from beneath furrowed brown eyebrows in which small, wiry gray hairs twisted.

"You're gonna kill him, ain't ya?" Miller blurted out the question.

"Boy," Battles said with menace, "don't make me wish I was hauling you belly down over your horse, too."

With that he turned, trotted his horses and the other two horses out to the two-track wagon trail paralleling the river. He turned right onto the trail and galloped off to the west.

Behind him, Miller whistled and shook his head. He heard footsteps behind him and turned to see the half-breed barman standing in the shack's open doorway.

"Be fun to see, wouldn't it?" Miller asked.

"What would be fun to see?"

Miller stared at the dust plume that was all he could see of Battles now. "Them two old wildcats goin' at it—head to head." He spat to one side, shook his head again, almost dizzy with the prospect of witnessing such a showdown. "Yessir, that'd be a thing to see and tell your grandkids about, sure enough."

CHAPTER 3

"What do you say we step in here and belly up to the bar, Junior?" Ben Stillman, sheriff of Hill County, asked his one-year-old son.

Benjamin William Stillman, gussied up in a gold-buttoned coat, white shirt with ruffled sleeve cuffs, wool knee breeches, and buckled shoes, flopped around in the crook of his father's left arm. His little black shoes dangled along the side of Stillman's brown leather vest to which the sheriff's star was pinned and a silver watch chain drooped.

On the boy's brown-haired head resided a pancaked watch cap the same color as the coat. Around his neck was a wide, black bow tie.

The middle-aged father, still beaming with the flush of first-time fatherhood, pushed through the batwings of the Drovers Saloon on First Street in Clantick, Montana Territory, only a few doors down from Stillman's office and jailhouse. He and the boy headed for the elaborate bar and backbar running along the room's right side.

Stillman's rangy deputy, Leon McMannigle, stood at the bar with a beer and a ham and cheese sandwich from the free lunch platter on a plate in front of him. A former buffalo soldier and Army scout, the easygoing, good-natured McMannigle lived at Mrs. Lee's Place, formerly named simply Rooms-By-the-Hour, one of Clantick's three parlor houses over on French Street. He enjoyed the ministrations of the soiled doves, all of whom

22

adored him, in return for him watching over the girls and ridding the place of troublesome customers as soon as they became trouble.

Stillman stepped up to the bar and flipped a nickel to the beefy, sandy-haired barman, Elmer Burk, who'd been arranging clean shot glasses into a pyramid beside a jar of pickled pigs' feet. "Elmer, we'll have a beer. Just one. If we ask for another, you're to summon my wife."

McMannigle reached over to gently caress little Benjamin Stillman's smooth, plump cheek with the side of his index finger. "I'll be hanged if that boy don't look more like his mother every day, Ben."

"You think so?" said Stillman, scrutinizing the boy, who was trying to grab the brim of Stillman's broad-brimmed, cream-colored Stetson, the crown of which was encircled by a snakeskin band. "Here I been thinkin' he favors me . . ."

"Got Fay's big, brown eyes," McMannigle said, leaning in closer to gurgle back at the boy, who giggled his delight while trying now to touch the black man's billowy, red and white polka-dotted neckerchief. "And his nose is straight. Ain't crooked like yours."

"Mine didn't *come* crooked," Stillman said, miffed. "It was *punched* crooked, several times."

"Has Fay's high forehead, too, and look at that thick hair. I'll wager it'll turn dark brown, just like hers, in a couple of years."

"My hair's dark brown," Stillman said. "Leastways, it was before working with you started streaking it gray."

McMannigle, ignoring his boss, continued beaming at the toddler. "Yessir, that boy's gonna grow up to be one dark-haired, brown-eyed handsome lad. One of them aristocratic-lookin' gentlemen of the Beaumont clan." Fay's father, Alexander Beaumont, had been a wealthy French rancher from down along the Powder River near Milestown. "Ben, in a few years you're gonna have to fight the girls away with a stout oak branch!"

"Galldangit, Leon—I had to fight 'em away, too, when I was younger," Stillman grumbled, though he wasn't actually annoyed in the least. Ben Stillman loved his exotically beautiful French wife more than anything, and it was just fine with him that their child favored Fay, though any objective observer would have attested that the child resembled them both.

The sheriff adjusted his hold on the boy, who was looking wide-eyed around the impressive-looking drinking hall with its stout timber ceiling support posts, beams, gas chandeliers, and two dozen or so tables. An oil painting of a naked woman lounging on a green velvet fainting couch hung over the backbar mirror. There was a gambling area through a door beneath the stairs, with a half-dozen baize-covered tables and a roulette wheel. Game trophies stared down from the walls of the main drinking hall, and Little Ben probably thought they were staring at him.

The place smelled of tobacco smoke, sweat, and liquor.

Burk set Stillman's beer on the bar.

"Much obliged, Elmer. Now, I reckon we'll investigate what my deputy left of your lunch platter, if anything." Stillman left the beer where Burk had set it, and moved down the bar, the boy pointing at and scrutinizing his own image in the backbar's polished mirror.

Or was he admiring the naked woman?

"Lunch is still free with a beer," Burk said, returning to his half-built pyramid. "Though your deputy's appetite is puttin' a mighty big dent on my overhead."

Before McMannigle could respond to the customary cajoling, Burk turned to Stillman. "You want me to fix up the little man there with a sarsaparilla or somethin'?"

"Fay don't let him drink sarsaparilla," Stillman said, plopping some slabs of ham onto a thick slice of coarse, dark-brown bread. "She says he don't put down well for his afternoon nap if he's given sugar."

"Speaking of Fay," McMannigle said, narrowing a skeptical eye at his boss, "she know you're here? I mean . . . with, uh . . . Little Junior there?"

"We Stillman men have always been introduced early to the delights of stellar drinking establishments," Stillman said, adding cheese to the sandwich. "I see no reason to dally. It's a big world, and the way I see it, a boy might as well get started as early as he can appreciating it."

"Yeah, but let me ask again," McMannigle said ironically, brushing a fist across his nose and sharing a conspiratorial look with Burk as Stillman slid a sliver of yellow cheese between his son's red lips, "Fay know you're . . . uh . . . introducin' Little Ben to his first drinkin' establishment?"

Stillman sighed, felt his cheeks warm a little with genuine chagrin. "No, she doesn't." The sheriff winked at his deputy as he headed back to where he'd left his beer on the bar. "And if she finds out I brought him in here, we'll both most likely be taken to the woodshed. So I'd just as soon you kept it under your hat, Deputy."

McMannigle and Burk chuckled.

"Fay's over at Mrs. Osterweiler's house for her weekly sewing circle." Stillman took a long drink of his beer. The boy was trying to grab the glass, as though he wanted an introduction to amber ale, as well. "So the boy's all mine for an hour. Lord knows that's about all the time the woman ever gives me with him."

"Why's that, Ben?" asked Burk.

"I don't know," Stillman said. "I reckon she's afraid I'm gonna corrupt him. Imagine that!"

He chuckled and took another deep swallow from his beer mug.

"Oh, look—it's the sheriff's *bay-beeee!*" came a delighted screech from above.

Stillman licked foam from his mustache and turned to see three soiled doves, half-dressed in skimpy nightclothes, descend the stairs from the second-floor balcony. None was wearing much more than a corset, their gauzy night wraps billowing out around them. They all looked as though they'd just rolled out of bed and weren't quite awake. None was wearing face paint, stockings, or shoes, and their bare feet padded down the stairs and then across the floor as, in a line, they strode past McMannigle to where Stillman held Little Ben in the crook of his arm.

Little Ben stared at the three twittering damsels as though mesmerized.

"Sheriff Stillman, it's about time you brought your son by for an introduction!" cajoled the smallest girl—a buxom, blond little coquette named Nancy.

"We've heard soooo much about him!" squealed another whore—a brunette with a mole just left of her wide, pretty mouth. Stillman thought her name was Kansas Kate or something like that.

The third one, a mulatto from the French Quarter in New Orleans who went by the name Miss Versailles, playfully tugged McMannigle's hat brim down as she passed the black deputy, and then turned to Little Ben and clapped her hands as she bent forward, snapping her lustrous hazel eyes wide and intoning, "Oh, myyyy—now, ain't he just the cutest little thing you every did *see?*"

"Would you mind if we held him, Sheriff?" asked Kansas Kate, extending her hands to little Ben Stillman.

The boy bounced around in his father's arm and held his own arms out to the girl, leaning forward and gurgling loudly, excitedly. McMannigle slapped the bar and laughed. "Looks like little Junior already got *his* mind made up!"

Stillman hesitated.

He glanced at Burk, who hiked a shoulder noncommittally, and then glanced over his shoulder to see if Fay, by any chance, was looking in a window. "Oh, well, I did say we Stillman men like to get an early start on enjoyin' life, and I reckon there ain't much more enjoyable than a jaunty bosom." Trying to keep his eyes off the girl's breasts, which were just barely covered by her frilly cream corset, Stillman let Kansas Kate sweep little chattering Benjamin, Jr., into her arms and clasp him tight to her bosom.

The girl turned with her prized package to the other two girls, and then they were all cooing and exclaiming and practically fighting over him. Little Ben didn't seem to mind the attention. He chattered away incoherently, drooling and pointing a crooked, wet finger at Miss Versailles's substantial cleavage.

With a father's pride, Stillman watched the three girls fawning over the seed of his loins. He reflected with an inward chuckle that while he'd lost his innocence at a relatively young age to a prostitute named Mississippi Delta, just before he'd run off to join the War Between the States on the side of the Union, his son had him beat by quite a few years.

"Why, that little devil," McMannigle said, shaking his head in amazement while he watched the whores hugging and kissing and caressing the happy, bouncing infant. "Look at him—he's a natural!"

Stillman muttered, "I reckon that's something else he got from the French side of the family."

Taking advantage of the girls' ministrations and the boy's preoccupation, he returned to his sandwich. He had come over to the Drovers for his usual lunch, not merely to show his son around, though he had to admit he had become a bit of a show-off since the boy's birth.

The sheriff had taken only a couple of bites when hooves

drummed in the street outside the saloon. He turned to see Crystal Harmon, wife of his late best friend's son, Jody Harmon, turn her sorrel gelding up to the hitch rack just beyond the large, front window to the right of the Drovers's batwing doors. The horse was dusty and sweat-lathered. Crystal had ridden him hard. She was trailing a second horse, a buckskin that Stillman recognized from the Harmon remuda.

Stillman's heart thudded. He glanced at the three doves still cavorting around his son. The mulatto girl was laughing and bouncing the boy in her arms. Stillman looked out the window to where Crystal Harmon was throwing the reins of both her horses over the hitchrack.

Stillman glanced at Leon, who shot him a wide-eyed look of sympathetic anxiety.

Crystal was like a daughter to Stillman. She was also good friends with Fay. They were like sisters, in fact, since Fay was only a few years older than Crystal. The women had such a close bond that they discussed everything new and noteworthy in their lives. Just how noteworthy would it be that Stillman had brought Little Ben into Drovers to be fawned over by three, mostly naked whores?

Would Crystal inform Fay of her rough-hewn husband's indiscretion?

If so, the sheriff might find himself sleeping on one of his jailhouse cots for a few nights.

Stillman's anxiety grew when he heard Crystal's boots thumping on the boardwalk just outside the batwings. It was too late for him to do anything. He'd been caught. Stepping out away from the bar in a futile attempt to block Crystal's view of Little Ben and the whores, Stillman squared his broad shoulders at the batwings.

Crystal pushed through the doors, her tanned cheeks flushed from the long ride, her eyes bright with urgency. She wore a green plaid cotton work shirt, cowhide vest, and denim jeans. Her legs were long and lean, with the strength and power of a practiced rider. A man's Stetson was pulled low on Crystal's forehead, to just above her lucid blue eyes.

Crystal and her husband, Jody, worked a small ranch along White-Trail Creek, about twenty miles south of Clantick. Crystal had a child of her own, and she ran a tight cabin, but she also rode the range with the gritty gusto of any cowboy.

She was a sturdy, pretty, practical girl, and Stillman loved her as much as he loved Jody, the son of his old partner, Milk River Bill. But he wished to hell she wasn't standing before him at just this moment.

"Well, hello there, honey," Stillman said, feeling his cheeks turn as hot as branding irons. "What brings you to town in the middle of the week? Boy, you sure blew that sorrel out!"

Crystal stopped just inside the batwings, doffed her hat, and ran her hand through her long, straight, blond hair. As she did, she swatted her hat against her left thigh, and dust wafted from her faded denims. "Hi, Ben. Yeah, I rode hard. Had to get here fast. There might be trouble out at . . ."

She let her voice trail off as her gaze scuttled over Stillman's right shoulder toward the three whores powwowing around little Benjamin William. She glanced at McMannigle behind Stillman, whom the sheriff couldn't see from his vantage but whom he assumed was probably looking a little tense. As was Elmer Burk, no doubt.

Crystal looked back at Stillman and arched her brows. "Startin' him out a little early, aren't you, Ben?"

Stillman hiked a sheepish shoulder. "Is it ever too early?" He was happy to change the subject though he did not like the anxious light in Crystal's eyes. "Honey, what's wrong?" he asked her.

"It's the doc."

29

"Evans?"

"This mornin', early, Jody was out moving some of our two-year-olds to the government range west of our place, and he saw the doc—at least he *thought* it was the doc—riding with two other men along Three-Witch Creek. They were heading toward the old Stanley place in Three-Witch Valley."

"I didn't realize Evans had left town." Stillman glanced at McMannigle, who shrugged as if to say he hadn't, either. "Hell, he hardly ever rolls out of bed till halfway between sunup and high noon."

"Maybe it wasn't him, but from a distance Jody thought it *looked* like him, and he was on a beefy, old chestnut like the doc's gelding. He had a bag hanging from his saddle horn."

"Like the doc's medical kit," Stillman said, nodding thoughtfully. "Maybe Mrs. Stanley's going to have another baby."

"That'd be kind of hard for her to do, Ben, since she got bit by that rattlesnake two summers ago in her springhouse, and died. Heck, Stanley took his four kids and moved off the ranch. He's tending bar in Big Sandy. His cabin's been sitting abandoned, with weeds growing up through the porch, ever since. I ride through the place every now and then on my way to sell eggs to Matt Parrish at the Circle P."

"That's right—I forgot," Stillman said. "So, why would the doc and them two other fellas be headin' toward the Stanley Ranch, and why are you all worked up about it, Crystal?"

"Because last week when I rode through the Stanley head-quarters, the cabin was no longer abandoned. Four or five men were living there."

"So someone bought the place from Stanley," Stillman said.

"Or took over his lease," added McMannigle.

Crystal shook her head. "I don't think so. The men I saw looked like trail scrubs of the human variety. They're not runnin' any cattle, and they haven't done anything to fix up the place. They're just livin' there. Maybe *holin' up* there for a time. I didn't like the way they looked at me when I rode through, if you get my drift."

She fixed both Stillman and McMannigle with a significant look. "Jody said that when he saw the doc—if it was the doc he saw earlier this morning—he wasn't sure why but the doc didn't look any too happy. And by the way the other two men were riding—one in front of the doc and one behind—he didn't seem to be riding there because he wanted to be."

Crystal wrinkled the skin above the bridge of her nose as she slapped her hat against her other thigh, causing more dust to waft. "Jody an' me—we think the doc's in a tight, Ben."

CHAPTER 4

"Does sound like the doc might've got himself in a bad box," Stillman allowed, thoughtfully raking a thumbnail along his jaw as he and Crystal rode their horses along Beaver Creek, which flowed out of the Two-Bear Mountains humped against the southern horizon ahead of them.

"That wouldn't be like him at all," Crystal said with a sarcastic snort. She was riding her second horse, a buckskin she called Banjo, just off Stillman's right stirrup. She'd stabled her blown-out sorrel in Auld's Livery & Feed Barn in Clantick with the intention of retrieving the sorrel later.

"Nope, sure wouldn't." Stillman's tone was wry. Doc Evans was known for the trouble he often got himself into, though most of it was due to drinking, gambling, or women. Sometimes, all three.

As Stillman and Crystal slowed their horses to rest them after having loped for a quarter mile, the sheriff studied the trail beneath him closely. There were only a few fresh tracks now just after midday and in the middle of the week, when there wasn't much traffic on the trails, but there were a few. The three sets that Stillman figured belonged to Evans's party and that were heading south had been made several hours ago, probably sometime during the night. *Probably the middle of the night.* Whoever had fetched the doc had done so most likely because of an emergency.

There was little doubt in Stillman's mind that Jody Harmon

had been right about having seen Evans earlier that morning. Having left Little Ben with Miss Versailles, Nancy, and Kansas Kate in the Drovers Saloon, and knowing the little tyke was in good hands—he'd been around a long time and he'd never found anyone more trustworthy than a working girl—Stillman had hurried home to saddle his long-legged, deep-bottomed bay, Sweets. He'd ridden the spirited stallion up to the doctor's sprawling, dilapidated house on a bluff overlooking the Milk River on the west end of Clantick. The doc hadn't been home, and neither had been his hammerheaded chestnut, Faustus.

(Evans may have been a drunkard, a hapless gambler, and an overly precocious whoremonger, but on the rare occasion he wasn't indulging his sundry indiscretions, he had his nose buried in classical literature.)

As he and Crystal continued riding, following willow-sheathed Beaver Creek into the verdant mountains, Stillman felt a worry burr raking him under his shirt. For all his weaknesses, Doctor Clyde Evans was a good friend and a colorful, entertaining character. He was one of those folks who enrich your life in ways you don't realize until you're confronted with the possibility of their being removed from it.

Evans had been one of Stillman's strongest allies when Stillman had come to Clantick several years ago to investigate the murder of his old friend, Milk River Bill Harmon. Before, Stillman had been languishing in a Great Falls rooming house, drinking, whoring, and gambling away his life or what he'd thought was left of it after a drunk whore had shot him in the back by mistake in a Virginia City brothel.

Working as a deputy United States marshal out of Great Falls at the time, Stillman had been arresting the jake whom the whore had been "entertaining." Apparently, Stillman's prisoner hadn't compensated the girl for her services, and she'd snapped off a pie-eyed shot at him, hitting Stillman instead.

The wound, which had nearly paralyzed the lawman, had caused him to retire and to begin languishing away in that boardinghouse, plunging into a deep abyss of alcohol-fueled self-pity, awaiting, *encouraging,* his miserable end.

Ironically, the death of Stillman's best friend, a man he'd first come west with after the War Between the States, had saved him. Jody Harmon, having heard his father's stories of Stillman, the legendary lawman and former buffalo hunter and Indian fighter, had ridden down to Great Falls to fetch Ben out of that boardinghouse, urging the retired lawman to investigate his father's murder. Little had either Jody or Stillman himself known that Bill's boy had been leading Stillman out of the darkness and back into the light of a new life.

A new life complete with a new career, marriage to the beautiful French rancher's daughter whom the lawman had long loved, and, most recently, first-time fatherhood . . .

All that despite the tragedy that had befallen Milk River Bill and his devoted son, Jody. It was a tragedy that had befallen Crystal, as well, because it had been Crystal's own crazy-drunk father, Warren Johnson, who'd killed Bill for no better reason than Johnson hadn't wanted Jody, a half-breed whose deceased mother had been a full-blood Cree Indian, to marry his daughter. Jody and Crystal had married anyway, and now they had a good life together with little William Ben—named after Milk River Bill and Stillman himself—on their horse and cattle ranch along White-Tail Creek.

Stillman and Crystal turned down the gulch through which White-Tail Creek twisted along a shaggy two-track trail, but they did not follow it as far as the Harmon Ranch headquarters. Instead, with Crystal taking the lead, they headed through a little spur in the southern ridge and followed a coulee past a spring and up a steeper ridge through pines, box elders, and aspens.

The small portal of a long-abandoned mine shone in the side of the ridge, sheathed in boulders and brush. As Stillman followed Crystal along a trail up the slope, Ben saw a big roan horse standing tied to the brush to the right of the mine, switching its long, cinnamon tail. Glancing over its shoulder at the newcomers, the roan twitched its ears and switched its tail faster. The latigo of the roan's saddle wasn't cinched but hung toward the ground. Stillman recognized the Harmon brand on the roan's right wither.

A lean, darkly tanned young cowboy stepped out from behind a fir tree growing on the slope above the timber-framed mine portal. Jody Harmon waved the Winchester carbine in his gloved right hand. He didn't say anything and neither did Stillman or Crystal as they rode up to the right of the roan. They were near the Three-Witch Valley and their voices might carry on the warm, early-autumn breeze to the old Stanley cabin.

Stillman and Crystal dismounted, quickly uncinched their latigos to give their horses room to breathe, and then Stillman slid his Henry repeating rifle from his saddle scabbard. He fished out his spyglass, which was tucked into a tanned moose hide sheath in his saddlebags, and hung it by its rawhide thong around his neck. He removed his spurs and dropped them into the saddlebags.

Crystal slid her own Winchester from her saddle boot—Stillman had seen her target shooting with Jody, and she could shoot as well as any man Stillman had ever known—and followed Stillman up a well-worn trail climbing the ridge beside the mine portal.

Jody watched them from above. The middle-aged Stillman was breathing hard by the time he'd reached the flat area on which young Harmon was standing, and Jody said, "You oughta stop smoking them hand-rolled cigarettes, Ben."

"You think it's the hand rolling that's bad for my wind?"

Stillman said, lifting his hat to run a hand through his thick, longish, salt-and-pepper hair as he caught his breath. "I reckon I'll have to start buyin' ready-mades, then." He was a large, craggy-faced, raw-boned man, nearly six-feet-three inches tall. A bushy mustache mantled his mouth. It was the same salt-and-pepper as his hair and the shaggy brows over his eyes.

He snugged his hat back down on his head and turned to young Harmon—a well-set-up, handsome lad who had his father's husky, long-legged build, with long arms and thick hands. But Jody also owned his Cree mother's dark, chiseled facial features with a long, broad nose and deep-set, soulful eyes.

At least, Stillman assumed those features came from the boy's mother. Ben hadn't had the privilege of meeting Bill's wife. As Stillman recalled, Bill's light blue eyes had flashed with high-spirited humor. Jody took life more seriously than his father had, and his dark-brown hair was cropped short beneath his tan Stetson to which was sewn a Cree talisman of beaded and dyed porcupine quills—a nod to the spirituality practiced by his mother, whom he'd lost to illness long before Arthur Johnson had killed his father.

"What ya got, son?" Stillman asked.

"Come on," Jody said, and they started climbing again.

This trek up through fragrant pines was longer than the first one but less steep. Soon Stillman, Jody, and Crystal crouched behind boulders on the far side of the ridge. Stillman doffed his hat to peer around the left side of the covering boulders and into the gulch opening below. He couldn't see much from this angle so he got down on his belly and crabbed forward around the rocks until he could see the old Stanley ranch headquarters on the gulch floor about sixty yards up the cut to Stillman's right.

The sun had angled over to the west, and shadows bled out

from the gulch's southwest wall. Still, the ranch yard with the box-like, weathered log cabin and the barn and stable to the rear were mostly bathed by golden sunshine. So was the windmill sitting in the front yard, near the creek, the splintery wooden blades creaking lazily in the slight breeze that also rattled the leaves of the aspens along the creek.

There was no movement around the cabin except for a thin tendril of gray smoke lifting from the brick chimney thrusting up the cabin's left wall. A narrow stoop, propped on stone pylons, fronted the place. Behind, a half-dozen or so horses milled inside the corral, one rolling on its back and causing dust to rise in a heavy cloud around it.

The chestnut was watching the rolling horse as though deeply interested. The beefy chestnut looked very much like Clyde Evans's mount, broken to both saddle and buggy harness.

Stillman removed his spyglass from its sheath and used it to more closely survey the ranch headquarters. Still, no movement. The horse had finished rolling and was now lumbering to its feet. Stillman counted seven horses, including Evans's chestnut, inside the corral. Jody and Crystal were staying back behind the covering boulders to Stillman's left.

The sheriff closed his spyglass and scuttled back behind the rocks and rose to one knee.

"You think the doc's in trouble?"

"I don't know, Ben," Jody said. "But the Stanley place hasn't been occupied till recently. If it sold, someone in town would have told me. And the way them two riders seemed to be hazin' the doc along earlier . . ." Jody shrugged. "I don't know. I think there's a good chance. And one of the fellas occupyin' the cabin is hurt pretty bad."

"What make you think so?" Crystal beat Stillman to the question.

" 'Cause just after I sent Crystal to fetch you from town, and

I got back up here, someone was screamin' and cursin'. And for a long damn time, too." Jody gave his head a wag. "Turned my backbone to jelly, hearin' that."

"Most of the doc's patients scream," Crystal quipped. "His bedside manner is lacking."

"Just the same," Stillman said, pulling his Colt Army .44 from the plain California holster angled for the cross-draw on his left hip, "I'm gonna go down and check it out."

"You're gonna need a hand, Ben," Jody said. "I'll go with you. Crystal, you stay here."

Crystal tugged Jody's hat brim down over his eyes. "Don't boss me, Mr. Jelly Backbone. Maybe I'd better go, Ben. I'm a better shot than my husband on his best day."

"Crystal, damnit!"

"Both of you are staying here," Stillman growled, not amused by the younger folks' customary, generally good-natured ribbing. He flicked open his Colt's loading gate and filled the chamber he usually kept empty beneath the hammer with a fresh cartridge from his shell belt. "And neither one of you go down there, no matter what you hear. Understood?"

Stillman spun the Colt's cylinder, dropped the revolver back into its holster, and, fastening the keeper thong over the hammer, gave each of the young Harmons a level, commanding look. They were nervous. Stillman could see it in their eyes. They weren't accustomed to dealing with a cabin full of possible owlhoots, and they were worried about Stillman. He was the closest thing to a father that either of them had now, with both their own fathers dead.

"Don't worry, young'uns," the veteran lawman said, crooking a smile at the pair kneeling side by side behind the boulder. "This ain't my first do-si-do."

He rose and grabbed his Henry from where he'd leaned it against a rock.

"Just make sure it ain't your last!" Crystal hissed as Stillman swung around and began running at a crouch along the ridge, far enough back from the gulch that he couldn't be seen from the ranch yard.

"I swear—a fella packs on a few years, and everybody thinks he's an old mossy horn due for the slaughterhouse," Stillman grumbled under his breath, as he continued jogging along the ridge crest, parallel with the gulch.

When he'd run what he figured to be fifty or so yards, he drew up behind a chokecherry snag at the edge of the ridge. The cabin was nearly straight beneath him now. Still, no movement. He looked along the slope beneath him for a way down the ridge that was relatively covered. There was a large chokecherry and hawthorn snag about twenty yards farther on.

He stepped back out of the small snag he was in, the wiry branches dark with the ripe, bitter fruit raking his jeans cuffs. He continued jogging along the ridge crest, sweating through his blue chambray shirt and vest, only to drop flat when he heard a wooden scrape from below. He crawled over to take a gander into the gulch.

The cabin door had opened. A familiar figure moved across the narrow stoop, down the three steps, and out into the sunlit yard. He was moving gingerly, trying to put little weight on his right foot on which he wore a brown half-boot. The man was short, thickly built, with broad shoulders, and he was dressed in brown suit pants, a white shirt, and a checked brown vest. He wore spectacles on his broad, swarthy face framed by dark-red sideburns. A thick, dark-red mustache drooped down over both sides of the man's mouth.

Stillman had little doubt that the gent in the suit, built like a boxer, which the doctor had been at one time, was Clyde Evans.

As Evans limped out into the yard, heading toward the windmill, Stillman raised his spyglass to his right eye, and adjusted the focus. Through the sphere of magnified vision, he watched the doctor scoop a bucket of water up from the stone stock tank at the base of the windmill. Evans turned and began carrying the bucket back toward the cabin, water sloshing over the sides of the bucket to splatter in the well-churned dirt of the ranch yard.

Evans was facing Stillman now, and the sheriff could see that one of the doctor's eyes was swollen. The lens over that eye appeared to be cracked. He had a cut on his lower lip. He was limping badly on his right foot. His thick, rust-red hair was badly mussed.

Stillman snarled a curse as he lowered the spyglass. They'd roughed the doc up a bit. Not real bad. But bad enough to rile Stillman's dander. Enough to assure Stillman that the doc was not out here of his own free will. The men in the cabin were likely long coulee riders of one stripe or another. They had an injured man. Maybe the man had been shot by a stagecoach guard, maybe by a posse.

But the injured rider meant enough to the others for them to have fetched Evans from Clantick in the middle of the night.

Boots thumped on the porch. Stillman turned to see another man stepping out of the cabin. He was tall and lean, and he was cradling a carbine in his arms. He wore no hat, and his wheat-colored hair was long and shaggy. On his hips were two pistols. The handle of a long knife jutted from the well of his right boot, which rose nearly to his knee.

"Vermilion," Stillman muttered, scrutinizing the tall man through his spyglass. "Johnny Vermilion." He recognized the face from one of the wanted dodgers he had hanging in his office.

Vermilion said something to the doc. He was facing away from Stillman, so the sheriff hadn't heard what he'd said. He could hear Evans say, "I'm comin'," in an angry, gravelly voice.

As Vermilion turned to follow the doc into the cabin, Stillman heard the notorious Montana bank robber say, "My brother dies, Mr. Pill Roller, *you* die!"

Stillman lowered the spyglass and returned it to its pouch, muttering, "Shit."

CHAPTER 5

Stillman picked his way carefully down the ridge, shuttling his gaze between the cabin below, its north wall nearly straight ahead of him, and the deer trail he was following through the chokecherry snag.

There were two windows on the side of the cabin facing him. Curtains showed in both windows, but both were only about half-closed. It helped that there were three box elders between Stillman and the cabin, and heavy brush to both sides of the trail he was on. They helped screen him.

Still, anyone keeping an eye on the ridge from either window facing him would spy the big man in the blue chambray shirt, brown leather vest, and broad-brimmed cream Stetson moving down the slope toward them. He realized now that he should have had his deputy, McMannigle, backing him, but he hadn't known how severe the danger out here was.

He liked to keep either himself or Leon in town, as the Clantick bank was always a target in this half-wild country. The parsimonious town council hadn't seen fit to hire a town marshal, so Stillman's jurisdiction included Clantick as well as the entire county around it—a lot of territory for only two lawmen to cover.

Stillman gained the bottom of the slope, feeling as though rocks were grinding in both knees. He wasn't accustomed to this much footwork. And, as much as he hated to admit it, he wasn't getting any younger. He was still on the uphill side of middle age, but he'd squeezed the sap from every year, just as every year had squeezed the sap from him. He still had the whore's bullet in his back, as it had lodged too close to his spine for any doctor he'd so far seen to dare dig it out and risk paralyzing him. The bullet often bothered him, as well.

No point in thinking about that now, you old fool, he silently admonished himself, as he moved out away from the slope, crouching low. He dropped to his least sore knee behind the largest of the three box elders. Sucking air into his lungs, hearing it wheeze out, sweat dribbling down his cheeks and into his mustache, he mopped a sleeve across his forehead.

He stared at the cabin from around the right side of the tree. He could hear voices echoing inside. The shutters were pulled back from both windows facing him, and he thought one or two of the voices was emanating from the window nearest the front. The others seemed to be coming from another place in the cabin.

The curtains over both windows billowed out in the wind. And on that wind he thought he could hear the laughing voice of a girl or a young woman amidst the lower tones of a male.

Stillman drew a deep breath and set his hat back on his head. He glanced once more at the horses inside the corral. Six of the herd probably belonged to the men in the cabin. Six men. Maybe five men and one woman. Steep odds, but Stillman had seen steeper.

Of course, he'd been younger, then.

There you go again, you copper-riveted fool. If you're gonna start doubting yourself, you might as well turn tail right now. Let your friend Doc Evans fend for himself and you head on back to Clantick and turn your badge in to the town council. Go on home to Fay and Little Ben, fish and raise your boy and your chickens.

Stillman drew another breath, adjusted his hat brim, took his rifle in both hands, and ran out from behind the box elder. He shifted his gaze between both windows, both growing larger before him, the man's and the woman's voice growing louder in the one nearest the front. He kept that window on his right as he gained the cabin wall, left of a low pile of rotting wood against which an old, moldering wheelbarrow had been upended and abandoned.

The wood smelled of rot, as did the cabin. Stillman could also smell tobacco smoke as it wafted out the nearest window.

"Shut up, you dumbass," said the woman's voice. Her low, husky voice was so clear that she seemed to be speaking to the sheriff himself from only a few feet away. "Try to concentrate a little here, will you, please?"

Pressing his back against the cabin as he faced the ridge, Stillman looked over his left shoulder and over the woodpile at the open window with its buffeting curtain. As in most crude cabins, the window was low, and the stacked wood had been arranged so as not to block it.

He crawled along the piled wood, doffed his hat, and risked a peek up beneath the billowing curtain and into the room beyond. Stillman widened his eyes at a woman's bare torso standing or sitting in profile to him. The young woman's long, straight brown hair was held back behind her forehead with a blue calico bandanna. Judging by the smoothness of her skin, at least that which Stillman could see, she was in her early twenties, maybe younger.

The girl was rocking back and forth, causing what was likely bedsprings to squawk beneath her. Stillman could see the curve of a full, pale breast behind the hair spilling down her right shoulder, only a few feet from the window. As she rocked on the bed, she rolled her head and shoulders luxuriously, groaning and speaking, sometimes chuckling around a loosely rolled, smoldering quirley protruding from between her full, red lips.

"Charlie, I like that idea—truly I do—but if you don't stop blowin' and put forth a little more effort here, I'm going to find Vermilion, and diddle him, instead!" Cigarette smoke billowed around her head.

The man, whom Stillman couldn't see from his angle, chuckled. All Stillman could see of the man was his brown hands reaching up and closing around the girl's breasts, kneading them, causing at least one nipple to jut, as the girl chuckled again and threw her head back on her shoulders and began turning her face toward the window.

Stillman jerked his head back down beneath the window and behind the woodpile as the man cursed and said, "Ole Johnny cain't get it up even when he ain't drunk, Hettie darlin'. Too many whores, too much clap. Oh, Johnny talks a good game, but I heard from a whore down in Deadwood. . . ."

The girl laughed at that, drowning out whatever else the man she was straddling was saying.

Stillman's ears rang. For a second he thought the girl might have seen him out here, peeping through a window into a love nest, like a twelve-year-old boy. But when the girl gave no indication she'd discovered the lawman out her window, but continued groaning and causing the bedsprings to complain, Stillman saw her face again in his mind's eye, and muttered under his breath, "Hettie Styles."

Stillman recognized the name of an ex-dance-hall girl from Colorado, and slid it into the same mental pigeonhole with other names associated with the Vermilion bunch, a medium-sized gang of mining camp predators that, last he'd heard, were drifting east out of Idaho. They'd started out robbing gold and silver shipments and occasionally banks in Montana before heading to Idaho. That's where the girl, Hettie Styles, also wanted for confidence schemes, had joined Vermilion's crew and had been associated with several members of the gang.

Now, obviously, they were back in Montana.

Stillman hadn't heard of any banks or mines that had been robbed recently in the area, but sometimes the word was slow to make its way through the U.S. mail and the telegraph wires.

He'd developed a good memory for names over the years, and several names that comprised the Vermilion bunch rumbled in his ears: Johnny Vermilion, Hettie Styles, Charlie Birdsong, Lyle or Lester Stanton . . . and an older man, maybe Stillman's age, named Warner. John or George Warner. There were probably more men inside the cabin, but those were the only names Stillman remembered from the wanted dodgers he'd hung in his office. Besides, gangs were switching members all the time—losing some, acquiring others.

At the moment, the sheriff's primary concern was for Evans's safety.

With that in mind, he crabbed ahead, squatting low, and investigated the other window on this side of the cabin. Discovering that there was nothing in that room but a dilapidated dresser and a broken mirror lying amidst dirt and leaves that had blown through the window, Stillman made his way around the cabin's rear, which had no window but a lone, closed door in it, to the cabin's other side.

There were three windows on this side of the cabin. Stillman could hear voices emanating from the one up near the cabin's front corner, but the two nearest him were silent.

As he crabbed ahead, wincing against the creek in his bent knees, he scrutinized the window before him. There were curtains over this one, too, and they were also half-closed, but they weren't moving. Stillman lifted his head to peer over the sill and into the room, and then jerked his head down slightly when he heard a boot thump close by. He continued gazing over the windowsill to see a thick, pale hand with a ring set with a square black stone reach past the window to wrap itself around the neck of a plain, brown bottle standing on a crude shelf on the room's front wall.

Stillman's heart quickened. He recognized the ring on the hand that was lifting the bottle high and tipping it back. He also recognized the profile of the man drinking from the bottle, but as he lifted his head a little higher and was intending to call out to Clyde Evans, he saw another man in the room behind the sawbones.

This man was sprawled on a low bed against the room's opposite, plankboard wall. The man had a ratty Army blanket drawn up to his waist. A large, thick bandage encircled the man's chest and belly. Blood broadly stained the bandage in two places.

The wounded man appeared to be asleep. His lips were stretched with a wince even as he slumbered. A ragged hat hung from a peg in the wall above him.

Stillman could hear other voices through the room's front wall. They sounded like men raising and calling, playing poker. There was a good bit of ribbing going on, as well.

Evans gave a sigh and smacked his lips as he set the whiskey bottle back onto the shelf. His half boots thudded as he swung away from Stillman and the window to walk back toward the hide-bottom chair angled beside the bed on which his patient continued to slumber. A wooden bucket sat on the floor near the chair. On the chair was a porcelain washbowl in which a bloody sponge floated.

Stillman lifted his head higher and quietly cleared his throat to gain the doctor's attention. He'd been too quiet. Evans hadn't heard above the splattering of the water in the porcelain bowl as he rung out the bloody sponge in his hands. Stillman glanced at the man on the low bed once more. Anxiety rippled through him. He didn't want to awaken the wounded man, who might call out to the others. But he wanted to get Evans out of the cabin and out of harm's way as fast as possible.

"Doc!" Stillman rasped.

Evans half-turned toward the closed door in the wall near the foot of the bed, and said in a peeved tone, "I told you—I'm doin' all I can."

Stillman winced. Then, seeing that the voice hadn't come from the door, Evans swung abruptly toward the window. Stillman pressed two gloved fingers to his lips.

"Ben!" Evans said, quieter but still too loud.

The man on the bed stirred but did not open his eyes. Evans glanced at his patient and then walked on the balls of his feet to the window and crouched down. He blinked his good eye, which was sharp with anxiety. The other, behind the cracked lens of his glasses, was swollen nearly closed.

"How in the hell did you find me?" Evans whispered.

Stillman shook his head as if to say, "Never mind." He said, "Gonna get you outta here, Doc," as he reached through the window and grabbed his friend's wrist.

"Wait," Evans said. "My medical kit."

Evans stepped away from the window, to Stillman's left, and the sheriff hissed, "No—leave it!"

Again, the man on the bed stirred, muttered. Stillman poked his head through the window to see Evans squatting over his leather medical kit, which sat open on a blanket spread on the floor near the chair. He was tossing some small bottles and instruments inside. Stillman raked out a curse and ground his jaws anxiously, returning his gaze to the man on the bed, who was turning his head back and forth and lifting a hand to his bloody bandage.

As Evans started for the window, the wounded man lifted his head and looked around groggily. He was obviously drugged, probably still under the influence of ether.

"Hurry up, Doc," Stillman whispered as Evans approached.

"Hey," the man on the bed said, blinking his eyes exaggerat-edly. "What the hell's . . . what the hell's goin' on?"

He'd said it so loudly that one of the men in the front room said, *"Shhh!"* The others fell silent.

Evans shoved his kit at Stillman, who took it and set it on the ground and then reached through the window to help the doc-tor through. As he did, he heard a man yell from the other side of the room's front wall, "What's goin' on in there?" A slight pause. Evans got a leg over the windowsill. "Evans?" the same voice called. "What the hell's goin' on in there?"

"Someone's here, Johnny!" the man on the bed bellowed. "Johnny—someone's here!"

The man on the bed raised a revolver from under the blanket. Stillman grabbed the doc and pulled, falling back, and he and Evans dropped beneath the level of the window as the gun inside the room exploded. The bullet chewed through the top of the sill, spraying slivers in all directions. Evans groaned as he rolled onto his back. Stillman heaved himself to his feet and loudly pumped a cartridge into his Henry's breech as the wounded man's revolver thundered again.

That bullet hammered the side of the window casing.

"Johnny, someone's here!" Vermilion's brother bellowed.

Stillman aimed his Henry through the window, drew a hasty bead on the center of the young man's chest, and squeezed the trigger, blowing a fresh hole through his bandage and slamming him up against the wall behind him. The young man screamed and triggered his revolver into the ceiling before dropping the gun with a thud as he died.

Then Stillman withdrew his rifle, yelled, "Stay here, Doc!" and took off running toward the front of the cabin.

He heard Doc say wearily behind him, "All that work for nothing . . ."

CHAPTER 6

Stillman ran around the cabin's front corner and leaped onto the veranda. The front door was closed. Beyond it, Stillman heard men stumbling and stomping and yelling. The lawman did not wait for them to get their bearings, but kicked in the front door and stepped inside as it bounced off the wall to his right, and stopped it with his right boot.

There were two men in the room, both with pistols drawn, both partly turned away from Stillman and staring into the narrow corridor running from the front kitchen and parlor area into the back room. Neither man was Vermilion. The hall was obscured by a half-drawn gingham curtain wearing a coat of dust and cobwebs and printed with orange and black flowers. Raising his Henry to his shoulder, Stillman shouted to be heard above the din of raised voices and stomping boots, "Stillman— County Sheriff!"

The two men standing around the small table littered with playing cards, coins, and paper money swung toward him, wide-eyed with anxiety beneath the brims of their hats. "What the *hell?*" the one on the right shouted, red-faced with fury.

Two or three more men and the girl were yelling down the corridor. Vermilion had likely found his brother's bullet-riddled corpse.

The two facing Stillman slid their eyes around. Their feet were moving as though the floor were sliding around beneath them. The one on the right snapped up his pistol, and Stillman's Henry stabbed smoke and flames at him. While that man was being thrown up off his feet and straight back, Stillman dispatched the other gent, as well, his empty cartridge casings clinking onto the floor behind him and rolling around his boot heels.

The second man screamed, triggered one of his two drawn pistols into the table, shattering a whiskey bottle, and then flew back out the window to Stillman's right.

A man shouted loudly. A gun flashed in the hall. The bullet curled the air to the right of Stillman's head as it winged out the door behind him.

Stillman fired into the hall, blowing the man who'd just fired at him through a door to the man's right. Another shadowy figure moved. Possibly two. Light from the door behind Stillman partially limned a bearded, tanned face with two pinched eyes beneath a black hat brim. The man raised a pistol; sunlight glinted on the barrel.

Stillman's Henry bellowed three more times, the empty cartridge casings arcing over Stillman's right shoulder, powder smoke wafting in the air around his head. The curtain leaped wildly as one or two of the sheriff's bullets tore through it. He heard two shrill yells down the hall, and saw what appeared to be two shadows leaping and twisting and then falling down to lie in dark lumps on the floor.

A man groaned. There was a thud as though a gun or boot had struck the floor. A heavy silence descended. Gun smoke hung in heavy, gray, gently undulating ribbons.

Down the hall, a floorboard creaked faintly.

Stillman pumped another cartridge into the sixteen-shot Henry's chamber, snugged the brass butt plate up against his shoulder once more.

"That's enough," a woman's slightly raspy voice said. "Stop shooting! You got us!"

Stillman said, "Step into the hall with your hands raised. If you think I won't shoot a woman, you'd best think again."

Hettie Styles stepped out of an open doorway on the right side of the hall. She stepped over a dead man's leg, and turned to Stillman. She was as naked as the day she'd been born but a hell of a lot better filled out. Her long, brown hair tumbled over her shoulders to partly screen her breasts.

She smirked at Stillman as she raised her hands to her shoulders. She shrugged.

"See?" she said. "Not armed."

"Get out here."

"Where?"

Stillman didn't respond. He kept his Henry's sights lined up on the deep cleft between her breasts.

"Do you mind if I get dressed first?"

"Get your naked ass out here and have a seat at the table."

The woman stepped forward, the floorboards creaking faintly under her bare feet. Her breasts jiggled slightly behind her thick hair as she padded slowly into the kitchen. Her cheeks were mottled pink with anxiousness, but her eyes were cool. She looked around at the dead men around her and then, as she reached the table, turned to Stillman.

Her eyes flicked to the five-pointed star riding high on the left flap of his vest.

"You did some damage here, Sheriff."

Stillman heard footsteps behind him, recognized the doctor's tread. Evans mounted the stoop, stopped in the open doorway, and cleared his throat.

Stillman continued facing the cabin, in case any of the outlaws still had some life, as he said, "You all right, Doc?"

"A little worse for the wear, but I'm kicking."

Stillman lowered the Henry, reached across his belly to slide his Peacemaker from the holster on his left hip. He turned sideways, extended the revolver butt-first to Evans, and said, "You hold this on Miss Styles here. If she makes a try for a gun, shoot her." He glanced at his friend, who was looking beleaguered as he continued to stand in the doorway. "You think you can do that?"

Evans took the gun as he looked at Hettie Styles standing off by a corner of the table. "Yeah," he said. "Yeah, I think I can do that."

"Sorry for the black eye, Doc," Hettie said. "Johnny gets mean when he's drunk, and he's been drunk since Arthur got shot in Sulphur." She paused, turned her head slowly to stare down the short, dark hall. "At least, he used to . . ."

Stillman kicked a chair out from the table. "Have a seat."

Holding Stillman's gaze with a subtly defiant one of her own, lips quirked in an ironic half-smile, Hettie sank into the chair. She glanced at Evans holding Stillman's revolver on her from the door, and winked. She lifted her hands, cupped her full breasts, and sighed.

"If she moves," Stillman said, "shoot her."

"He heard you the first time, Sheriff," Hettie said as Stillman moved around the table to inspect the first man he'd shot—he appeared to be Zeke Lancaster—who lay on his back, broken glass, spilled whiskey, and his own blood matting his chest. His mouth and eyes were open, but he wasn't breathing.

The other man who'd been in the kitchen was hanging out the window. Only his legs, hooked over the windowsill, were visible. Neither leg was moving. Deeming him a corpse, as well, Stillman walked down the hall, extending his Henry straight out from his right hip. He hadn't realized it until now, but his rifle was growing heavier in his right hand. That forearm was starting to tingle and ache.

Stillman shoved the discomfort into the back of his mind as he stopped at the end of the hall. In the room to his right, a man clad in only longhandles lay belly down near the dilapidated dresser and the broken mirror. Dead leaves scuttled around his shaggy head in the breeze pushing through the window.

Stillman heard a grunt and a scrape, and turned to peer into the room on his left—the room in which the doc had been tending Vermilion's brother. Vermilion wasn't dead. He was crawling toward the rear wall, leaving a trail of smeared blood across the floor behind him. He was grunting and groaning. He was heading for his brother's pistol on the floor near the hide-bottom chair.

Stillman spread his boots inside the door and aimed the Henry at the back of Johnny Vermilion's head. "Nuh-uh."

Vermilion stopped. He turned his head toward Stillman. His eyes were pain-racked, tendrils of his long, sandy-blond hair pasted to his cheeks, carpeted in a thin, scraggly version of the hair on his head. Stillman held the Henry on him. Vermilion looked at the rifle in Stillman's right hand.

Stillman looked at it, too. It was shaking. The barrel was slanting toward the floor.

Vermilion smiled.

The outlaw turned his head forward and lunged for the pistol under the chair.

Stillman's rifle thundered. The bullet only creased the top of Vermilion's head, pluming the outlaw's hair. Vermilion cursed shrilly as he fished his brother's .44 out from under the chair. He gritted his teeth as he clicked the hammer back and swung the gun around.

Stillman triggered the Henry again . . . and again . . . and again . . . until Vermilion lay flat on his back, staring up at the ceiling, blinking wildly, limbs twitching as he died.

Stillman looked down at the smoking rifle. He was holding it in both hands now. It was still shaking. His right arm was cramping badly. The pain extended around his hip and into his ass and down the back of his right leg. That knee had long, sharp pins in it.

"Goddamnit," Stillman said, bunching his lips as he stared down at the quivering rifle in his hands.

The bullet in his back was getting way too cozy with his spine . . .

"Goddamn whore," Stillman raked out. How many times would he be forced to relive that fateful night in that smelly, Virginia City brothel?

He took the Henry in his left hand only, dropping the right, nearly useless one to his side. He moved into the room, glanced at Arthur Vermilion lying on the bed spread-eagle, his head against the wall, chin angled sharply to his chest. Arthur's older brother lay on the floor beside the bed, his lower jaw half-blown away.

Blood was leaking from the left side of Johnny Vermilion's neck, from his left arm and from that hip. The shot that had finished him had been Stillman's last try, the one he'd finally managed to drill through the outlaw's heart.

"Christ," Stillman said, tucking his right thumb into his pocket to try to keep that hand from visibly shaking. He didn't want Evans or anyone else to see the pathetic state he was in.

"You all right in there, Ben?" the doctor called from the front room.

Stillman heard Hettie Styles say with an ironic air, "I think he's having trouble. Better go and help him, Doc. Maybe Johnny shot him."

Stillman turned and, trying not to limp on his right foot—that boot felt as though it were filled with rocks—left the room and walked back up the hall. He stopped near the door to the room from which the girl had surfaced, and glanced inside. There were several piles of clothes on the floor around the bed with the mussed Army blankets. A filled coffee sack had served as a pillow for the man Hettie had been straddling.

"Get in there and get dressed," Stillman ordered the girl.

The thuds of fast-moving horses rose in the distance. Still-man looked past the doc still standing in the doorway and then said to Evans, "That's Jody and Crystal. Keep 'em outside—will you, Doc?"

"You all right, Ben?"

"Yeah, I'm fine."

Hettie had stopped in front of Stillman, letting him get a good look at her. She wasn't shy. She raked him up and down and said, "I don't know—you don't look too good, Sheriff. You sure you're all right?"

Stillman waved his rifle, and she stepped into the room.

As Evans turned to walk outside, Stillman filled the bed-room's doorway with his big frame, holding his rifle in his left hand. Hettie had just bent forward to pick some clothes up off the floor. Stillman glanced away from her as he said, "Keep your hands off those guns."

Near the clothes lay a shell belt with two filled holsters.

"I know, I know," Hettie said in her mocking tone. "You're not adverse to shooting a woman."

"You got it."

"How about to running away with one?" She turned to Still-man. "Are you adverse to that?" She was holding a tobacco-brown blouse in one hand, a thin, cream-colored chemise in the other. She canted her head toward a pair of well-filled saddlebags leaning against the wall. "There's nearly twenty thousand dol-lars in those pouches. We could go a long ways, for a long time, on that much money. If you think you're up to it."

"I'm not up to it."

"How old are you, Sheriff? Sixty?"

He knew it shouldn't burn him, but it did. Maybe because he was feeling so damn old suddenly, and because a girl like this could get under any man's skin. Even a man who was happily, gratefully married and had a child he would have given his life for. "Not quite that old," he growled. "Just get dressed. I don't have time to stand here and chin with you. I'll be taking you back to Clantick."

"You're a handsome man, for an older one. You think I'm pretty?"

Hettie held the blouse and the chemise beneath her breasts, giving him a good, long look at her wares. He had to admit, she was impressive. She was also dangerous. A girl like her cut a wide swath. He had to get this wildcat to Clantick and in a cage as soon as possible.

Just then Stillman's right knee buckled. Pain rippled through his back and down his arm as that forearm and hand seized up, both spasming. Stillman fell back against the doorframe. Hettie lunged toward him, reaching for the rifle. Stillman raised the Henry in his left hand, glaring at her from beneath the brim of his Stetson.

Hettie froze. The Henry's barrel was two inches away from her naked belly. Her eyes were shrewd.

"You're not well, Sheriff," she said, shaking her head slowly, jeeringly. "You're not well at all."

"Ben?" Evans called from the front yard. "You all right in there?"

Hettie chuckled. She turned around and bent over again to pick up the chemise, which she'd dropped when she'd lunged for the rifle. She shook the thin, low-cut garment out in front of her. "Don't worry, Sheriff."

She winked as she dropped the chemise down over her breasts. "It'll be our little secret."

CHAPTER 7

Fay Stillman set little Benjamin William into a wheelbarrow mounded with quilts and heavy blankets, kissed the boy on the top of his beautiful head, and said, "You gonna help Momma hang up the bedding, Little Ben?"

The boy gurgled an incoherent response and held up the little wooden horse he had in one hand as if to show her something he hadn't been showing her since Leon McMannigle had carved and given the horse to the child over a month ago.

"Horsey!" Fay intoned, lifting the wheelbarrow by its wooden handles with a grunt, and pushing it forward, blowing a lock of her long, chocolate brown hair away from her face.

"Wishyswishy!" the boy exclaimed, laughing delightedly and flopping his hands in the air.

It was a beautiful, relatively cool early-autumn day, with a faultless Montana sky sprawling over the little town of Clantick and the chalky buttes of the Milk River flanking the settlement. There was just enough breeze, rife with the smell of mown grass and wildflowers, for airing out Mrs. Stillman's stockpile of autumn and winter bedding, getting it ready to place on their bed as well as in little Ben Junior's crib.

While it was still warm and sometimes hot during the day, the nights were getting cooler, the stars brighter. Soon the air would be sharp and crisp. The leaves would be turning on the cottonwoods and box elders rolling up and down the hills surrounding their little chicken farm at the edge of town, and the nights would be crystal clear, with a sharp autumn bite that would foretell the long, cold, snowy winter ahead.

Fay didn't mind the looming dramatic season change. The winters weren't all that harsher up here in northern Montana than they were in southern Montana, where the former Fay Beaumont had grown up on a vast ranch stretched across the stark, rolling bluffs of the Powder River country. Ben was home more in the winter, as the owlhoots weren't as busy. And Fay liked to have Ben at home. Especially now, since young Benjamin William had blessed their lives, filling their shared life's cup all the way to its brim.

Besides, Fay liked the coziness of the cabin with a hot fire blazing in the hearth, and her man's masculine arms wrapped around her in their soft, comfortable bed deep with heavy quilts. She loved to feel the heat of Ben Stillman's body ensconcing hers in the winter, when it was so cold outside that sometimes pine trees exploded up in the Two-Bears, and the stars were so bright over the snow-mantled hills that they resembled campfires.

As Fay pushed the wheelbarrow toward the clothesline at the front of the house facing the town, on the opposite side from the old buggy shed and the chicken coop, Little Ben flung his wooden horse into the grass. The boy laughed again with unabashed delight and flapped his arms wildly.

Fay set down the wheelbarrow with a sigh. "Now, why did you do that, you little rascal?"

Benjamin William laughed and clapped his hands and pointed at the horse lying in the spare wheat grass that grew around the Stillman place, mixed with sage, yucca, and needle grass. Fay retrieved the horse, galloping it through the air toward her delighted boy, who couldn't quite follow it with his flopping hands.

"Here it comes, Little Ben—get ready to saddle up and *ride*!"

When the laughing boy had possession of the "Wishyswishy!" once more, Fay continued to push the wheelbarrow over to the clothesline strung between the two wooden posts she'd labored to sink into the ground. As she did, she scoured the ground for rattlesnakes, which were known to slither up out of the Milk River, twisting through the buttes only a hundred yards to the north.

Fay had shot several sand rattlers and diamondbacks over the past two years, since she and Ben had arrived in Clantick. The vipers made a succulent stew—Fay had been taught growing up on the ranch to waste nothing edible—but she'd prefer they remained down in the barrancas along the river, especially now with Little Ben's ability to crawl around and to potentially get himself into trouble.

He'd be walking soon—in fact, he was already starting—and Fay knew that when the boy gained full control of his legs, she'd have a devil of a time keeping up with him.

When she'd looked carefully around once more, and saw no rattlers sleeping in the shade of a sage bush, she set the boy with his horse on the ground, and kissed him on both pudgy cheeks. While Little Ben played with the horse, Fay began to hang the bedding on the line, securing the blankets, quilts, and afghans with wooden pins. She hummed as she worked and considered what she'd cook for supper. She also found herself worrying about Doc Evans, for she'd learned earlier from Leon about the possible trouble out near Jody and Crystal's place in the Two-Bears.

Would Ben be home in time for supper? This was such large country, and his jurisdiction covered so many square miles of it, that when he was called away from town, he was often gone for days. Sometimes, he'd been gone for weeks, and that had always filled Fay with grinding worry. She loved her husband no end, and if anything ever happened to Ben . . .

She was almost glad to have her dark turn of thought interrupted by the loud squawking of a chicken issuing from the backyard. Then another one squawked, and another . . .

"You stay right there, Little Ben!" Fay said, wheeling away from the clothesline, and, holding her Mother Hubbard's hem above her ankles, took off running toward the rear of the house. As she ran, she glanced back at Little Ben waving the horse in the air and staring at her, wide-eyed. "Stay right there—don't move a foot for Mommie, okay?"

Then she was on the far side of the house and could see the chickens, which had been foraging freely in the yard, leaping and running and trying to fly. One made a mad dash toward the buggy shed, and, through the thin cloud of billowing dust, Fay could see the small, red fox in pursuit.

"Get out of here, you devil!" Fay shouted, reaching through the small, neat, frame house's open back door for her Winchester carbine.

She raised the rifle, cocking it, and aimed hastily, not so much trying to hit the fox as trying *not* to hit the chicken, whose tail feathers were between the fox's jaws.

Bam! Bam-Bam!

The fox released the barred rock rooster as the bullets blew up dirt beside it. It gave a startled, dog-like yip. The fox swerved so abruptly away from the chicken that it fell and rolled and then dashed off through the brush along the old buggy shed, which had been part of the small chicken farm when she and Ben had bought the place and the eighty acres surrounding it. They'd owned a little place on French Street for a year, not far from the brothels, but after Fay had become pregnant, they'd bought the farm, wanting a little more room in which to raise a family.

Fay took another shot at the fox's thick, shaggy tail, which appeared half the size of the rest of the scrawny beast, and then lowered the carbine, ejecting the last spent cartridge.

"Nasty devil!" Fay barked in French. The language she'd first spoken at home seemed to surface when she got excited.

The chickens—mostly barred rocks and Rhode Island reds with a few leghorns and bantams—had all spread out around the side of the yard opposite the coop, which was enclosed with chicken wire, and the buggy shed, near where the trail led down the buttes and into Clantick. The barred rock rooster, which Ben called Clancy, for some reason—Ben, who'd loved chickens since raising them back in Pennsylvania as a young boy, had named nearly the entire flock—was skip-hopping around and clucking indignantly, his feathers literally ruffled. Fay walked over to the scene of the attack and looked around to make sure the fox hadn't killed or seriously injured any of the chickens.

But then she remembered she'd left Little Ben out by the clothesline, and quickly leaned the Winchester against the rear of the house, beside the back door, and ran around the house's west side.

"Benny!" she called, suddenly afraid the boy, left to his own devices, might have encountered a rattlesnake.

Knowing a mother's keen fear at imagined catastrophe, her heart racing, Fay flew around the house's front corner, stopped, and looked around. Her heart flip-flopped painfully. Little Ben was nowhere in sight. There were only the half-dozen quilts, blankets, and the two afghans buffeting like flags on the line.

"Ben!"

Fay started forward but stopped when she saw the little, wooden horse lying on the ground where she had placed the boy.

"Ben!" Fay screamed, bounding forward. "Ben—where are you, Little Ben?"

She whipped her gaze to both sides of the blankets buffeting on the line and then pushed through a large star quilt, and, as the quilt flapped back down behind her, she stopped dead in her tracks. She took a startled step backward as she slapped a hand to her chest, blinking as though to clear her eyes.

No, he was there, all right. Not thirty yards away from her, where an old buggy trail curved along the shoulder of the bluff.

A man in a black cutaway coat, brown wool vest, and string tie was holding Little Ben. A large, broad-brimmed, black slouch hat shaded the stranger's deep-set eyes.

The stranger—tall and saturnine, maybe in his late-forties, early fifties—was talking to Little Ben, smiling, jostling the boy in the arm that ended in a steel hook. Little Ben was studying the hook. He was leaning forward, pointing at the menacing steel contraption, and gurgling his fascination.

"See there," the man cooed. "That's my hand. What do you think of that, little one? A little different from what you're used to seein', isn't it?" He gently caressed Little Ben's cheek with the side of the hook, the boy reaching for it as though trying to grab it and study it more closely.

Fay started forward. "Ben!"

The stranger looked up at her, feigning a look of surprise. At least, he must have been feigning it. He had to have heard Fay calling for her son, and seen her push through the quilts.

"This yours?" the man called, flashing Fay a fawning smile. "He was just a minute ago crawling after a gopher."

Fay hesitated, glancing at the revolver holstered on the man's hip and at the butt of a rifle jutting above the other side of a smoky gray horse, a grulla that stood behind him, tearing grass along the buggy trail.

"Yes, he's prone to doing that."

"I hope everything's all right . . . ?"

"What's that?" Fay frowned. She'd been so worried about Little Ben, and then so startled by the stranger, that the fox had slipped her mind. "Oh . . . yes, it was only a fox after the chickens," she said, continuing forward and wrapping her arms around the boy, pulling him away from the stranger's hook.

As she did, she glanced to her right. She'd vaguely noted the three horses forming a small pack train behind the stranger's grulla, but now she gave them a closer scrutiny. Revulsion rippled through her. She turned slightly away from the horses, so Little Ben wouldn't see the two dead men lying belly down across two of the mounts' backs.

The men were not covered. Their heads hung toward the ground on the near side of the horses, hair dangling. Bees and flies hovered over the bodies.

Fay scowled at the tall man still smiling down at her and Little Ben. "Lawman?" she asked, looking for a badge but not finding one. "Or bounty hunter?"

Fay knew that Ben often had to deal with such men who hunted other men for money. Most were outlaws themselves, or had been.

"Neither."

"Well, my husband's not home," Fay said, preparing to turn away and head back to her work. The man and his cargo appalled her, and she didn't want Little Ben around it either.

"So, you're Mrs. Stillman," the man said in his oily way, still smiling down at her, but his demeanor now seemed more supercilious than unctuous. "My Lord,"—his snake-like, blue-gray eyes raked her up and down—"you are a beauty."

Fay backed up another step, clutching Little Ben more tightly to her bosom, partly to protect the boy, partly to cover herself. She'd been the target of bold male stares before, but there was something especially repellent in the stare of this man. She felt as though he'd stripped her and she was standing naked before him.

Chicken flesh rose across her breasts and down her back and

arms. She was glad she was wearing a loose, high-necked housedress.

"Who're you?" she asked, unable to keep her disdain from her voice.

The bold-eyed stranger removed his hat with his right hand and gave a gentlemanly bow. "Jacob Henry Battles, Mrs. Stillman. I am deeply honored to make your acquaintance. I am a . . . uh . . . a former *acquaintance* of your legendary husband. In fact, I was looking for him at his office just now, and found the place empty, the door locked. I enquired at a shop across the street and was told that he might have come home for lunch."

The man's eyes flicked toward the house behind Fay and Little Ben and the bedding buffeting on the line. "Might he be here or was I misinformed?"

Fay detected a Southern accent though it had grown more exaggerated the more the man had spoken. His bearing was as much condescending, Fay thought, as pompous.

"No, he's not here," Fay said, wrinkling her nose against the stench of fresh blood she thought she could smell rising from the dead men draped over the horses. Maybe she'd imagined the smell, because she could hear the flies hungrily buzzing around them. "He was called out of town unexpectedly."

"Ah, I see. I do apologize for coming to your home with my . . . uh . . . my grisly cargo, Mrs. Stillman. It's just that these two fellas are a matter I'm in a bit of a hurry to get cleared up with your husband."

Despite her wanting to get away from the man, Fay was curious. "I'm not sure I understand you, Mr. Battles."

"Please, call me Jacob."

Fay just stared at him, her disdain clear in her French brown eyes.

Seemingly unfazed by Fay's lack of response, Battles continued with: "You see, Mrs. Stillman, your husband and I

65

have a history. I guess you could call it a professional one. In fact, this arm here"—he held up the hook—"or the lack of one, I should say, was the result. As was twelve years in a federal prison. So, you see, with my rather checkered past, I wanted to report the killings of these two men to your husband before anyone else could and maybe not tell it the way it actually happened."

"You mean, how the killing of these men happened, Mr. Battles?"

"That's right. Yes, ma'am. I want to make sure your husband understands that I killed these men in self-defense. That if I had not done so, I myself would surely be nestling with diamond-backs."

"That's very honorable, Mr. Battles."

As though he had not heard the sarcasm in the woman's voice, Battles said, "Yes, well, honor has gained importance in my life, ma'am. Uh . . . would you mind if I called you 'Fay,' Mrs. Stillman? 'Ma'am' seems such a crude way to address one so feminine and beautiful."

He was smiling straight at her, but no warmth touched his eyes. They were, instead, as hard as marbles in their red-brown sockets spoked with deeply carved age lines.

Again, Fay merely stared at him, giving him nothing. For his part, while she felt no immediate danger from the man, he did inspire cool witches' fingers of dread to tap a dour rhythm along her spine.

"Well, as I was saying . . . uh . . . *Mrs. Stillman*—informing your husband of the way these men died is important to me because I do not ever wish to spend another twelve years behind bars. Or even one or two years, for that matter. I came to this country up here in northern Montana to settle down."

Battles removed his hat, hung it on his hook, and ran his hand over his nearly bald head as he stared out over the little town of Clantick to the south. "I heard it was quiet here. Still a little rough around the edges, like I myself am, but generally quiet and unhurried"—he turned back to Fay with that snake-oil salesman smile—"with a railroad running through in case a man grows restless and requires a trip to either coast."

Fay blinked, both dubious and apprehensive. "So . . . you've decided to settle down in Clantick?"

"Yes. It is a nice town, isn't it? I read a railroad brochure, and—"

"That's how you picked it?" Fay asked, skeptically. "A railroad brochure?"

"Yes, exactly."

"So, it's just a coincidence that my husband, whom I assume was the lawman who put you in prison, and possibly caused you to lose your arm, is sheriff of Hill County?"

"Oh, your husband is not the one who put me away for all those years, Mrs. Stillman. No, that was done by a judge and a jury. And rightfully so, I might add. I was guilty of what I'd been accused. Your husband was merely the man who, while fulfilling his duties as a deputy United States marshal, took me into custody. And, in so doing, yes, he caused me to lose my arm."

Battles ran his gloved right hand over the hook as though polishing it. "But let me assure you, Mrs. Stillman—I harbor no grudge. In fact, it might not even have been Ben who fired the bullet into my arm, shattering the bone above the elbow until it looked like several bloody toothpicks and small knives poking out of my shirt."

Fay wrinkled her nose and placed a hand on the back of Little Ben's head, though the boy, apparently bored by the conversation, and it being time for his nap, had fallen asleep against her shoulder. The mild way Battles spoke of grisly events was chilling, but she tried not to show it, because she had a feeling that appalling her was the man's intention.

She also had a feeling that Battles's presence here in Clantick was not as innocent as he wanted her to believe.

"There were three lawmen after me that day," Battles said. "Ben, or . . . uh . . . *Sheriff Stillman* was only one of them. I have no idea who fired the shot that took my arm. Anyway, I've taken up enough of your time, Fay—or, I mean *Mrs. Stillman*. I'll get my grisly cargo out of your yard. Oh, look there, the boy's asleep. Little Ben, is it? Ben, Junior, I assume? What a beautiful child. Aren't they innocent at that age? And so terribly vulnerable. You shouldn't leave him out in the yard unattended, you know." Battles winked. "Never know when a rattlesnake will happen by."

With that he climbed into his saddle, turned the horses around, pinched his hat brim to Fay, and rode back down the butte toward Clantick.

Fay carried Little Ben back into the house, shuddering.

CHAPTER 8

Stillman reined Sweets up at a fork in the trail and poked his hat brim off his forehead.

The left tine of the fork led over to White-Tail Creek and the Harmon Ranch while the right tine would take Stillman, Doc Evans, and Stillman's prisoner, Hettie Styles, back to Clantick. It would also take Hettie's dead cohorts back to Clantick for probable burial in the potters' field northwest of town. All five men were tied belly down across their saddles, their horses tied nose to tail, with the first horse tied to the tail of Hettie's mount, which Stillman was leading by its bridle reins.

"You two best get on home and see to that godchild of mine," Stillman told Jody and Crystal. "I appreciate the help. Kiss that boy for me."

"All right," Crystal said. "Kiss Little Ben for me and greet Fay for us, Ben."

Jody glanced back at Hettie riding behind the doc, the woman's cuffed hands tied to her saddle horn. Stillman had tied her ankles to her stirrups, as well. She sat her saddle with a rancid look on her otherwise pretty, brown-eyed face, her hair badly mussed, giving the female outlaw a wild look.

"You sure you don't want me to ride to town with you, Ben?" Jody said. "Help you get Miss Styles locked up in your jail?"

Stillman said, "I wouldn't be much of a sheriff if I couldn't get one prisoner to town—now, would I?"

"It ain't that," Jody said, glancing at Crystal. They shared a fleeting, concerned look, then returned their gazes to Stillman. "It's just that . . . well—"

"You sure you're all right, Ben?" Crystal finished for her more reticent husband, pulling her horse out in front of Stillman's bay and swinging it around so that she faced the sheriff. "We noticed you were favoring that right arm . . . and you're lookin' a little peaked."

"Peaked, am I?" Stillman grunted, feeling peeved.

"It ain't a sin to be feelin' colicky, Ben." Crystal looked at Evans. "Tell him, Doc. And tell him again how he oughta get that bullet dug out of his back, like you been tellin' him."

"I'm tired of talkin' to a brick wall," Evans said, shrugging and shaking his head in defeat.

Stillman looked from Evans to Jody and Crystal. He was feeling more and more riled. "I think all three of you oughta just mind your own damn business," Stillman said. "If I think I need that bullet dug out of my back, I'll have it dug out of my back. In the meantime, I'd just as soon not discuss it." He gave Crystal an especially pointed look. "And I'd just as soon neither of you goes behind my back to discuss it with my wife, neither!"

Crystal flushed guiltily, telling Stillman that he'd been correct in his suspicion that she and Fay were getting together and palavering over his health. That made his cheeks and ears burn even warmer despite his knowing that he was damned lucky to have people in his life who were concerned about him. A few years ago, before he'd come to Clantick and met Fay for a second time, that hadn't been true.

Back then, he could have died in a privy, drunk, and been buried in the same kind of cemetery as the one the dead men he was trailing now were headed for.

Still, the lawman didn't want to think about the bullet in his back. He wanted to think about only good things—about being a good lawman, husband, and father. Being forced to think about a possible surgery that may cure the spasms or possibly confine him to a wheelchair for the rest of his life put a fist-sized bee in his hat.

It made him feel weak and old—two of the worst feelings that Ben Stillman could think of.

"Now," he continued, shifting his angry gaze between the two Harmons, "I'm feelin' fine as frog hair, goddamnit, so you're to stop worrying about me. Now, if you'll excuse me, I have a prisoner to take to Clantick." He glanced at Evans and gave Hettie's horse's reins a jerk. "Come on, Doc!"

As Stillman, Evans, Hettie Styles, and the horses packing the dead men continued on up the trail, swerving onto the right fork toward Clantick, Crystal rode out into the trail behind them, and yelled, "Ben Stillman, you're the most bullheaded man I ever met in my life, and you can go to *hell*!"

Stillman couldn't help laughing at that. Crystal had more gravel than her dearly departed father-in-law, Milk River Bill. The sheriff hipped around in his saddle, trying not to wince at the pain in his right side, and yelled, "I love you, too, sweetheart! Now, go on home and tend your boy!"

He chuckled again as he turned forward, putting Sweets into a spine-jarring trot and then a lope.

"Just one big happy family out here!" Hettie yelled behind him, scowling caustically over her horse's bobbing head.

When they slowed the horses to rest them as they continued along the trail hugging Beaver Creek, Hettie said after a while, "Doc, you know how much money is ridin' in them saddlebags behind the sheriff's gimpy back?"

Evans glanced at Stillman. "Those fellas riding behind that angel-faced succubus are much better off than they were a couple of hours ago, Ben. You did them a favor."

"How's that, Doc?"

"Yeah, how's that, Doc?" the abrasive girl wanted to know.

71

To Stillman, Evans said, "You should have seen how she was playing them, one off another. I have a feeling that each of the five firmly believed that she and he was going to kill all of the others and ride off to Mexico together with the stolen money. She had them all so hornswoggled and love-drunk, they didn't know which end of the bottle was the lip. Speaking of which," Evans added, wincing against his own sundry infirmities as he reached back to pull a flat, hide-sheathed metal flask from one of his saddlebag pouches, "I need some soul balm and pain-killer."

"I'd take a drink of that, Doc."

Evans looked at Hettie. She wore the tobacco brown blouse, breasts jutting hard from behind it, and tight denims held up by a wide, brown belt. She had a young, heart-shaped face with broad cheekbones and wide-set brown eyes—eyes that would have been pretty without their perpetually shrewd, mocking cast. She was long-legged, with nicely curving hips, and a ripe, full bosom.

"I see no reason to waste good brandy on the worms," Evans said, glancing at Stillman. "Which I hope will be dining on her soon. Do you think she'll hang, Ben?"

"I don't know, Doc," Stillman said. "I reckon we'll have to find out if she killed anybody. I 'spect there's a good many lawmen who'll be vying to take her into custody and fill a courtroom for her. And maybe several judges chompin' at the bit to build her a gallows and throw a necktie party in her honor."

"I can hear you two up there!" Hettie yelled above the clomping of the horses and the trickling of the creek through its cottonwood- and box-elder-lined bed off the trail's right side.

Evans glanced back at her, then turned forward again, and shook his head. "Nah, they'll never hang her. But they should."

"Why's that?"

"Dangerous," Evans muttered. "Damned dangerous, a girl like that. I hope you can get rid of her soon, Ben. Send her off to some other lawman's jurisdiction."

"You think she's that dangerous?" Stillman said, narrowing a skeptical eye at his friend.

"Yes, I do, Ben," Evans said, shifting his position in his saddle, adding in a pinched voice, "Yes, I do."

"Hey, Doc!" This from Hettie, who'd been listening to the men's conversation.

"Don't talk to me," Evans growled. "You're a bad girl, pure crazy to boot, and no balm to a weary man's soul at all. Not at all, Miss Styles."

"Oh, come on, Doc. Throw me a bone. Hear what I have to say!"

Evans did not respond.

"Just so you know," Hettie said. "There's damn near twenty thousand dollars in them saddlebags."

"*Those* saddlebags," Evans corrected the girl. "A young lady so charming and pretty should use the King's English, Miss Styles."

"You and me could have a good time on that much money, Doc."

"Oh? And how would we get it away from Sheriff Stillman?" Evans asked her.

"He's old and stove up," Hettie said. "You could probably knock him over with a rock." She laughed wickedly at that.

Evans looked at Stillman.

Stillman chewed back his annoyance at the insult, admonishing himself for his thin skin. "Don't worry, Doc," he said. "I know you're not considerin' anything untoward. Besides, you and Widow Kemmett are fixin' to get married. Everyone in the county knows that. You'd have to knock her over with a rock, too." He cast the doctor a lopsided smile. "And she's not half as stove up as I am. And from what I hear tell about her conversations with the ladies from the church, including my own dear wife, you've done stole that woman's heart."

Stillman winked at the sawbones.

Evans muttered something that Stillman couldn't hear. The doctor was staring straight ahead through his good eye; above his spectacles, his dark-red brows were furled with what appeared grave consternation.

"Doc?" Stillman said. "You ain't, uh, havin' second thoughts, are you? I mean, about hitchin' your team to the Widow Kemmett's wagon?"

"Hey, Doc," Hettie said. "You and me could have a good time in Mexico together. You think I'm pretty—I know you do. I seen how you was lookin' at me when Stillman had me runnin' around naked back at the cabin. I bet this old widow hag can't stoke your fire box as hot as I could . . . given half a chance."

Evans continued scowling over his chestnut's ears, seeming deep in thought. His thick, boxer's neck had turned bright red.

Stillman was starting to grow a little worried. Not because he thought that the doc would do anything against the law. But if Clyde Evans was known for one thing aside from being a capable jaw-setter and pill-roller, it was his weakness for women. Especially sexy, buxom young women.

No man in Clantick frequented the town's whores more than Evans did—aside from possibly Leon McMannigle, but that was mainly because Stillman's deputy lived in a whorehouse.

Stillman was growing worried because he was wondering if Clyde Evans hadn't started thinking that Katherine Kemmett might be a little too old and staid in her ways for the more carefree, liberal-minded doctor. The widow had been married to a Lutheran minister, and headed up the Clantick Lutheran Women's Society. While she'd been much younger than her deceased husband, and was a handsome woman in her mid- or

late-thirties, she was a far cry from the sexy wildcat Stillman
had tied to her saddle and was trailing behind Sweets.

And who, understandably, was turning the doctor's head.
Hell, she'd even turned Stillman's head a time or two . . .

Mrs. Kemmett was as crisp and prim as many women twice
her age. It was often said around Clantick that butter wouldn't
melt in the Widow Kemmett's mouth, and that if she somehow
attained the power, Heaven forbid, she would board up all the
whorehouses, lock the whoremongers in their houses with their
families every Friday night, and tax the sale of spirituous liquids
to such a high degree that a man would have to mortgage his
house for a happy hour shot of Who-hit-John!

Stillman himself had sporadically wondered if Evans would
really go through with the wedding, despite the sheriff's
certainty that the doctor sincerely loved the widow and that she
would be a wholesome influence on his life and an inspiration
to his soul. That she would, in fact, make Evans a better man.

Because Katherine Kemmett was truly a good woman.

But was Doc Evans ready to marry and settle down in the
widow's spit-and-polished, whitewashed life?

"Hey, Doc," Hettie said in her mocking way behind Stillman.
"I speak French, if'n you get my drift!"

Evans reined Faustus up suddenly. Stillman did likewise.

"Ben, I know she's your prisoner, but there's something I
must do."

Evans gigged his horse around Stillman's bay. As he did, he
withdrew a red handkerchief from the back pocket of his shabby
broadcloth trousers.

Hettie eyed him suspiciously. "What the hell you think you're
doin'?"

"Something we should have done when we first started out."

Evans may have been a doctor and a connoisseur of fine
brandy and literature, but he'd been a boxer in his younger

days. He was fast, and he was strong. Before Hettie knew what was happening, he'd grabbed the woman by her hair, steadied her, and wrapped the neckerchief around her head, inserting it into her mouth as a gag, and tied it.

Hettie jerked around furiously and snapped like a rabid dog against the cloth in her mouth.

"There, now we should have a quieter ride," Evans said, putting Faustus back up beside Sweets. "Shall we continue, Sheriff?"

"I like your bedside manner, Doc," Stillman said, touching spurs to the bay's flanks.

CHAPTER 9

"I admire a man who takes such pleasure in his toil that he hums while he works," quipped Doc Evans as he, Stillman, Hettie, and the outlaw woman's deceased gang pulled up in front of Auld's Livery & Feed Barn on First Street in Clantick.

It was six o'clock, and the sun was low, but the flies were out, buzzing around the two cadavers sprawled atop makeshift counters comprised of planks stretched across sawhorses against the large, gray barn's front wall, right of the open double doors that fairly blew the smell of hay, straw, horse flesh, and ammonia into the street. As Stillman drew Sweets up in front of the opening, he peered into the barn's interior, the thick, early evening shadows of which were relieved by two flickering lamps hanging by ropes from rafters.

Auld, a big, bearded German liveryman who doubled as the town's undertaker, was hunkered over a half-made casket propped on sawhorses in the barn's broad main alley, about six feet from the entrance. Auld's fat tabby cat, Gustav, sat atop a large, portable tool chest and workbench on casters, which sat against a ceiling support post behind the big German.

As Evans had noted, Auld was whistling happily as he hammered a sideboard onto the casket atop the sawhorses. Nails bristled from the tangle of beard around his bearded lips.

Auld, being hard of hearing, apparently hadn't heard the horses pull up in front of the barn. Gustav studied the newcomers dubiously, blinking his yellow eyes, which were touched with tiny crescents of reflected lamplight, and then jumped down off the workbench with a mewling groan. The cat, who served as the liveryman's ears, rubbed up against the big German's left ankle. Auld turned to look at the cat and then jerked his head toward the front of the barn.

"Ah, Sheriff Stillman!" said the big German in his heavy accent. "What you got there?" He was turning his head this way and that, trying to get a look at the horses behind Stillman and Evans.

"I was about to ask you the same thing," Stillman said, swinging down from Sweets's back.

"I'm hungry, Sheriff," Hettie said from her perch on a gelding. "I'm so hollowed out I feel like my backbone's carvin' notches out of my belly. I know my rights. You gotta feed me. I'll warn you right now—I might not look like it, but I got the appetite of a Russian mule-skinner."

Stillman, who'd removed Evans's gag from the girl's mouth a half hour ago, so she could drink water, only half-heard the girl. He was more interested in the two dead men in front of the barn than Hettie's sundry complaints. As he walked over to where they were laid out, Evans dismounted his chestnut and followed him. Auld limped over, as well, the fat tabby cat now riding on the German's thick right shoulder.

Stillman inspected the two dead men, recognizing neither one. Both wore empty holsters, however. Both had died from lead poisoning. At least two shots apiece. Judging by the apparent stiffness of their limbs, the opaqueness of their eyes, the waxiness of their skin, and the blue of their lips, they'd both been dead for a good day, possibly two days.

"You hear me, Stillman?" Hettie said in her snotty tone.

"Hobble your lip or I'll let Doc gag you again," Stillman said distractedly, turning from the dead men to Auld. "Who're these fellas and who shot 'em?" Since he'd cleaned up the town two years ago, there'd only been a handful of killings, but Stillman took each killing as a personal insult. Every killing in his town meant he wasn't doing his job.

"Ja, they come in earlier," the big German said, scratching the back of his head beneath his narrow-brimmed, conical, canvas hat with the claw end of a hammer. "Tall man in a black suit brought them in. Was lookin' for you. Leon—he got called out to the old Paulson place. Old Leo Paulson's hired man, Ernie, came in to fetch Leon quick. Old Paulson was drunk and threatenin' to hang himself in his barn again, and the hired man and Mrs. Paulson were fit to be tied."

Auld was absently stroking the fat tabby on his shoulder and shuttling his gaze between the impressive albeit wild-looking girl sitting the horse behind Stillman, and the five dead men sprawled over the saddles of their horses lined up in the street behind Hettie. The German's eyes didn't seem to know where they wanted to settle more, though prospective business seemed to win out, at least momentarily.

"Son of a biscuit—what you got there on them horses?" he asked, widening his eyes with unconcealed jubilation. "More business for Auld?"

The cat seemed happy, as well, for it shook itself and then lifted its left front paw, licked it, and scrubbed barn dirt from its ear, as though the new business required a celebratory bath.

"Have you ever seen a happier businessman?" Evans asked Stillman, who was still inspecting the two dead men.

"They're all yours, Emil," Stillman told the German.

"Two dollars for the coffins and another dollar for burial?" Auld wanted to clarify his terms.

Evans chuckled. "If you can call dropping a cadaver into an unmarked, three-foot hole 'burial.' "

Auld wrinkled his nose at the sawbones. "Those are my terms. The town council—they better not squawk!"

"Oh, they'll squawk, but I'll see you're paid," Stillman said, turning to the big German. "I wanna know a little more about the man who brought those two into town. Bounty hunter?"

"Ja, I think so." Auld frowned and tugged at the thick, spade-shaped beard drooping from his chin. "Or, no. I don't know who he was. He was tall and he had a hook for an arm. About your age, maybe, I don't know."

"A hook?"

"Ja. Said to tell you he was over at the Drovers." Auld had said this last while strolling over toward the five horses bedecked with dead men, the German's dark-blue eyes sparkling with the eager anticipation of a child on Christmas morning. "Who you got here, Sheriff?"

"Them are my boys, Mr. Auld," Hettie said. "Best gang a girl could ever hope to ride with though they couldn't play poker for beans. And they never could shoot straight while intoxicated, either. Thus, their current condition. You treat 'em right, you hear? That's Johnny Vermilion there, and his brother, Arthur. I'm Hettie Styles, and I'm right nasty, and I'll get nastier if I see you layin' my boys out in the street for everybody to gawk at, like you done with them other two."

"Doc?" said a young woman's distant voice. "Doc Evans, is that you over there?"

Stillman turned to see a young woman in a plain, cream-colored dress trimmed with a spray of brown print flowers, and a white apron, approaching the livery barn from the east, coming at a slant from the other side of the street. Her dark-blond hair piled into a bun atop her head but with several sausage curls dancing along her cheeks, glittered in the day's rapidly weakening salmon-green light.

A short, full-hipped, round-faced girl—plain but not unattractive—she was Evelyn Vincent, the waitress from Sam Wa's Café. Evelyn, mid-twenties, was one of those vivacious people whose natural curiosity dictated they keep a firm finger on the pulse of their town, so that if you wanted to know the news and didn't have the most recent edition of the Clantick newspaper, *The Courant,* near at hand, you need only drift over to Sam Wa's for the day's special and a chat with the busy, pragmatic, loquacious, and curious Miss Vincent.

Although she had a troubled past, one which Stillman had helped her put behind her, as he'd put his own behind him, Evelyn knew every person in town and probably in the county, as well. And Stillman didn't know a soul who didn't like her.

"Who's that?" Evans asked, probably having trouble seeing in the dusk with only one good eye and the other obscured by swelling and a cracked spectacle lens.

"Doc?" The girl came running, holding her skirt above her ankles.

"Evelyn—is that you?"

"Oh, Doc!"

The horses fidgeted and started as the girl rushed past them. Stillman quickly grabbed Sweets's reins to hold the mount, and the others tied to him, in place. Evelyn threw her arms around Evans's back, hugging him tightly, briefly.

"I heard from Leon what happened! Oh, look at you! Look what they did to your face!"

"I'm fine, Evelyn," the doc said, chuckling and giving the girl's cheek a brotherly peck. "I'm just fine, thanks to Ben and the Harmons. What I need is a belt, a bath, another belt or two or three, and a good night's sleep. Think I'll lock my doors tonight," the sawbones added, giving Stillman a wry glance.

His sleep had been interrupted the previous night by Johnny Vermilion and Zeke Lancaster, who'd come to town to fetch the doctor for Arthur.

"That eye looks terribly sore, Doc," Evelyn said, reaching up and gently placing an index finger on the swollen area. "Oh,

Doc, your poor glasses."

"Yes, well, I will be needing a new lens, won't I?" Evans said, unhooking the bows from his ears to inspect the lens. "Fortunately, I have a spare pair at home."

"You come on back to Sam's with me right now," Evelyn ordered. "I have a bottle of that brandy you like. You can have a few belts of that while I fetch some steak to put on that eye. And that bottom lip could use a stitch or two!"

"Ah, hell, the lip's fine," Evans said.

"I can stitch it for you, Doc. Remember how you taught me?"

"No stitches," Evans said. "I promised myself I'd never allow my flesh to be pierced again once I'd left the boxing ring. But that brandy and steak sound fine as frog hair."

The doctor glanced from Stillman to Hettie. "Ben, do you need any help here . . . with your prisoner?"

"He's gonna need all kinds of help if he doesn't feed me soon," Hettie grumbled, threatening Stillman. "That sure as hell doesn't look like any old widow, Doc. Does that old widow know about *her*?" She arched a brow at Evelyn.

"Who is this?" Evelyn wanted to know, favoring Hettie with a reproving scowl.

"Best not look at me, Missy," Hettie said. "I'm the devil in a brown blouse. I'm evil. Even my folks told me so. But you go ahead and pass it around town all you like." She raised her voice, looking around. "I'll pay five hundred dollars to any man who thinks he's got the *cojones* to bust me out of Stillman's jail. Five hundred dollars! Five hundred dollars for cutting me free of Stillman's picket pin, and I'll throw in a couple of free pokes, to boot!"

"Good Lord," Evelyn said.

"Close your ears, my good girl," Evans told Evelyn.

Evelyn turned to Stillman. "You all right, Ben?"

"I'm fine, Evelyn. And I'll *be* fine."

"Fay was looking for you awhile ago. She came into Sam Wa's. She was upset. Stemmed from a visit she got."

"Visit?"

"Apparently the man who shot those two dead men over yonder came to your place looking for you. He gave Fay quite a chill. She wasn't all that fond of remaining in the house alone afterwards, so she brought Little Ben down here to town, and she and I had pie and coffee together."

Stillman had tied Sweets to a hitching post. He squared his shoulders at Evelyn and poked his hat off his forehead, worry raking him. His voice low, pitched with dread. "He didn't hurt her, did he?"

"No, nothing like that."

Hettie said, "I'm bored and hungry, Sheriff."

Ignoring his prisoner, Stillman said, "Did Fay have a name for this visitor she had up at the house, Evelyn?"

The waitress looked pensive. "Battles. Jacob Battles. Used a middle name, but I can't remember what it was."

"Henry," Stillman said, half to himself, tendrils of foreboding wrapping around him. "Jacob Henry Battles."

"And just who is this Jacob Henry Battles?" asked Evans.

"Clyde!" Another woman called for the doctor.

"Oh, no," Stillman thought he heard Evans say as he turned to see a chaise, top down, behind a large sorrel gelding, rolling toward the livery barn from the west.

Stillman recognized the horse and buggy as belonging to Katherine Kemmett. Leon McMannigle was riding along beside the wagon on his willowy steeldust, the wan light glinting off the badge on the deputy's black leather vest.

"Clyde!" the widow exclaimed as she drew the chaise to a halt near where Evans and Evelyn Vincent stood.

Stillman saw the waitress sheepishly remove her hand from

the doctor's coat sleeve.

"Katherine, I'm fine," Evans said as the woman set the buggy's brake and then stepped down into the street. She wore a pink dress and crocheted red shawl as well as a small, black straw hat trimmed with silk flowers. A paisley-patterned reticule dangled from her gloved right wrist. "Oh, Clyde—Leon told me you'd been kidnapped!"

"Well, I wouldn't exactly call it 'kidnapped,' but I was strongly urged to—"

"Oh, my goodness," Katherine exclaimed, looking around, her even-featured face with round, practical eyes and stalwart nose becoming pale, "look at all these *dead men*! My God, what happened here? And, oh, Clyde—look at your face!" the woman intoned, rising up onto her tiptoes, sandwiching the doctor's jaws between her gloved hands, and inspecting his sundry scrapes, swellings, and bruises.

"Oh, gosh! Oh, my gosh, look what they *did* to you!" Katherine turned to the waitress, who now stood a ways back from Evans. "Evelyn, did you *see*?"

"Yes, I saw, Mrs. Kemmett. It's terrible what they did to poor Doc."

"I'll be all right, Katherine. Evelyn was just going to—"

"Nonsense. You won't be troubling young Evelyn anymore. I'm here now. You trained me to take care of folks, Clyde, and now I reckon I'm going to have to take care of you. Climb up into the buggy, and I'll drive you home and get you bathed, fed, and fixed up good as new."

As Katherine hooked her left arm around Evans's right one, and began leading him to the buggy, Evans glanced over his shoulder at the waitress and said, "Thanks, Evelyn. I reckon I won't trouble you for that steak. I got a side of beef out in the keeper shed at home."

Stillman absently ruminated that it probably wasn't so much

the steak but the brandy that the doctor was concerned about. Katherine Kemmett had done—and was no doubt continuing to do—everything in her power to render the sawbones a teetotaler before they were married next month. Despite hearing that Jacob Henry Battles was in town, the sheriff couldn't help but chuckle wryly to himself over Evans's predicament.

"Oh, it was no trouble at all, Doc," Evelyn said. "Just wanting to lend a hand. I know you're in good hands with Mrs. Kemmett. You go on home and get a good night's sleep."

"Thank you, Evelyn," said Katherine Kemmett, as she released the buggy's break and sank into the quilted leather seat.

As Katherine slapped the reins against the sorrel's back, Evelyn waved and called, "I'll stop by sometime tomorrow and see how you're doin', Doc!"

Evans doffed his bowler hat to the girl as he passed.

Still mounted on and tied to her horse, Hettie stared after the chaise and said, "There goes a sad man. I'd have bet silver cartwheels against navy beans he was wantin' to go home with you, Miss Sugar Honey." She grinned lasciviously at Evelyn.

"Don't mind her," Stillman told the young waitress. "She said it best herself—she's bad. Prides herself on it. And I apologize for her still being on the street. I intend to get this polecat locked up straightaway."

Evelyn's mind seemed elsewhere. It was as though she'd only half-heard, half-understood what Hettie had said. She gave Stillman a wan smile, and said, "I'd best get back to Sam's. Still got some cleanin' up to do before I head on back to the boardinghouse. Good night, Ben."

"Good night, Evelyn," Stillman said, frowning as the waitress turned and retraced her steps to the other side of the street, heading to Sam Wa's little frame eatery two blocks east.

If Stillman hadn't been so preoccupied with more important

matters, he would have ruminated longer on his vague suspicion that Evelyn might have been more disappointed than she was letting on about the doc riding off with Katherine Kemmett instead of joining her, Evelyn, over at Sam Wa's.

"Well, I see you made out all right," Leon said, inspecting the dead men sprawled across their saddles. He glanced up at Hettie. "She one of these . . . uh . . . fellas?"

"As you can see, Deputy," Hettie said, "I am no 'fella.' "

Leon stared up at her, shaking his head, "No, you ain't at that. You ain't at that."

"Be careful of this one," Stillman warned his deputy.

"Oh, you don't have to tell me twice. I just seen her and I can already recognize trouble, despite the purty packagin'."

Hettie told the black deputy to do something physically impossible to himself. McMannigle merely sighed, brushed a fist across his nose, and shook his head.

"Everything all right out at the Paulson place?" Stillman asked him.

"Yeah, we got ole Leo to bed without hangin' hisself. Me and his hired kid got all the weapons and rope out of the cabin. I declare, every time Leo goes on a drinkin' tear, he threatens to kill himself, and sends his poor ole wife to the rafters! I asked Mrs. Kemmett to ride along and counsel the poor woman, since they're good friends from church."

"Good thinkin'," Stillman said, handing Leon the reins of Hettie's horse. "Take her over to the jail and lock her up good and tight, will ya?" He removed the loot-filled saddlebags from over Sweets's back and draped them over the back of McMannigle's steeldust. "And lock these up in a separate cell. Loot from the Sulphur Bank. I'll send a telegram to the lawman down there in the morning."

"Where you goin'—home?"

"Eventually," Stillman said, sliding his Henry rifle from his saddle boot. He pumped a fresh round into the chamber and lowered the hammer to half-cock. "But first I gotta see a man over at the Drovers."

He told Auld to tend all the horses, and then he headed for the saloon where he hoped to find Jacob Henry Battles.

CHAPTER 10

"What's with all the fresh beef out there, Ben?" asked Elmer Burk as Stillman pushed through the batwing doors and walked into the Drovers Saloon.

Stillman looked around. It being a weeknight, and relatively early, there were only a handful of regulars either occupying the tables or standing in a single clump at the bar. Stillman stared through the wafting tobacco smoke toward the back of the drinking hall, where a lone customer sat at a table behind and to the right of the cold, potbelly stove, which hadn't been fired since last May.

It was nearly as dark inside the saloon as it was outside. Burk, being a skinflint, was slow to light his kerosene lamps. Only one flickered against a ceiling support post near the bar. The lone drinker was mostly in shadow, but Stillman knew he was the man he was looking for.

Burk and the other customers watched Stillman with mute interest as the lawman strode forward, spurs chinging. He kicked several chairs out of the way before he stopped in front of the table at which the lone drinker slouched, one boot propped on a chair, his hat covering the breech of the rifle resting on the table near his right elbow.

"Marshal Stillman, hello. Er . . . but it's not marshal, anymore, is it? You're a county sheriff, now, I understand."

Stillman rested his rifle barrel on his shoulder and glared down at the smiling face of Jacob Henry Battles, the man's gray-blue eyes reflecting the few, flickering rays of lantern light that reached this far back in the room. "What's a hydrophobic old stock-killin' dog like you doin' running off your leash, Battles?"

Battles turned his half-filled shot glass in his fingers and canted his head toward the open bottle of Sam Clay on the table near the '66 Yellowboy Winchester. "Can I buy you a drink, Ben? You don't mind if I call you Ben—do you? I mean, after all we've been to each other, I certainly think we should be on a first-name basis."

Stillman glanced at the stiff arm angled across Battles's belly. The arm ended in a metal hook curving down out of the sleeve of the man's black wool coat so old that it owned a dull copper sheen.

"Answer the question, Battles? How come you're not still penned up in Deer Lodge? The judge gave you a thirty-year sentence and would have given you life if more folks had been willin' to testify against you."

"It's called parole, Ben. I did twelve of the thirty years. Territorial parole board let me out on good behavior. I suppose they figured I was too old to do much harm." Battles raised the hook. "An old man with only one arm can't cause much trouble. Why waste the money on keepin' him locked up? Hell, I couldn't even work in the rock quarries."

Stillman tried to fathom that a parole board would release a man who'd killed as many men as Battles had. There'd been twelve—mostly stockmen—that Stillman knew about. Fifteen and twenty years ago, Battles had been a favorite regulator hired by large, corrupt stock associations to "weed out" other, mostly smaller cattlemen or sheep men whom the associations had considered to be encroaching on the territory of the associations' members.

But Battles, trained as a sharpshooter during his time fighting for the Confederacy in the War Between the States, had killed more than stockmen. He'd killed anyone—small-town mayors or city council members and local lawmen—anyone the large cattle syndicates had deemed their enemies. He'd used a Sharps Big Fifty for long-range work, and an Allen pepperbox revolver for close encounters in dark alleys or shadowy hotel hallways.

It had taken Stillman three years, once he'd been assigned to Battles's trail, to run the man down. Jacob Henry Battles had been as slippery as smoke on the wind.

"Rest assured I'll be checkin' that out first thing in the morning, Battles." Stillman had a frustrated feeling that the man was telling the truth. If Battles had escaped from the territorial pen down at Deer Lodge, he'd have a pile of telegrams informing him so. However, no one informed local lawmen when notorious killers were freed from their cages. "Till then, I'd like to know what the hell you're doin' here in my town and county, and what, especially, you think you're doin' *up at my house terrorizin' my wife.*"

"Oh, I wasn't terrorizing Fay, Marsh . . . I mean, Sheriff. No, no, not at all. That was never my style. When I rode into town with those two carcasses that I'm sure you've seen by now, and discovered your office unoccupied, I heard that you might have gone home for lunch. I was in a hurry, which I think is understandable, given our history and my recent incarceration, to explain the dead men as soon as possible. I merely went to your house to find you and assure you that those two men out there in front of Auld's barn were killed in self-defense. They were out to long-loop reputations for themselves."

He chuckled and sipped his bourbon. "I certainly don't want to risk having to spend even another day behind bars."

Stillman set his Henry on the table and leaned over it. "Well, that's where you're goin', you sonofabitch."

Battles frowned.

Stillman grinned. "That's right. I'm lockin' you up, Battles . . . until I can thoroughly investigate the shooting you were involved in. My lawman's intuition tells me that just as soon as you were let out of your cage, you went back to the only thing you know—killin'. That intuition tells me you killed those men in cold blood. Leastways, till I have time to give the matter a thorough investigation, I'll be turning the key on you, Battles." No better way to keep an eye on the man until he could send him on his way, if not back to Deer Lodge.

"That won't be necessary, Sheriff."

Stillman looked to his right as one of the men standing at the bar had turned around to face him. He was a young man, a few inches under six feet, in a brown and white steer hide vest. He wore a black hat and black denims, and he had a black holster thonged low on his right thigh from which a Colt Lightning .38 revolver with staghorn grips bristled.

The kid smiled, eyes twinkling, cheeks dimpling. He had a permanent dimple on his chin. If he'd been standing there earlier, Stillman hadn't seen him. Kansas Kate was standing close beside him, one of her stiletto-heeled feet propped on the brass bar rail.

The kid wrapped an arm around the girl's bare shoulders, drawing her close beside him, grinning, and said, "I seen the whole thing, Sheriff. Just happened to be there in Big John's place. I'm sure you know that little, rat-infested waterin' hole southeast of here, in the Breaks? Don't think it's gotta name. Just the same, I was there when those two no-accounts attract-in' flies out by Mr. Auld's Livery thought they was gonna gun down Mr. Battles there—er, the Devil's Left-Hand Man, I should say—and get their names in the newspapers."

"The Devil's Left-Hand Man, huh?" Stillman straightened as he appraised the grinning youngster. "Who're you?"

"Name's Miller. Gandy Miller. Cowhand when I can get the

work." Miller raised a beer mug to Stillman and took a sip from it. He grinned even while drinking and licking the foam from his clean-shaven upper lip. "I was driftin' through the Breaks, lookin' fer work."

"And you saw the shooting?"

"Sure did. Stopped for a beer. Then two saddle tramps challenged Mr. Battles there—I recognized him from the illustrated newspapers—and drew on him. If he hadn't got his rifle raised before they got their pistols drawn, it'd likely be Mr. Battles lyin' face up on a pine plank, waitin' for his wooden overcoat to be fitted."

The kid chuckled at that and squeezed Kansas Kate tighter. The girl looked up at him, and then she laughed, too, giving the boy's arm a playful slap.

No one else in the place said a word. All conversations had stopped when Stillman had approached Battles's table. The bystanders were standing or sitting, shuttling their gazes from Stillman to Battles and over to the kid standing at the bar with a beer in one hand, his other arm wrapped around the whore, smiling an innocent, unctuous grin.

"Will you be willin' to sign an affidavit?"

"Well . . . I don't know . . . what's an affa . . . um, what'd you call it?"

"A written testimonial. You write it and sign it. If you lie on it, you get punished the same way you would if you lied under oath at a court trial. Lyin' on it would be called perjury, and it could cost you a year behind bars."

"Sure, sure. I'll sign one o' them. I wouldn't have no reason to lie, Sheriff Stillman. I'm just tryin' to do the right thing— that's all." Miller glanced around the room, grinning his pride in himself and looking for approval.

Still, no one said a word.

Miller raised his glass again to Stillman, and drank. The kid's slurps were the only sounds in the room.

Stillman stared hard at Miller. There was something about the kid he wasn't swallowing. But maybe it was only because Stillman didn't want to believe him. At any rate, there wasn't much Stillman could do under the circumstances except take Gandy Miller's affidavit. In the meantime, he had no legal excuse to turn the key on Battles.

Stillman felt his ear tips burn with frustration and anger as he turned back to the old killer, who sat staring up at the sheriff with a smug half-smile on his mustached mouth.

"You clear out of town tomorrow, Battles. Tomorrow, you hear? By noon."

"I heard you, Sheriff."

"By noon."

"Yes, I heard. You want me out of town by noon tomorrow. Are you sure I can't buy you a drink? You seem to still have your neck in a hump. Nothin' like a shot of good bourbon to settle a man's hackles."

Stillman leaned forward against the table, sliding his face to within three feet of Battles's. "In the meantime, if I see you anywhere near my house or my wife or child again, I'm going to kill you. No warning, nothing. Just a bullet through your forehead and a grave in potters' field."

Battles sighed his dismay. "I'm sorry we can't be friends, Ben. I was really hoping we could."

Battles raised his shot glass to his mouth. Fury burned through Stillman. He thought of Fay, Little Ben, and imagined Battles riding up to the house with the two dead men draped over their horses. As Battles touched the shot glass to his lips, Stillman swept his left hand across his body and then back, smashing the back of that hand against Battles's hand holding the glass. The glass flew across the room to smash against the far wall beneath a hanging wooden clock, making the clock's silver pendulums clatter and clang.

Stillman continued to glare at Battles. Now the old regulator was glaring back at him, the complacent smile gone beneath the thin mustache mantling his lip.

Someone paced a hand on Stillman's right shoulder. Behind him, Leon McMannigle said quietly, reasonably, "Come on, Ben. You've had your say. Let it go for tonight."

A renewed wave of fury, this time directed at Leon, swept through Stillman. He had enough self-control not to act on it. Instead, he took a second to reflect, and, not only realizing that his deputy's advice was wise but feeling grateful that McMannigle had voiced it, the burning inside him subsided. He straightened, picked his rifle up off the table, and rested it on his right shoulder.

"Noon tomorrow," he repeated to Battles, who merely stared at him, his gray-blue eyes still hard.

Stillman glanced at the grinning Gandy Miller. "I'll see you in my office tomorrow morning."

"You got it, Sheriff," said the annoyingly affable young drover.

Stillman walked with Leon through the batwings and into the street.

"You got some history with that stranger," Leon said, scratching a long, black sideburn. "Had me a feelin'."

"It's an old story," Stillman said. "Twelve years old. Keep an eye on him, will you?"

"Sure thing."

"You get that pretty polecat locked up?"

"Yeah, but she sure gave me an earful. I learned some new words tonight."

"Lucky you got a thick skin."

They were standing in the street, which was dark now, out front of the saloon and staring off in the direction of the jailhouse. "I hope your skin's thick enough to deflect bullets, Ben."

"Why's that?"

"Apparently, that girl's done put a bounty on your head. I heard a couple of saddle tramps talkin' about it on my way over here. Five hundred dollars and a free poke!"

"Yeah, well, I'm insulted. I figured my head would be worth at least a thousand dollars and two or three pokes. Just one poke? Pshaw!"

"That's gonna be all over the county by sunup tomorrow."

"I'll worry about that bridge when I cross it." Stillman reached into his shirt pocket for his makings sack. He took his Henry under his left arm, and began building a smoke. He needed one. "You best stay in the jailhouse tonight. Them girls over at Mrs. Lee's are gonna have to go it alone. Should be quiet, it bein' a weeknight."

"Go on home and get some rest, Ben. You look tired. Maybe a little peaked."

That annoyed Stillman for no reason except that it reminded him that he *felt* yellow around the gills, and that his right arm was still feeling as though he were holding a ten-pound chunk of lead in his hand.

"Nothin' my wife can't cure," Stillman said.

"Good night, Ben." Leon strode along the street toward the jailhouse.

Stillman leaned against an awning support post until he'd finished rolling the quirley closed and had lit it. He inhaled the bracing smoke deep into his lungs, blew it out on the cooling night air, and rested his rifle on his shoulder once more. Since he'd left Sweets with Auld, and didn't feel like saddling the horse again, he'd have to walk home.

That was all right. It was a cool night.

And he had much to mull over before he got back to his and Fay's little house on the butte overlooking Clantick.

CHAPTER 11

Gandy Miller watched Stillman and his deputy leave the Drovers. The young man's heart was beating heavily. It was pumping a strange elixir through his veins.

He turned to the pretty brunette whose name he had not yet learned, and said, "I'll be right back, Sugar. Don't go takin' up with no one else now, hear?"

He took another sip of his beer, trying to slow his heart, and strolled over to the table at which Jacob Henry Battles continued to sit. Battles had been staring at Miller since Stillman had left the saloon.

The other customers had returned to their drinks, smokes, and conversations.

Battles continued to stare obliquely at Miller.

Miller said, "Mind if I sit down, sir?"

Battles voice was a low, resonate growl. "What the hell are you doin' here, Miller?"

Gandy hiked a shoulder and continued standing where the old bull buff, Stillman, had been standing, glaring down at his old enemy, Battles. Miller looked around carelessly and said, "Oh, I don't know. I figured I'd ride up and see if any of the ranchers in this neck of the Two-Bears is needin' an experienced cowhand."

"You're no more cowhand than I am, Miller."

"Why, sure I am," Miller said, chuckling. He pulled the chair out and slowly sank into it. Doing so, he kept his hands above the table, so Battles wouldn't mistake his intentions and send him flying out the batwings in a hail of hot lead.

"You followed me," Battles said. "Why?"

Miller sipped his beer and glanced at the pretty brunette whore standing with her back to the bar, watching Gandy with an expression ranging from curiosity to concern as though he'd just entered a corral containing an unbroken bronc. Which, in a sense, Miller thought he had. Of course, the whore hadn't known Miller until he'd walked into the saloon a few minutes ago, just before Stillman had. The girl's primary worry was most likely that trouble might break out and interfere with her night's earnings, not for the health of a young man she didn't know.

"Yeah, all right—I followed you, Mr. Battles. Good thing I did, too—don't you agree?"

Battles turned his head a little to one side and furled his brows as he sized up Gandy Miller. Miller thought the old bull buff from the wrong side of the law looked more concerned about him, Miller, than he had about Stillman.

"Oh, don't worry," Gandy said, lifting Battles's bottle up off the table and tipping it over the old regulator's empty shot glass. "I ain't gonna try nothin' like what Queen and Two-Dog tried. I seen what happened to them. No, sir, I ain't lookin' for no reputation. At least, not the kind you might suspect."

"What kind, then?"

"Oh, it's nothin' like that!" Gandy said, raising his hands, palms out. "No, no—make no mistake, Mr. Battles. My only interest is in you and your life in general, and, well, maybe . . . I might have just a little interest in seein' how things turn out between you two."

"Between whom?"

"Why, between you and Sheriff Stillman, of course. You see, I done read about the both of you when I was still a kid, hidin' them old yellow-covered books under the cot in my side-shed bedroom back home in St. Paul so's my ma wouldn't find 'em and take a willow switch to my bare ass."

"I see." Battles threw back half his bourbon. "You think I've come here to tangle with Stillman."

"Ain't ya? Just now I thought you was gonna go at it like Kilkenny cats!"

Battles shook his head and then threw back the last of his shot. "My intentions were just as I told the good sheriff himself. I'm merely here to settle down and start a new life for myself up here in this big, open country far from the madding crowd."

"Even if that was true, Mr. Battles," Gandy said, "you heard what the sheriff done said about noon tomorrow."

"Yeah, I heard," Battles said. "But don't mind Stillman. He's still livin' in the old days, when lawmen could do that sort of thing and get away with it. Times have changed. He can't tell me where I can or can't sink a taproot."

Gandy's eyes were fairly popping out of his head. "You don't intend to obey!"

Battles stood and donned his hat.

"You don't, do ya?" Miller persisted, unable to keep the glee from his voice. "There ain't no way Jacob Henry Battles would take an order from a county sheriff. 'Specially not the same one that shot his arm off!"

Battles adjusted the angle of his hat and then hiked his rifle onto his shoulder. He adjusted a bulge under his coat near his right side, which was probably the old Allen pepperbox revolver he'd been known to carry for close-up work, and kicked his chair back under the table.

"Boy, you're startin' to put a bee under my saddle."

Miller raised his hands higher above the table. "I do apologize, Mr. Battles!"

"From now on, stay away from me, hear? My life is no spectator sport." Battles arched his brows with menace. "Makin' like it is, you're gonna crawl my hump."

"Ah, hell, now you're angry. Here let me make it up to ya," Miller said, remaining in his chair and looking up at the old gunman, who was beginning to look a little weary now at day's end, his leathery cheeks sagging slightly and some red showing around his eyes. "Can I poke my hand into my vest pocket for a dollar? I'd like to buy you a mattress dance with that purty brown-haired dove over yonder."

Miller glanced at the dove, who scowled back at him.

"It'd be an honor for me to do that for you, sir—to buy a whore for none other than Jacob Henry Battles himself!"

Battles stared at the kid for another two beats. Then he wagged his head and gave a rueful chuckle. He sized up the whore. "No, thanks. She's purtier'n a speckled pup, but . . ." Battles grabbed his bottle off the table, and stuffed it into a coat pocket. ". . . I don't go in for saloon girls." He pinched his hat brim to the girl, who angrily crossed her arms on her corset. "I do apologize, dear. I just prefer the parlor house variety of *dove du pave.*"

He moved around the table, holding his rifle on his shoulder. Glancing back at Miller again, he said, "Kid, I don't trust you any farther than I could throw you uphill in a Gulf Coast hurricane. So you take my advice and keep your nose out of my business." He spread his lips back from his large, yellow teeth. "Or I'll be carvin' another notch on my old pepperbox."

Caressing the hammer of his old Winchester with his thumb, he strode out of the Drovers, the batwings clattering back into place behind him.

"Jesus jump—did you hear that?" Miller asked the girl as he sidled up to her again at the bar. "Jacob Henry Battles just threatened my life!"

The whore looked at him skeptically. "I'll be damned if you

don't look delighted."

Miller chuckled and squeezed her hand. "Let's go upstairs. I'm purely brimming over with need of bleedin' off some sap."

She pulled her hand out of his, scowling. "I don't know if I should after you tried to palm me off on that old regulator."

Miller stared at her with incredulity and wonder. "Why, you just don't understand, do you? That there was Jacob Henry Battles—the Devil's Left-Hand Man. Why, you should feel honored to pleasure such a legend!"

The pretty little brunette crossed her arms on her ample breasts again, and wrinkled her nose toward the batwings. "Old killers make my skin crawl. I've entertained my share. Takes two baths to rid me of the death stench afterwards, and several nights for the nightmares to fade. You'd best abide by what your Mr. Battles done told you and stay away from him, or you're liable to be pushin' up rocks and cactus on Boot Hill."

Stillman was tired and his right leg felt as though it were half-asleep.

That made his tramp along the trail that wound up the butte on which his little farm sat harder than it otherwise might have been. He wished he had held onto Sweets. Sometimes he stabled the bay at the farm, sometimes at Auld's. Tonight, he should have ridden him home, but he'd had too much on his mind to think about the quarter-mile walk.

The windows of their small, tight, neat frame house on the hill above him glowed beneath the dark sky sprinkled with twinkling stars. The stars looked like sugar spilled on black velvet. They looked so close that they were nearly touching, but there were millions of miles between each, he'd heard—vast, empty distances between each bright, turning world. Sometimes Stillman enjoyed looking at the stars; he enjoyed the childlike wonder with which they filled him. Sometimes, when he felt old and there was too damn much on his mind, they made him feel too small and fleeting for comfort.

He shouldn't be feeling this old, he thought, as he followed the trail up into the yard, heading for the front porch, breathing hard. He had a young wife to provide for, a child to raise . . .

He turned the doorknob. Locked. Fay often didn't customarily lock the doors, as Clantick was mostly a quiet, peaceful town. Stillman wanted her to keep the doors locked when he wasn't around, but she often forgot. Tonight, she had not. He remembered her visit from Battles.

There was a light tread inside the house. Through the window left of the door he saw a shadow slide across the living room floor half-lit by a light from the kitchen at the house's rear. The bolt slid free of the hasp, the door opened, and Stillman stepped into his young wife's open arms. Fay wrapped her arms around his waist, pressing her head against his chest.

Stillman held her tightly, moving his hands around on her back, feeling her warm breasts mashed against his belly. He kissed her forehead, smoothed her hair back from her cheeks as she looked up at him, brown eyes wide and lustrous between long, curling tendrils of her thick, chocolate hair.

"So glad you're home," she breathed.

"You all right?"

Fay nodded. She was wearing a low-cut gown with a thin wrap over her shoulders, against the night's early-autumn chill. The gown was for him, he knew. Fay often changed out of her frumpy housedresses when he was due home. She enjoyed her man's delight in her exceptional body. She also enjoyed giving him as much access to it as possible.

Far from a vamp, Fay had an earthy, hearty appetite for giving and receiving pleasure with Stillman, and she did not do so tentatively, with the lamps out, but with a frankness, adeptness, and ingenuity Stillman attributed to her French heritage as well as being raised around lusty cowpunchers on a remote horse and cattle ranch. Given Fay's dignified public persona, Stillman doubted that anyone suspected such sweaty doings in the Stillman house after sundown, and he often gave an inward chuckle when he pondered the contrast while enjoying the sweet torture of his young wife's Montana boudoir.

"Where's Little Ben?" Stillman asked her.

"Asleep."

"Did Battles frighten him?"

Fay shook her head and gave him a crooked smile. "He was probably still too distracted by his tussle with the saloon girls."

Stillman's ears warmed, and he looked down in chagrin. "I'd forgotten about that. You wouldn't have wanted me to leave him with Leon, would you?"

Fay chuckled. "Leon would have him chewing plug tobacco. No, I'm sure the girls were quite entertaining. At least, when I found him upstairs in the Drovers with his harem, Little Ben looked downright enchanted."

Stillman laughed. "Chip off the old block."

Fay took him by the hand. "Come on into the kitchen. I have a plate on the warming rack."

Stillman grabbed her. "I have other ideas." He kissed her, pressed his hands against her back, and then slid them around her waist and up her flat belly to her full, ripe breasts. He could feel the cool curve of her flesh beneath his calloused palms. He felt her nipples begin to swell beneath the thin, low-cut frock.

Fay entangled her tongue with his, nibbled his mustache, and pulled away, breathing hard. "Later. You have to eat."

As she tugged on his hand, leading him through the parlor toward the kitchen at the house's rear, he said, "And then—"

"And then a bath," Fay said. "And, *then* . . . !"

While Stillman washed at the stand in the rear mudroom, Fay set out a plate of thickly sliced pot roast, mashed potatoes covered in gravy, and fresh peas and green beans from Fay's irrigated garden, the vegetables swimming in a thick, lightly spiced cream sauce. While Stillman ate hungrily, his sleeves rolled up his corded forearms, Fay sat across from him, a glass of chokecherry wine in her hands. She leaned forward against the table, which pushed her breasts up in her corset edged with black lace.

She watched him with an amused, loving light in her coffee-brown eyes.

He knew that sooner or later she would broach the topic. It had been hanging in the air around them since the moment she'd opened the door. He didn't have to wait long. As soon as he'd cleared his plate, she set before him a large wedge of juneberry pie mantled by a thick dollop of freshly whipped cream. Fay poured herself a fresh glass of wine and sat back down across from him as he dug into the pie and took occasional sips of black coffee from a heavy stone mug.

Fay, never known to mince words, didn't bother doing so this evening. "He's here to kill you, isn't he?"

CHAPTER 12

Stillman swallowed the pie he'd had in his mouth, took one of Fay's hands in his, and squeezed it. "No. He is not here to kill me."

"You lie, monsieur."

"Nope." In fact, Stillman didn't know if it was a lie or not, because he didn't know Battles's true intentions. He knew what the man had said, but he didn't believe him. So, he supposed, he really was lying. But keeping Fay from worrying was worth a lie or two.

She arched a skeptical brow across the table at him.

Stillman continued eating his pie. "He's just passing through. I'm not sure why he brought those two dead men up here—prison must have addled his brain—but he merely wanted to see me to explain the shooting."

Fay kept her brow raised, chin dipped, as she said in a wry, shrewd tone, "He told me he'd come here with the intention of taking up residence, monsieur."

"Yeah, well, I changed his mind. He'll be pulling foot on out of Clantick by noon tomorrow."

"Did one of your bullets take his arm?"

"I don't know whose did. There were two other lawmen riding with me, both federal boys from Dakota Territory. Battles started shooting as soon as he saw us, and rode into a box canyon. Tried shooting his way out." Stillman swallowed another bite of pie. "He didn't make it. Shouldn't have lived with all the lead in him. None of us was hurt."

"Who let him out of the pen?" Fay asked as she rose to retrieve the coffee pot.

"No, I'm done, honey," Stillman told her, dropping his fork onto his empty plate and shoving the plate and his cup away as he leaned back in his chair.

The sudden move of his right arm sent several rods of fiery pain shooting from his elbow into his wrist and up into his shoulder. He made a face, then quickly relaxed it. Fay had her back to him, but she turned away from the range to cross her arms on her breasts.

Stillman sighed, blowing his cheeks out. "That hit the spot. Hit several, in fact. As for who let the old jail rat out—I reckon it was the territorial parole board."

"So, he's on parole . . ."

"Likely will be for the rest of his life. Probably has to remain in the territory where his parole officer can keep a hackamore on him. No doubt, he's still feelin' a little shackled and off his feed. Especially since he's missin' an arm and all. If he makes the slightest misstep, he'll be back behind those strap-iron bars of Deer Lodge Pen before you can say, 'I ain't worried anymore, Ben—please take me to bed!' "

Stillman grinned.

Fay tempered her smile by chewing her lip. "All right," she said, throwing her hair back from her shoulders, giving him a good look at her well-filled corset. "But before you'll be welcome in my bed, Sheriff, you'll be taking a bath. Go on into the bathroom. I've already filled the tub with cold water. I'll be there in a minute with hot."

She had a copper kettle steaming atop the range, and as Stillman slid his chair back and rose with a wince, she turned to it and opened the stove door to add another log.

"Damn slave driver is who I'm livin' with," he grumbled.

"Con artist, more like. This is blackmail!"

"Shhh!" Fay hushed him from behind. "If you awaken Little Ben, you'll be rocking him back to sleep and you *will not* be taking my clothes off!" Her French accent, mostly undetectable, became pronounced when Fay's passions were aroused.

Stillman winced again. As he strode past the stairs, he bent an ear toward the second story, and was relieved not to hear any stirrings from above. He continued into the washroom under the stairs, and took his clothes off.

He'd converted the little room, once a pantry, into a modern bathroom with a large, porcelain tub. He'd run a pipe from the windmill on the house's east side through the bathroom wall. The pipe was capped with a small, metal trapdoor, which, once lifted, allowed cool, fresh well water to run from the windmill and stock tank into the tub. He'd outfitted the tub with a drain connected to a pipe that ran back through the wall and out onto the ground.

Stillman lowered himself into the cool water. He'd taken so many cold-water baths in his life that he didn't bother to wait for the warm to be added. He dunked his head and, moving gingerly so as not to cause any more lightning strikes in his right side, though he felt a constant, heavy tingling in that arm and leg, used a cloth and a cake of castile soap to wash his face and neck and behind his neck and ears.

As he did, he hoped that during the imminent bedroom festivities, Fay wouldn't suspect the trouble he was in. He felt inclined to make love to his wife despite his physical discomfort, for Fay could stoke his stove like no other woman he could imagine. But he didn't want her to know about the spasms.

She'd known the bullet had grieved him before, and they'd discussed the surgery that Doc Evans had suggested and that would have to be performed by a special surgeon from Denver. Stillman had agreed to the procedure, though it was risky, and even if it cured the spasms, it would lay him up for a good two months at least. It would keep him out of the saddle for half a year, but there was also a strong possibility that he'd never be able to ride a horse again.

What's more, the operation was costly and would likely wipe out what little money he'd saved.

Having agreed to make the trip to Denver, he'd then decided to postpone it until after Little Ben was born. Since the child had come into the world, he and Fay hadn't discussed the surgery. Ben had a feeling that she, knowing the risk, had suppressed the idea as much as he had, unconsciously willing it away, though of course that wasn't possible. Today had been the first time the spasms had assaulted him in nearly a year.

Would they assault him again when he was making love to his wife?

Fay came in holding a lamp. She set it on a shelf and then knelt beside him, soaked and lathered a brush, and scrubbed his back. He reached back, grabbed her arm, and pulled her over beside the tub. He drew her to him, kissed her, and slid the straps of her dress down her arms.

She groaned as she continued kissing him, dropped the brush on the floor, and reached into the tub. While she teased him, manipulated him gently, his blood rose.

"Do you like that?" she whispered in his ear, tauntingly, so close that he could feel her saliva crackling.

"Oh, yeah."

"Such sweet pain, is it not, monsieur?"

Stillman leaned back in the tub and dug his fingers into the sides.

"Shall we continued this upstairs?" she asked very quietly, so that he could barely hear her above the crackling, wet sounds she was making with her hand half in and half out of the water.

He turned to her, his heart thudding. He stared at her short, refined nose, her wide-set eyes, which were slightly crossed now as she tortured him with her soft, warm hand. He looked at her wide mouth, her lips slightly parted, showing the pink, wet tip of her tongue. The dimple in her chin was touched with shadow. He leaned farther over in the tub to lick a small mole on her neck, his rising blood growing hot.

"Yeah," he said. "Upstairs . . ."

Upstairs, by candlelight and while their baby slept in a crib near the open door of their room, he watched her shed her dress slowly, teasing him, watching his desire grow once again. Her body was long-limbed, smooth as ivory, curved in all the right places. The shape of her face, her playful brown eyes, short nose, and full lips were all distinctly French, as was the passion he could feel burning inside her, revealed by the swollen breasts, the lights in her eyes.

When her dress and the few undergarments she'd been wearing were on the floor, she laughed, jumped into bed, breasts jouncing, and winced at the crib, hoping she hadn't awakened Little Ben.

When the infant didn't stir, she pressed her lips to Stillman's.

He massaged the ripe orbs, ran his hands down her belly, which had been so full with their child a year ago. What a miracle that had been. He'd never loved her, wanted her more. Her stomach was nearly flat again due in no small part to the hard work she put in around the farm, inside and out of the house, tending the chickens and her garden, and the horseback riding she enjoyed whenever she got the chance. A couple of times since the baby was born, she'd ridden out to White-Tail Creek to ride with Crystal in the Two-Bears; sometimes she rode alone in the buttes along the Milk.

"Shall we put another one in there?" she asked as Stillman kissed her belly button and then slid his tongue down lower.

She gave a shudder of pleasure, and touched him.

Stillman groaned as lances of sheer pleasure spoked in all directions.

"Might be a good idea," he said, gently shoving her onto her back, watching her thick, chocolate hair fan out across her pillow. "Let's put it on the warming rack. Tonight, let's just enjoy tonight, huh?"

She gave him a mock military salute and then welcomed him into her arms, wrapping her legs around his own.

As they made love, he vaguely considered the idea of them having another child. That led to a vague consideration of the spasms, which he was no longer feeling. There was a slight tightness in his right forearm, maybe a little numbness in that knee, but that was all.

Hopefulness swelled in him as did his endless love and desire for the beautiful woman groaning beneath him.

"Oh," Fay cried softly, turning her head on the pillow, closing her eyes.

Later, when she'd bathed them both with a sponge, she returned to bed and wrapped herself around him, resting her head on his chest.

"French women have an expression to describe lovemaking like that," Fay said quietly. "My mother shared it with me when I became a woman. *J'ai couché avec le diable*. I feel as though I have just lain with the devil."

Stillman lifted his head from his pillow. "Huh?"

Fay chuckled and nibbled his mustache. "Don't worry. It is a compliment."

"Oh," he sighed.

"What's wrong?" she whispered.

Again, Stillman frowned. Then he chuckled. "What makes you think somethin's wrong?"

"When you make love like that, monsieur, with such intensity even after a hard day's work, I know something is eating you." She rose up onto an elbow and ran her fingers threw his chest hair. "What is it?"

As Stillman opened his mouth to speak, there was a strange tinkling sound. Almost simultaneous with the curious, eerie noise, a rifle's shrill bark reached his ears from outside. There was the loud *whump!* of a bullet tearing into the wall over the dresser on the left side of the bed, and then Stillman saw the round hole in the window to his right.

Little Ben began shrieking in his crib, and Fay screamed.

CHAPTER 13

Stillman leaped out of bed and plucked Little Ben out of his crib, holding him against his chest and backing away from the window that was sporting a hole in it. Fay dashed toward him, ignoring his shouted warning to, "Stay down!" She took the boy from Stillman and began rocking the crying child against her breasts.

Stillman shielded them both from the window and shoved Fay down to her rump on the floor, ordering her to stay down and away from the window while he went after the shooter. Fay cooed to the crying boy, continuing to rock him, as Stillman grabbed a pair of balbriggans out of a bureau drawer, and stepped into them. As he pulled the longhandles up his arms, he glanced at the window over which the bullet-torn curtain was drawn.

The red lace curtains were ominously still. Outside, Stillman could hear nothing beneath his son's crying.

He reminded Fay to stay down as he ran through the bedroom and into the hall, Fay yelling behind, "Ben, you be careful!"

Once he'd donned his boots and his hat and his Henry rifle, Stillman hurried to the mudroom door, kicking a table leg and a kitchen chair in the darkness, and stopped, tipping his head toward the door, listening to the night beyond it. The shooter would know he'd rush outside, and might be waiting.

Beyond the door, the night was eerily quiet.

Stillman slowly turned the porcelain doorknob, drew the door open, quickly bounded outside, and, crouching low, stepped to the left. He pressed his back up hard against the house's rear wall. He extended the Henry straight out from his right shoulder, ready to shoot at the first flash of a gun.

Gradually, his heart racing, he eased the tension in his trigger finger. The flash didn't come. As his eyes adjusted to the darkness relieved by starlight and a moon rising low in the east, he was able to make out the chicken coop with its surrounding wire fence and the buggy shed, which he used as a stable, fifty yards straight out from the house, beyond the privy. He could see no one anywhere around him.

To his far right rose a dull thud, as though someone had kicked a stone.

Stillman ran out from the east side of the house. There were some scraggly cottonwoods, about sixty yards from the house. Stillman drew to within twenty feet of the trees, and slowed, holding the rifle out again from his right shoulder. He was beginning to feel a sharp tightness in his arm and leg and down his back. It was as though a winch inside him were being cranked, tightening a rope holding all his muscles and nerves together.

The rifle grew heavy. It sagged in his arms. He nudged it up, urging strength back into his arm and hand. He was sweating under his longhandles.

As he gained the trees, his left boot clinked on something. He stooped and picked up a .44 cartridge casing. Holding it up to the starlight, he saw that it was a rimfire cartridge, a common type used in Stillman's Henry but also used in a .66 Winchester Yellowboy repeater, which was the rifle that Stillman had seen on Battles's table in the Drovers earlier. Most newer rifles used the center-fire cartridges that could also be used in the more common revolvers.

The butte dropped away beyond the trees to a crease that wound and twisted down to the Milk River just north. Down the slope, a horse whinnied. Stillman raised the rifle again. The thud of shod hooves drifted up the slope. The thudding increased until Stillman could hear the horse galloping down and away from him, out of the buttes.

"Come back here and face me like a man, you bushwhacking tinhorn!" the sheriff shouted, surprised by how loud his voice sounded in the quiet night. It echoed over the town hunched darkly beyond the pale buttes to the south.

The only response was the dwindling thuds of the horse galloping away, out of sight down the buttes and in the direction of Clantick.

Stillman lowered the rifle. He swung around, looked up at the second-story window of his and Fay's room. Light shone beyond the red curtain. He could no longer hear Little Ben crying.

Fury surged through Stillman as he walked heavily, half-dragging his right foot, back through the yard and into the house. He slipped his Colt out of the holster hanging from a peg by the parlor door, kicked out of his boots so not to make noise on the stairs and reawaken his son, and carried both the revolver and the Henry upstairs.

Fay appeared at the top of the stairs.

"It's all right," Stillman said, breathing hard.

His head was swimming from lack of oxygen. Exertion, he figured. And nerves. And he was old and stove up from that bullet in his back. He dug his fingers into the stairwell to keep from falling backwards. He hoped Fay didn't notice, but she must have, because she came down the stairs, draped his right arm over her shoulders, and helped him up the stairs and into their room.

Little Ben lay fidgeting in his crib but no longer crying. He seemed content. Fay took Stillman's hat and his guns, set them aside, and then helped him into bed and drew the covers over him. He lay back, resting his head on the pillow. His nerves were leaping like frogs beneath his skin. His right side felt like hot mud.

Fay crawled under the covers, rose onto an elbow, and stared down at him, her wide eyes filled with fear. She was breathing hard, her breasts rising and falling heavily behind the covers.

"It'll be all right," Stillman said, sliding her hair back from her right cheek, caressing that cheek with his thumb. "I'll get him. Tomorrow, I'll get him."

Fay sniffed. She slumped down against him, wrapped her arms around his neck, and cried.

She cried for a long time and all Stillman could do was rub her back and repeat over and over, in a voice even hollow to his own ears, "It'll be all right."

But it wasn't all right, for another rifle shot cleaved the night wide open.

"No!" Stillman grunted, eyes snapping wide as he jerked his head up off the pillow. He was about to reach for his rifle leaning against the wall beside him, but stopped and looked around, frowning, blinking. His racing heart slowed.

Gray light pushed through the bedroom's two windows. Thunder spoke—a single boom followed by a good ten seconds of loud, echoing drumming. Fay was not in bed beside him. Her covers were throw back and her pillow still held the indentation of her head. Her distinctive odor—similar to black licorice and cherry blossoms—lingered, as well. Little Ben's crib was empty. The smell of coffee brewing and bacon frying ebbed into the room from downstairs.

Stillman rose from the bed and slid the curtains away from the window. Around the ragged hole and the cracks branching away from it, raindrops splattered and dripped. Beyond, the morning was gray with low, sooty clouds tumbling this way and that. Lightning flashed over the buttes, which appeared the color of flour under the gunmetal sky.

Stillman heaved a sigh of relief. He went over to the washstand, splashed his face with cool water, rubbed water through his thick, dark-brown hair liberally sprinkled with gray, and then dressed in his traditional denims, blue shirt, and brown vest, dropping his silver Waltham pocket watch into his vest pocket. The inside of the timepiece's lid sported a small photograph of him, Fay, and Little Ben taken just weeks after the baby had been born. He gave his mustache a quick combing, wrapped his shell belt and single-action Colt around his waist, donned his hat, and picked up his rifle, checking it to make sure he hadn't pumped a round into the action.

He was extra careful about everything now with Little Ben in the house. He reminded himself that soon, when his son started walking in earnest, he'd have to lock up his guns every night, maybe keep a pocket pistol under his mattress for protection from possible intruders.

He looked at the bullet-rendered window he'd have to replace.

And from bushwhackers . . .

Anxiety mixed with rage swept through him once more, as did the memory of Little Ben's wailing. The bullet must have passed only a few feet over the child's crib before tearing into the papered wall about four feet above the pine wainscoting. Stillman went downstairs, opening and closing his hand to loosen it as well as the stiff muscles in the forearm and elbow. His leg ached but the stiffness would no doubt leave after he'd moved around a bit.

Thunder continued to rumble, and lightning flashed in the windows. He could hear the rain on the roof.

In the kitchen, Fay stood clad in her brown and gold gingham Mother Hubbard, a matching ribbon securing a thick tress of her hair back in a long, loose chignon, holding Little Ben on her hip while she forked bacon around in a cast-iron skillet. As Ben moved around the table and leaned his rifle against the wall by the mudroom door, she turned to him, the anxiety still bright in her eyes.

"Breakfast's almost ready."

"You should have woke me when you got up." Stillman kissed her, squeezed her, and kissed Little Ben, who appeared a little fussy and fidgety this morning. He wasn't crying, but tears were rolling down his smooth, plump cheeks, which owned the same vanilla hue of his mother's. The nubs were mottled red.

"I thought you could use the extra sleep. Breakfast's almost ready." Fay had a half-dozen fresh eggs lined up beside the bacon skillet, ready to be fried in the grease.

"I'm skipping breakfast this morning," Stillman said, caressing the back of Little Ben's head. "Is he all right?"

"I think the storm's bothering him," Fay said. "Probably reminds him of last night."

Stillman kissed the boy again. He gave Fay a lingering squeeze and kissed her cheek again, warmly, as she worked at the range. "Fill me a plate. I'll eat it for lunch." He shrugged into his yellow oilskin duster, pulled on his boots, and picked up his rifle.

"You should eat something, Ben."

"I'm not hungry." He could think only of Battles, of locking the old killer up as soon as he ran him down.

"Ben?"

Stillman turned from the door.

Fay gazed at him with obvious worry. "You're not . . . you're not well, are you?"

"I'm fine, honey."

He opened the door and went out and started slogging down the butte toward town. It wasn't raining hard, but what rain had come down had turned the trail to wet cement, causing the chalky clay to stick to Stillman's boots. The rain freshened the air, touched it with the tang of sage and the piñon smoke of breakfast fires. The wind had picked up, and as Stillman reached First Street, he could hear the jangle of shingle chains.

He mounted the stoop fronting the jailhouse, tripped the latch, and opened the door. Leon jerked his head up from his chest with a start, and dropped his boots, which he'd had crossed atop the roll-top desk before him, to the floor.

"Easy," Stillman said as his deputy automatically reached for the Schofield holstered on his hip.

McMannigle looked relieved, then sheepish. "Uh . . . sorry, Ben."

"Hope I didn't wake you."

The deputy chuckled. "That girl back there"—he canted his head toward the stout door at the rear of the room, which opened onto the six-cage cellblock—"she's like havin' a demon locked in a box. Caterwauled half the night. Pure poison comin' outta her mouth! Didn't get much cat-nappin' done."

"Good. And I'm glad to see you two didn't run away together," Stillman said ironically.

"A man'd be a fool to run away with *that,* no matter how pretty she is."

"I'd have to agree with you." Stillman stayed on the porch, as he didn't want to track mud into the office, and he didn't plan on staying here long. "Have you seen Battles?"

"The regulator?" Leon pursed his lips and shook his head. "Nah. Not since last night, anyways."

"When did you see him last night?"

"Seen him go into Mrs. Lee's place around nine or so, just after he finished up supper at Sam Wa's."

"He spend the night at Mrs. Lee's?"

"Couldn't tell ya, Ben. Never seen him after that. Say, this wouldn't be about that rifle shot I heard last night, would it? I thought it was probably that old Swede shootin' at skunks again just east of you."

"Someone triggered lead at the house last night between ten and eleven."

McMannigle sat up straight in the Windsor chair before the desk, causing the swivel to squawk. "I'll be damned! I shoulda checked it out, but I was worried about that catamount back there in the cellblock. She's got half the men in town prancin' around with their tails up. You think it was Battles?"

"Yes, I do," Stillman said, jutting his lower jaw. "Stay here. I'm headin' over to Mrs. Lee's."

CHAPTER 14

Mrs. Lee's place was a remnant of the old hiders' and fur trappers' camp and ranch supply settlement that Clantick had been back fifteen and twenty years ago, and even before the outbreak of the War Between the States. When Fort Assiniboine had been built west of town, the settlement became a hub for off-duty soldiers, as it still was.

Folks had toiled hard at their various jobs back in the camp's first wooly years. They'd fought Indians, prairie fires, and winter blizzards, and they'd often died bloodily and painfully. During their short spurts of free time, the men had come to Bullhook Bottoms, as the town had been known back then, to numb their minds with whiskey and women.

Stillman often imagined he could hear the ghosts of those old salts turning their wolves loose over here where Cottonwood Creek chewed through the west end of town, and where he remembered from passing through several times during those years that six rat-infested brothels were lined up along the creek like old, craggy women at a barn dance.

Mrs. Lee's was the one place left standing though it had been nipped, tucked, and expanded over the years until now it was one of the grandest buildings in the county—a large, sprawling, three-story Victorian with gingerbread trim and a wraparound porch. Mrs. Lee herself answered Stillman's knock on the door. Three colored glass chimes rang loudly as she did.

Holding a powder-pink velvet housecoat around her shoulders, she blinked skeptically at the big man standing before her. "Well, good morning, Sheriff. Fancy seeing you so early. I'd remind you that I don't open for business until noon except that I know you're not here on *that* kind of business."

Mrs. Lee lifted a beringed fist to cover a yawn. She had a different ring on every finger, including her thumb. Mrs. Lee was the only name that anyone, as far as Stillman was aware, knew her by. She was in her late thirties, early forties—a somewhat rotund, dishwater blond with large, blue eyes in an oval face that had no doubt been beautiful at one time, and she still was pretty despite time's indelicate touch and the woman's overdependence on rouge and too-long eyelashes even so early in the morning.

Stillman had heard that she'd once performed as a dancer in the Montana mining camps farther south, and that her husband, long dead, had once played the piano and driven a wagon in their traveling show.

"Nope, not that kind of business, Mrs. Lee. I'm lookin' for a man named Battles. Is he here?"

She didn't normally divulge the names of her clientele for obvious reasons, though Stillman knew she wouldn't hide anything from the law.

"Mr. Jacob Henry Battles?" she said, arching a brow and fingering the gold broach holding the collar of her robe closed. "Well, yes as a matter of fact, he is."

Stillman pushed the door wide and the woman sort of stumbled back on her pink-slippered feet. "I'll be seein' him."

"Well, of course, Sheriff," she said, startled, glancing down at his boots, which he'd given an obligatory scraping before mounting the porch. "Won't you please come—?"

"How long has he been here?" Stillman was halfway through the long entrance foyer, heading past a grandfather clock and an elegantly carved and brocade-upholstered armchair toward the carpeted stairs beyond. His voice boomed around the foyer like the thunder outside.

"Since last night," Mrs. Lee said as she closed the door.

"Where?"

"Top floor." The woman paused. "Sheriff?"

Stillman stopped at the first landing. She stood with a hand on the newel post, staring up at him. "Never mind. You'll see."

As Stillman continued up the stairs, he heard gradually loudening coughs. He gained the third story, peered down the hall carpeted with a wine-red runner. The only light was from a window at the far end of the hall, and it was murky. Voices sounded behind closed doors on either side of the hall.

Mrs. Lee came up the stairs behind him. "He's with Missy," she said. "Down the hall on the left."

As Stillman moved down the hall, holding the Henry in his right hand, a man's voice rose behind a door on his right. That door opened, and the man stepped out only to lurch back with a start.

"Oh . . . Ben!"

"Mornin' Mayor," Stillman said, walking straight on past the portly gent in a green three-piece suit with fawn vest, a dark-skinned girl milling behind him. "I see the missus is out of town again."

Mayor Wilfred Crandall laughed nervously. "Yes, she . . . uh . . . went to visit her ailing mother in Great Falls."

"Congratulations." Stillman stopped at the door, which a wooden block inset with a copper plate identified in elaborately etched cursive writing as belonging to "Missy." The man's hacking coughs rose on the other side of it. Stillman knocked once, twisted the knob, threw the door wide, stepped inside the room.

He caught the door on its way back toward him with his left boot.

The room was surprisingly large and well appointed, with a

thick, spruce-green carpet trimmed with an umber floral pattern and a canopied bed to the right. A girl sat on the edge of the bed. She was a small, curvy brunette, and she'd been sliding a wet sponge down her left arm when Stillman had burst in. Now she gasped, tossed the sponge into the washbasin on the bed beside her, crossed her pale legs, and covered her nubbin breasts with a black silk wrap.

She gave Stillman a bitter, angry look.

The sheriff ignored her. His attention was glued to the man sitting in an armchair on the other side of the room. Dressed in white balbriggans, barefoot, his curly, gray-brown hair tangled around the bald, pink crown of his skull, Battles half-faced a curtained window in which lightning flashed sporadically. Thunder boomed and peeled beyond it.

The old regulator was hunched forward in his chair. A long cheroot smoldered in an ashtray on the window ledge to his right. His Yellowboy rifle leaned against the window near the cheroot. A bourbon bottle stood open on the floor near the rifle's butt.

Battles's head bobbed violently as he brought a hand to his mouth, and coughed loudly—deep, raking spasms that seemed sure to kick out a lung. Stillman moved toward the regulator, aiming the Henry straight out from his right hip. When Battles stopped coughing, and drew another breath into his lungs with a gasp, Stillman pressed the rifle's barrel against the back of the man's neck.

"Hello, Ben," Battles said, staring at the sheriff's reflection in the window. "What're you doing in a place like this? You're married to one beautiful woman. Always was partial to brown-eyed, chocolate-haired women."

He glanced over his right shoulder, smiling. His face looked like crinkled parchment. His eyes were bright with tears left over from the coughing fit. The irises were thinly outlined in red. Stillman saw that the man was holding a porcelain-covered tin chamber pot in his hooked left arm. It was streaked with blood.

"I take it personal when folks shoot into my house, Battles."

"Don't blame you a bit."

"You, I take it."

"No." Battles shook his head, stretching his lips back from his blood-streaked teeth. "I would never shoot into your house, Ben. Unless I intended to kill you, of course. If I'd intended to kill you, you wouldn't be standing here now."

Stillman looked at the girl sitting on the edge of the bed with her bare legs crossed, holding the kimono closed across her breasts. "How long's he been here?"

"Since around nine o'clock last night, Sheriff." This from Mrs. Lee, who Stillman hadn't realized had followed him halfway into the room. "He hasn't left since. Every time the front door opens and closes, it rings those chimes, and I can hear them all over the house."

Stillman looked at Missy. The whore nodded.

Stillman stared down at Battles, his hard gaze belying his growing doubt. "A man like Battles would know how to leave a place without anyone knowin'."

"Yes," Battles said. "I would. But last night I did not." He turned his head forward and coughed into the chamber pot again. When he finished, he brushed a cambric handkerchief across his mouth and carefully trimmed mustache, and gave another ragged sigh. "This weather," he said despondently, staring out the rain-splattered window that looked out over the shake-shingled porch roof onto which large, white raindrops were splattering, the water zigzagging down through the crevices between the shingles.

"Consumption?" Stillman asked.

Battles nodded and glanced over his shoulder again at Stillman. "A gift from those cold, brick walls of Deer Lodge Penitentiary. The warden was right stingy with coal even during the coldest part of the Montana winter, blast him."

Stillman lowered the rifle. He reached over to pick up Battles's Winchester, and sniffed the barrel. The metallic, greasy odor was touched faintly with the smell of cordite. If the gun had been fired recently, the powder smell would have been stronger. Frustration bit Stillman as he leaned the rifle back down against the wall. He had to agree with what Battles had said. The man was too much of a cold-blooded professional to have made last night's errant shot.

Battles wasn't the sort who'd shoot through a man's window unless he knew he had a good chance of hitting his target. That fact coupled with Mrs. Lee's statement made it unlikely that the shooter had been Battles. The warmth of embarrassment mixed with Stillman's frustration. He hadn't thought it through, which he should have done before bounding in here like a bull out of a chute. Now he looked—and felt—foolish.

He remembered that broken window, the bullet hole in the wall not far from Little Ben's crib, and anger surged in him once more, its flames fanned by exasperation.

Battles took a pull from his bottle and said, "Ben, I fully intended to abide by your wishes and ride out of here by noon. However, with this weather and in my current condition, I'm afraid you'll have to grant me a little more time."

Stillman backed away, brushing past Mrs. Lee standing behind him. "You got till the rain ends. Then you saddle up and ride out. If I see you around town again, I'll turn the key on you. In the meantime, I'll be wiring the warden in Deer Lodge to make sure it was the parole board's idea to set you free."

Battles's smug smile infuriated him further. The man was laughing up his sleeve at him. Not openly. But he was mocking Stillman, just the same. He knew that Ben couldn't force a man with consumption onto a horse in this weather. He also knew that that fact had Stillman burning, as did the question of who had fired the shot into the sheriff's house last night.

Stillman repeated, "As soon as the rain ends." Glancing at Mrs. Lee he said with a sheepish air, "Sorry for barging in on you so early in the day, Mrs. Lee."

He pinched his hat brim to Missy, trudged out of the room, and moved heavily down the stairs. Absently, he'd taken his rifle in his left hand, leaving the right one free and flexing it.

As he dropped down into the long entrance hall, Mrs. Lee called behind him, "Sheriff Stillman?"

He stopped, glanced back up the stairs at her.

"Are you all right?" she asked, frowning and tipping her head to one side.

The grandfather clocked ticked woodenly, the seconds echoing around the hall. Rain splattered against the front windows on either side of the door.

"I'm fine, ma'am," Stillman said, and went out.

He moved across the porch to stand at the top of the steps looking out at the rain. He winced and raised his right, gloved hand. He opened and closed it, feeling the tight muscles all up his arm and into his shoulder. A few of those muscles were spasming, as was his right knee. Not enough to impede his walking but enough to make it a chore. Enough to make him wonder how much longer he could go on doing his job until every muscle affected by the bullet riding snug against his spine locked up and refused to move.

Stillman leaned against a stout porch post. He felt as hollowed out as an old gourd. Old and dried up and useless. Fay knew the trouble he was in. Despite their vigorous lovemaking last night, or because of it, she knew. And she was worried. And he didn't want her to be worried about him. It was he, her husband, who should be worried about her and their child. It was his duty to work and provide for them and protect them.

Not to attract trouble to his family's home.

Not to cause his wife to worry about him. To doubt him.

How much longer did he have before he'd be confined to a wheelchair?

The question almost caused his knees to buckle. He moved off down the porch steps and began slogging back in the direction of the Wells Fargo and telegraph office, intending to fire off messages concerning Battles, Hettie Styles, and the loot stolen from the Sulphur bank.

Stillman just hoped that before his time was up he'd found the man who'd fired the bullet into his home.

CHAPTER 15

Over at Sam Wa's Café on First Street, Evelyn Vincent finished scrubbing off tables soiled by the lunch crowd, and emptied the wooden bucket of dirty, soapy water into the rose and lilac patch she tended behind the small, wood-frame eatery. She counted out the money she'd hauled in over lunch, and returned ten dollars to the cash box for change. She locked the rest in Sam's safe in the small office area of the kitchen partitioned off by room dividers on which were painted corpulent Chinese men and women in flowing robes riding just-as-fat white geese over snow-tipped mountains under a sky of periwinkle blue and in which a fat green dragon flew, blowing streams of bright red fire.

Evelyn removed her apron and looked around the small but efficient kitchen, which she and Sam had cleaned just after Evelyn had turned the "Closed" sign over the front door. During the week, Sam always closed up for the afternoon, opening again for supper around five or whenever he made it in from his tiny shack behind the café.

Everything looked clean and orderly, pots and pans returned to their hooks over the range and dry sink. Evelyn had drained the large washtub, scrubbed the range, returned the flour, sugar and whatnot to their crocks, and sponged off the preparation table. The range was still ticking as the heat in the firebox dwindled, though the heat in the kitchen was still impenetrable, causing sweat to ooze from Evelyn's pores.

Evelyn covered her mouth as she yawned, removed her apron, hung it on its hook near the louver door to the main dining area, and called out the back door to Sam, who was in the keeper shed looking over some deer a market hunter had killed. Venison liver and fried onions was one of Sam's specialties. Evelyn told her employer that she was going home and that she'd see him again at five.

She didn't know if Sam had heard her or not—the Chinaman was growing hard of hearing in his later years—but Sam also had a habit of not rewarding cursory statements with obligatory replies. Evelyn always left the café this time of the day to go back to her rooming house.

Only, today she was swerving from that course, though she saw no reason why Sam would have to know about that part.

The waitress had prepared a wicker basket of food and covered it with an oilcloth. She removed the basket from the table and headed out the café's front door and into the street, which was still muddy and steaming from the rain earlier. The sun had come out between large, ragged clouds that appeared to still have a little rain left in them, and occasionally belched thunder, but the air had warmed and freshened.

It was time to saddle her horse, a three-year-old sorrel named May, which Doc Evans had given her last fall. Doc was not wealthy enough to routinely bestow expensive presents upon his friends, but when a rancher had paid off an appendix operation with the horse, which the doctor hadn't needed since he already had a horse, and one was enough, Doc turned the sorrel over to Evelyn simply because he'd known she'd wanted a horse to ride on occasion. And because they were friends.

That had been reason enough. And, while the doc could have sold the horse for cash, which he badly needed, he'd insisted she take it and had refused any sort of payment in return, though Evelyn had insisted on giving him a hug and had planted a heartfelt kiss on his cheek while he blushed and rolled his eyes.

That was the kind of man Doc Evans was—though few were allowed such glimpses through his crusty façade—and there were damned few around like him. In fact, Evelyn didn't know anyone else in town or even the whole county who could hold a candle to Doc Evans's warmth, humility, generosity, and intelligence. In all of her twenty-three years, she'd never known another man like him.

Which may or may not have been the reason why only a few weeks ago she'd awakened in her bed at the rooming house during one of her many recent restless nights and said aloud and with such steadfast certainty that it had shocked her: "I am in love with Doctor Clyde Evans."

Since that night, Evelyn's nights had been growing more restive. Having thought it over carefully, she realized now that she was, indeed, in love with Doc Evans. Despite her trying very hard not to, he was all she could think or dream about, and thoughts and dreams of him were keeping her awake nights. What made her attempts at sound sleep even more futile was her realizing that the doc was fifteen years older than she, and knowing full well that he had already promised himself to the Widow Katherine Kemmett, whom Evelyn also respected and admired!

It was a hopeless situation. And the last thing Evelyn wanted to do was to come between the doc and Katherine Kemmett. She wouldn't have hurt Katherine for anything. Still, she loved the doc, and she hadn't realized how much until she'd heard he'd been kidnapped from town yesterday, and hazed by gunpoint out to some outlaw shack.

The doc might have died, and she might never have seen him again!

Well, she could see him again now. No, they couldn't be

together, but today at least she could check on him up at his house west of town, and bring him a meal for lunch. Evelyn knew how much the doc liked his meals. Almost as much as he liked his brandy.

She'd tucked a nice bottle of Spanish brandy, which she'd bought at half the wholesale price from an itinerant liquor sales-man who was a regular at Sam Wa's—and who sparked Evelyn despite his being married—into the lunch basket beside the fried chicken, German potato salad, and coleslaw she'd prepared, all of which had been left over from Sam's noon lunch. The doc would appreciate the brandy. He usually bought the cheap stuff and sometimes settled for bourbon, which he despised.

Katherine Kemmett would not approve, of course, but what the widow didn't know wouldn't hurt her. The doc would know, and that's all that Evelyn cared about. That and seeing him again, hearing his voice and his droll jokes, seeing that boyishly sheepish grin on his broad, scholarly handsome face half-concealed by a thick carpeting of masculine, rust-red fur.

Evelyn's heart picked up its pace as she approached Auld's Livery & Feed Barn. She crossed the street by way of planks someone had laid as a makeshift bridge through the deep, mud-filled wheel ruts, and patted Mr. Auld's cat, Gustav, while the liveryman roped and saddled May. Auld always joked with Eve-lyn when she came to retrieve the sorrel, and today was no exception.

"Where you heading this time?" the liveryman asked.

Auld's part-time stableman, Olaf Weisinger, who was repair-ing a stable door, removed a nail from between his teeth and said, "Probably off to see a boy, huh? Sure, she's off to see a boy in the country. Them country boys got their eye on Miss Evelyn here." He winked at Auld. "I tried to get her to go to the Fourth of July horse race with me, but, no, she was too busy!"

He winked again and continued hammering a nail. Weisinger had been doing odd jobs around Clantick, including cutting and hauling firewood, since Clantick had been nothing more than a hiders' camp.

"I *was* busy, Mr. Weisinger!" Evelyn insisted, laughing as she held the big, purring tabby in her arms, the lunch basket at her feet. "Sam wanted me to sell sandwiches to the crowd that day."

"Pshaw," said Weisinger between hammer strokes. "We coulda gone that night. There were night races, too." Again, he winked, making sure Auld and Evelyn knew he was joking, though Evelyn suspected that, while Weisinger was pushing sixty, his having asked her to the horse races may have not been completely in jest. Someone had told Evelyn he'd been married once a long time ago to a Canadian woman but that she had died of measles.

"Maybe next year," Evelyn said, stroking the tabby.

"Ah, leave the poor girl alone, Olaf," Auld said, feeding the latigo through the cinch ring, the latigo whipping his overall-clad thigh. "She's taking lunch out to some cowpuncher. Look there. My, that's a mighty big lunch basket, Evelyn. Must be quite the good-sized lad!"

Evelyn glanced at the basket and felt her cheeks warm with a blush.

"Oh, sure—look there," Weisinger good-naturedly jeered. "Now we got her blood rising. Who is it, Evelyn? Come on— you can tell me and Auld. We won't tell no one!"

The two men chuckled.

"You'll just have to guess," Evelyn said, feeling the blush rising up into her ears. She would have told the men earlier that she was taking lunch to the doctor but now she was afraid that she couldn't do it without looking sheepish and giving her feelings for the man away. The problem with that was if someone saw her riding up to the doctor's place, and word got around like it always did in a town as small as Clantick, Auld and Weisinger would find out and, both being bored and snoopy and as gossipy as any women's sewing circle, might start to suspect that Evelyn's feelings for the doc were more than friendly.

No one could know that. Not ever. Evelyn didn't even want the doc knowing about it. The man was going to marry Katherine Kemmett, and there was no doubt about it!

The two men continued ribbing the waitress, who took the jeers as affably as she could under the circumstances, until Evelyn wrapped the basket's wicker bail over the saddle horn, allowed Auld to help her onto May's back, and rode on out of the barn and into the street.

Behind her, Weisinger yelled, "I bet it's that Hilzendigger boy, Ralph. Yah, it's Ralph Hilzendigger—that's who it is, all right!"

Evelyn touched the heels of her leather boots to May's flanks and she and the sorrel trotted to the edge of town and out past the Lutheran church, where the widow's husband had preached and where the rolling prairie opened and stretched toward the Continental Divide. Evelyn put the oat- and corn-boggy horse, whom she could tell was needing a good run, into a gallop along the trail that wove through the buttes along the Milk.

She intentionally passed the turnoff to Evans's place, which sat on a butte to her right. Someone from town might see her, and then word might get back to Auld and Weisinger. She felt foolish for doing so, but she'd ride for another half a mile, give May a good airing, and then turn off and head back to the doctor's place via the old river trail, most of which couldn't be seen from Clantick because of the buttes.

At least, she was sure the two old curious coyotes from the livery barn wouldn't see and get under her bustle about it.

She rode out to where she could see the river sliding milky-green between willow-lined banks and then picked up the old buffalo trail and followed it back downstream, toward Clantick. Now she was on the north side of the doctor's butte top house and barn, which had originally been built and owned by a mucky muck who'd helped plan the route for the still-fledgling Great Northern railway.

She turned the horse up the butte and watched the house loom into view before her—once obviously an impressive house with a mansard roof and a turret on each corner—it now resembled a place that children would deem haunted. Most of its red paint had long since flaked away, and woodpeckers had bored holes in the clapboard siding.

Evelyn crouched low and squeezed her knees against the horse's barrel as the sorrel lunged to the top of the hill. She pulled the horse over to the front of the house, which faced the river, and stopped in the high weeds growing up around the rod-iron hitch rack stretched between two stone pylons. Thick, green lilac bushes grew close to the house. They obviously hadn't been trimmed in years, for they were shaggy and sprawling, and their deep green was in sharp contrast to the lusterless brown of the mixed weeds and the tombstone gray of the abandoned-looking house.

Evelyn dismounted, vaguely opining that while the doctor was very good at his profession, he was not much of a caretaker. He needed a woman to move in and put a feminine touch to things. Katherine Kemmett, the industrious widow, was just the woman to get those bushes under control and to see that the house got painted. Spruce would look nice. And wine-red trim. Why, with a fresh coat of paint and a good mowing and trimming, the place would look as grand as it likely once had, capping this flat-topped bluff over the river . . .

Evelyn looped the sorrel's reins over the hitch rack and removed the lunch basket from the saddle horn.

"Doc!" Evelyn called, climbing the steps of the front porch that, cracked and pitted, squawked precariously beneath her weight. "Doc, it's Evelyn!"

The inside door was open. Evelyn peered through the rusty screen door and knocked twice, the rotting door rattling in its frame.

"Doc, you in there?"

No response. The doc was probably upstairs getting some badly needed sleep. Evelyn opened the screechy door and walked inside. She'd set out the lunch she'd made, and maybe clean up around the place a bit while she waited for him to stir. Then she'd take the food up to him, and surprise him.

He'd be thrilled. Katherine had probably fixed him a nice meal last night, but the doc had a hearty appetite.

Evelyn moved around the doc's clutter of stacked books and boxes and various paraphernalia that better belonged in a shed, and into the kitchen at the house's rear. She stopped just inside the door, frowning in surprise as she looked around. The kitchen was usually more cluttered than the rest of the house, and littered with moldy food scraps, cigar butts, and unwashed dishes, not to mention empty liquor bottles. One of the several half-wild cats that the doc fed often brought mice into the house, and they often stunk up the place, as well.

Today, however, the kitchen looked even neater than the one Evelyn had left at Sam Wa's. As she stood just inside the kitchen's arched doorway, holding the lunch backset in both hands before her, she felt a cold stone drop in her belly.

Katherine.

"Of course," Evelyn heard herself mutter in a dreadful tone.

Just then she heard footsteps and turned to see down the short hall to her left, beyond the kitchen and through a small mudroom, Mrs. Kemmett climbing the wooden steps beyond the rear screen door.

CHAPTER 16

Evelyn wanted to slip back out of sight and then flee out the front door, but she stood frozen in a sudden wash of anxiousness as the widow opened the screen door and slipped into the thick shadows of the mudroom, holding a large spray of late-summer wildflowers in her hand.

She stopped suddenly and said, "Oh, my—Evelyn, you startled me!" She clapped her free hand to her bosom. She wore a pale pink summer dress with a white collar and sleeve cuffs. Evelyn had rarely seen her in anything but dark or muted colors, rarely in anything so gay. The widow's hair was pulled back in a pretty French braid rather than in the usual, severe bun she wore at the top of her head and pulled so tight that it drew her eyes up at their outside corners, giving her a formidable, Slavic appearance.

If Evelyn's face had been glass, it would have shattered with her overly fervid attempt at a smile.

"Hello, Mrs. Kemmett," she said, trying to stroll nonchalantly forward and lifting the basket onto the doctor's dining table, which was now draped with a blue and white checked oilcloth and centered with an empty red, glass flower vase for which the wildflowers were no doubt intended. "I hope I'm not intruding. We had some food left over at Sam's place after lunch, and I was about to throw it out when I thought the doc might be hungry. Of course, I figured you'd probably taken him under your wing after yesterday, and all, but I figured if he'd already eaten, he might snack on this stuff later. Just some fried chicken and the fixin's, is all. If he doesn't want it, you can just throw it out."

"Oh, how thoughtful!" Mrs. Kemmett said, striding a little breathlessly into the kitchen. "Thank you, Evelyn."

She seemed a little subdued, self-conscious, glancing down at her dress and then fiddling with the braid. Katherine realized that her being here in the doc's house, alone with the doc, might indicate that she'd spent last night here, too, which would be more than a little indiscreet and prime fodder for the Clantick gossip mill. (As well it should, Evelyn thought snootily.)

Katherine set the wildflowers on the table and placed a hand on the covered basket. "I was going to heat up what I made for him last night, but I'll put that out for supper. If he ever wakes up, I'll lay your food out for lunch." She smiled a little woodenly, her pleasant face, which was probably pretty back when she was Evelyn's age, was touched with an embarrassed flush.

It was not to Evelyn's credit, the girl knew, that she was enjoying the widow's discomfort. It made Evelyn feel a little less self-conscious about her own reason for being here, which was, she had to admit with a sickening little twist of her heart, none other than her own love for the man who lived here. A love that would never, could never, be expressed lest she make an absolute sniveling fool of herself.

Still, an anguished voice was screaming inside her head, "No one could love him more than I do!"

"He's not awake, then, I take it?" Evelyn said, her smile in place, trying to conceal her disappointment.

"Sound asleep."

"Have you checked recently?"

"Oh, I don't have to, dear. If Clyde were awake, he'd be stomping around, likely looking for lunch. Again, Evelyn, thank you so much. I know Clyde will very much appreciate the food, as well."

"Well, like I said—I was just going to throw it out so I thought I'd ride it over and see if the doc was hungry."

"Yes."

"Well . . ."

"I'll see you to the door," Katherine said.

"I know the way," Evelyn said, turning and striding back through the house.

She slowed her pace halfway to the front door, remembering the bottle of brandy she'd placed in the basket. Her heart thudded. Katherine would find it. Everyone in town knew that the widow was a teetotaler and was trying very hard to make the doc one, as well.

The widow would probably throw that good brandy out!

"Anything else, dear?" the widow said behind Evelyn.

"No, nothing," Evelyn said with a start, throwing an arm out in a wave and continuing to the front door. "Nothing at all. I'll be seeing you, Mrs. Kemmett!"

Evelyn galloped down the hill from the doc's place toward the river. Once on the river trail, she galloped east, in the direction of town.

After a long, hard gallop, however, she found herself in the buttes on Clantick's north side, and couldn't remember steering the horse in that direction. Without realizing, she must have given May her head, and the filly had gone where her nose and the creases between the buttes had led her.

Now, on a low, flat-topped bluff, Evelyn reined the horse to a halt and released the dam inside her heart, letting her emotions off their leash in the same way that she'd given the sorrel free rein. She leaned forward over the horn, dropped her chin, and bawled.

She wasn't sure why she felt so wretched; her thoughts were many taut knots inside her. She just knew that finding Katherine Kemmett in the doc's house, when she'd wanted so badly to bring him lunch this day, to be alone with him and to talk with him like they often did at Sam Wa's or while strolling together along the river, had touched off a powder keg inside of her.

That powder keg, she knew now, allowing herself to look at it clearly and without reservation or hesitation, was her love for Clyde Evans and her deep, brooding yearning to be his wife.

What made that keg even more explosive was that Evelyn fully realized that she was a fool to feel this way. Doc was a mature man. A professional man. To him, Evelyn Vincent was a mere friend, albeit a doting one—an affable, curious, concerned young waitress who'd bent an ear to his troubles as she did for so many folks in Sam Wa's, which, in addition to the town's saloons, was a hub of social interaction. It had become that mostly because of Evelyn herself. That's where the friendship between she and the doc had begun three years ago.

Evelyn had been a mother hen since she was a girl and had had to raise her three younger siblings. Back in Iowa, her father had died when a dead tree he'd been cutting down for firewood had fallen on him. After that, Evelyn's mother's alcoholism had grown worse. Mrs. Vincent had always taken in sewing to help make ends meet, but after she'd buried her husband she mostly only drank and left the care of the house and farmstead and the raising of the other children up to Evelyn.

While the doc was older than Evelyn, in many ways he acted less mature, with his drinking and carrying on with doxies and his reluctance to commit himself to the widow, who obviously loved him. Ironically, it had been during this troubled time in his life, when he'd been mulling over whether to marry the widow and had been drinking heavily to numb his confusion, that he and Evelyn had become close friends and confidants.

Too close, the young waitress realized now.

At least, too close on her part.

The doc did not love her. He never would. She was too young for him, and the only young women he paid any intimate attention to were the doxies over at Mrs. Lee's place. At least, he had before the widow had put an end to all that when he'd finally promised to marry her.

Besides, while Evelyn knew that the doc liked her, he also probably saw her as uneducated and overly loquacious. That was a word she'd heard him use before about other folks, and he'd wielded the word with his usual sarcasm. The doc was a bookish man with a darkly caustic side. A loner who drank to quell the pains of his loneliness and for whom, until Evelyn, his closest allies had always been women of the professional variety, because he'd been deathly afraid of sharing his soul.

He was far different from Evelyn.

So, why did she love him so much?

Evelyn sobbed, tears rolling down her cheeks to splatter darkly on the saddle horn and pommel.

Because he'd shared his soul with her, and now in many ways she felt as though he and she were one. That was why.

Evelyn cut loose with a fresh round of sobs. Then she lifted her head, sniffed, and brushed the tears from her cheeks. She needed to talk with someone. In the past, she'd talked to the doc about her troubles, but of course she couldn't discuss her current problem with him. That she'd been the one who'd help convince him that he should get off the fence and marry Mrs. Kemmett almost made her laugh through her sobs.

Evelyn stared off over May's head. The world was bleary because of the tears still glazing her eyes. Slowly, her vision cleared like a spyglass being focused, and she saw, on a butte ahead and to her right, the Stillman house and chicken coop. A small, dark-haired figure who could only be Fay Stillman was moving around out in the backyard.

Evelyn sniffed again, staring at the Stillman farm splashed with stormy lemon sunlight and ragged, sliding cloud shadows. Occasionally, she could hear the clucking of the Stillman chickens. Evelyn's aching heart lightened; she brushed the back of a hand across her cheeks once more.

She had to talk with someone about how she was feeling or she feared her heart would literally explode in her chest. About the only person in town she could trust with such a secret and the venting of such overwhelming grief was Fay, whom she'd grown nearly as close to as she had the doc, though of course in a different way.

She clucked to the sorrel and brushed her heels against the horse's ribs.

"Come on, May," she said, her throat sore and her voice hoarse from crying.

"You stay right there, Little Ben!" Fay yelled in a jovial voice to the boy standing watching her through the wicker bars of his playpen, which Fay had set up in the parlor. Since her visit from the regulator, Battles, the other day, she no longer allowed the boy to roam freely while she went about her chores.

As Fay lugged several pine planks through the parlor toward the stairs, the boy screeched and hollered and banged his wood horse against the side of the pen. He was loud, as usual, but content enough to play with his horse, a canvas ball, a rag doll, and the several other toys she'd tossed into the pen with him, including an abacus whose colored beads he was fond of rattling.

"I'll be right back, Sweetie!" Fay said, lugging the planks up the stairs with a grunt.

She wasn't feeling nearly as cheerful as she sounded. In fact, she was downright terrified after someone had fired that bullet through the bedroom window last night, and then seeing the physical state that Ben was in. She wondered how long he'd been feeling gimped up again from the bullet in his back.

Silently, as Fay carried the planks into the bedroom and slid a chair over to the broken window, she castigated herself for her part in letting Ben go without having the surgery that Doc Evans had assured him had a 70 percent chance of curing the spasms. If left unattended, the bullet would continue to roll around inside its haven of scar tissue hugging his spine until it eventually caused him to lose the feeling in his right side, possibly even in both legs.

The doctor had convinced him to go ahead with the surgery, but then Ben had wanted to put it off until Little Ben was born . . . and then until Little Ben was walking . . . and then, distracted by the thrill of their first-born, he and Fay had stopped talking about it. Fay had even stopped thinking about it, because, she realized now, she had simply not wanted to think about the risk or the expense.

She and Ben had been so happy until last night. Now, she realized, that happiness had been mere fantasy. Ben was injured and there was likely an old killer in town, stalking him. And Battles might not be the only one wanting to draw a bead on Ben's back. Fay had heard via the Clantick grapevine, which was known to send out suckering roots all over the place, that a pretty young prisoner had put a reward on Ben's head.

How could the sheriff defend himself with the use of only his left side?

Fay had climbed atop the chair and was pounding nails through the board she'd placed over the window, and into the frame. They would have to order in a new pane from the mercantile, and it might not arrive for weeks. Fay wanted the window covered before Ben came home. He would insist on doing it, and she didn't want him straining himself. His work was enough of a strain.

She stopped hammering. She stopped breathing. She'd heard something.

Battles . . .

Fay stepped quietly down off the chair, lay the hammer on the bed, and replaced it in her hand with the revolver she'd set on the washstand loaded and ready. Her heart was hammering. It hammered harder when a long shadow slid into the room from the hall.

Fay gasped.

Quivering, she raised the pistol in both hands, ratcheted back the hammer, and yelled, "One more step and I'll blow your heart out, Battles, you *son of a bitch!*"

Silence.

A floorboard creaked.

A thin female voice said tensely, "Mrs. Stillman? Fay? Don't shoot. It's me—Evelyn."

CHAPTER 17

Three days later, Stillman sat in his office slowly rotating the cylinder of his Colt revolver and peering through the open loading gate at the brass caps of the cartridges rolling by.

Click, click, click . . .

Stillman had left one of the chambers empty. It rolled past the loading gate looking as black as the gap left by a missing tooth.

As he continued to roll the cylinder between his thumb and index finger, the sheriff glanced over the gun at the two yellow telegraph flimsies lying side by side on the scarred surface of his roll-top desk, each crowned with the black masthead announcing WESTERN UNION TELEGRAPH CO. He'd received both telegrams the day before—one in response to his query about Jacob Henry Battles to the warden of Deer Lodge Penitentiary. The other missive was in response to his note to the sheriff down in Sulphur simply informing the man that one of the thieves who'd robbed his bank was in Stillman's jail and asking him how he wished to proceed.

The sheriff's response had not been nearly as simple as Stillman's question. Neither had the response from the warden down in Deer Lodge been simple, though Stillman had found it far less troubling than the message from Sheriff Bill Parsons of Sulphur County.

Stillman glanced from the two flimsies on which the local telegrapher had penciled the responses from the sheriff and the warden, to the heavy stone mug sitting on the desk beside them.

Steam rose from the hot, black coffee he had just poured from the pot now chugging slowly on the potbelly stove, which Stillman had lit against the chill that had descended upon Clantick after the rainsquall. There was a metallic chill in the air, and that coupled with the changing cottonwoods down along the Milk and in the gullies spoking off of the river portended an early autumn. A cold one, Stillman thought, glancing out the window above his desk and noting the heavy strands of blue wood smoke wafting between the false-fronted buildings, as well as the gold and yellow leaves being shepherded along the still-muddy street by a northwest breeze.

Stillman shuddered inside his navy wool shirt, his fall shirt, which he wore over winter-weight longhandles. And then he leaned to his right, opened a drawer, and pulled out a small, flat bottle, and splashed a shot, maybe a shot and a half, of bourbon into the coffee. He returned the cork to the bottle, returned the bottle to its drawer, fished out a spoon, and stirred the liquor into the coffee as the peppery steam rose, touching the sheriff's nostrils.

He flipped the spoon into the drawer, closed the drawer, and leaned over the mug, drawing a good draught of the nicely scented steam deep into his lungs. The smell recalled times long ago, just after the war, when he and Milk River Bill were on their own, riding the coulees for game that they could sell to the railroads, which were just then beginning to stretch across the Mississippi; hunting buffalo or running a few head of their own steers to sell before the winter's first snow; and camping out along remote creeks and rivers, eating fresh meat roasted over open fires, and drinking coffee spiced with corn liquor they occasionally traded hides for.

Stillman smiled at the memories, lifted the mug in his right hand, the mug feeling heavier than it should have, and sipped the delicious brew. As he did, he knew a twinge of guilt. After having lost several years to hard liquor and gambling, he'd promised Fay he'd never take a drink of the strong stuff again. He'd drink only beer. Beer was merely sarsaparilla with a mild pop.

Stillman rarely went back on his word. Only on days like today when his body was grieving him, aggravated by the sudden cold snap, and he found himself with more trouble than he thought he might know what to do with, like the headache represented by the two messages currently lying flat on the top of his desk, near the coffee spiced with whiskey.

He took another sip of the bracing brew, picked up the message from the warden at Deer Lodge, and leaned back in his swivel Windsor chair, the chair's dry wood and the ungreased swivel both complaining beneath him. He ran his gaze across the telegrapher's penciled scrawl once more:

BATTLES RELEASED BY PAROLE BOARD JULY 1 STOP SICK AND DYING STOP SAW NO REASON TO BURY HIM AT PEN'S EXPENSE STOP

Stillman gave a caustic chuff as he worked the wrinkled paper, which he'd splattered with coffee, between his thumb and index finger, squinting at the words to clarify them. (He needed reading glasses, too, but they could wait.)

"Sick and dying," he growled, wrinkling his nose and flinging the flimsy against the overstuffed pigeonholes. The last sentence, "Saw no reason to bury him at Pen's expense," was Warden J. H. Greggson Davis's trademark gallows, albeit pragmatic, humor, which Stillman had encountered before.

Sick and dying.

Davis had turned him loose, and now the dying old regulator was Stillman's problem. The rain had cleared, but Battles was still in town. Stillman would have gone over again, and run him

145

out of town at the end of a cocked rifle, but McMannigle had told him that the man had been lying sick in bed since Stillman had last seen him. Sick and coughing up gobs of blood and medicating himself with pretty girls and whiskey, though Leon hadn't seen "how smoking as much as that old chimney is could be helpin' his condition none."

Stillman wanted Battles out of his town, but he didn't see how he could kick him out when he was as sick as he was. Stillman knew about being sick himself . . . and being old . . . and he doubted the man was any real threat to him, Stillman, and his family. Besides, Battles had become the least of the sheriff's problems.

Stillman had just shuttled his gaze to the other telegraph flimsy, the one on which the reply from the sheriff of Sulphur had been scrawled, when he heard the thud of boots on the stoop outside the jailhouse door. Instantly, he reached for the Colt but before he could bring the revolver up in his aching hand, the door opened and the liveryman, Emil Auld, stepped into the office, his cheeks above his heavy beard rouged by the chill.

"Got them boys all boxed up and ready to bury, Sheriff. Ground's dry enough."

Stillman released the pistol and slid his hand back to his coffee mug. With a note of irritation at the big German's intrusion, and at his own inability to raise his pistol as fast as he once had, the sheriff said, "What do you want—a silver sword? You'll get paid as soon as you fill out a request and turn it into the mayor. You know where his office is at as well as I do."

"I already done that!" was the German's indignant retort.

"What the hell you want, then?"

"You told me to tell you before I buried 'em, in case that sheriff in Sulphur wanted a look at 'em!"

"Well, he doesn't," Stillman said, "so go ahead and plant the sons o'bitches. They're not getting any sweeter smellin' lying over there in your livery barn!"

Auld hung his lower jaw, gaping. "What the hell's stuck in your craw, Sheriff?"

"Right now, you're—!" Stillman cut himself off as he shuttled his gaze over Auld's right shoulder and into the street behind the big German. The sheriff dropped his boots to the floor, rose slowly with his coffee cup in his hand, and walked toward Auld, who was nearly filling the doorway.

Auld glanced behind him. "What do you see out there?"

"Nothin'," Stillman grunted, his eyes locked on two horseback riders passing in the street fronting the jailhouse—two strangers wearing pistols on their hips, rifles jutting from saddle scabbards. The two strangers had their heads turned toward Stillman and were holding their gazes on the sheriff as they continued walking their horses on past the law office. "Nothin' important," he grumbled to Auld, pushing past the big-gutted German to step out onto the stoop. "Go ahead and bury them carcasses before they stink up the whole town."

"That's what I was gonna do!" Auld growled back, moving down off the stoop while glancing at Stillman as though the normally affable sheriff were a dog that had suddenly turned rabid.

As the liveryman slogged off across the street, heading back toward his barn, Stillman stood staring over the porch rail at the two riders who were now about a half a block beyond the jailhouse and were turning their heads forward, away from Stillman, to steer their horses through the midday, midweek traffic comprised of ranch wagons, farm wagons, wagons manned by soldiers from Fort Assiniboine, punchers on horseback, and miners down from the hills on supply runs with pack mules.

Stillman had a testy feeling about those two newcomers. He'd seen neither in town before, and the fact that they were strangers as well as *well-armed, flint-eyed* strangers, with guns prominently displayed, caused a bullfrog of unease to leap down his spine. Neither had tried to conceal his interest in Stillman. Three days had passed since the sheriff's sole prisoner, Miss Hettie Styles, had shouted out her bounty on Stillman's head. Stillman wasn't sure how many men had heard the offer for a five-hundred-dollar reward and a free poke to any man who killed the sheriff and turned Hettie free, but it didn't take that many to have heard it for word to have spread throughout the county and farther.

Stillman had made plenty of enemies in northern Montana, and for many of those enemies, a five-hundred-dollar bounty for his head would be most tempting. Some of those tough nuts with their necks in a hump might even see the amount as a bit extravagant. Throw in the offer of a poke or two from Hettie Styles, who'd made a name for herself as a saloon dancer in the gold camps farther south and then as a wild-and-wooly, pretty and sexy outlaw girl, and Stillman probably had something to be concerned about.

Those two hard-eyed strangers that had just passed in the street had sort of resembled Jacob Henry Battles in his day, before a wry humor kindled by age had tempered the flatness of the old regulator's gaze.

A scream emanated from the cellblock. It was muffled by the heavy cellblock door, but it was a scream nonetheless.

Stillman heard Hettie Styles cry, "Sheriff!"

"Ah, shit," Stillman said, limping over to the side of his desk from which the cellblock keys hung. He dropped his Colt into its holster, snapped the keeper thong over the hammer, and opened the cellblock door just as Hettie screamed his name again.

"What the hell is it this time?" Stillman asked, peering down the semidark alley between the six strap-iron cages, three on each side of the wooden-floored corridor. "The meatballs I gave you for lunch don't have enough salt in 'em? I'll fetch Sam Wa over so you can dress him down good an' proper."

Hettie was in the second cell down on his left, standing on her cot and pressing her back against the bars. She had two heavy blankets wrapped around her shoulders. She was staring toward the cellblock's opposite end. She jerked her head sharply at Stillman, eyes bright with rage.

"A rat! Sheriff, your cellblock is rat-infested!" She pointed across the cellblock. "It ran over there, and it's under that cot, eating something on the floor!"

"I'll fetch Auld's cat in here tonight. All the rats'll be gone by mornin'. Gustav's a prime rat killer."

"Shoot it right now! I will not stay in a rat-infested cellblock!"

"I don't see as how you have much choice." Stillman began to step back into his office, drawing the door closed behind him.

Hettie stopped him with: "Sheriff, I will scream all night. You know I will. And that deputy of yours won't get a minute's rest. I'll shout out the window and keep the whole town awake!"

"Oh, for Christ's sake," Stillman said, moving down the corridor and trying not to limp. "Where is he?"

"He's in the last cell. To the right." Hettie was breathing hard. She seemed genuinely afraid. "See him?"

Stillman slowed his pace about halfway down the corridor, near the ticking potbelly stove that was the cellblock's only source of heat. Crouching, he peered into the last cell.

"See him?" Hettie gasped.

"Yeah, I see him." Stillman raised the Colt, aimed, and fired.

The Colt's report was like an explosion in the cellblock, echoing off the stone walls. He had to fire three more rounds in frustration before a bullet finally hit its mark.

149

Powder smoke wafted amongst the purple shadows relieved by golden rays of cool sunlight penetrating the cellblock's three barred windows and pushing between the cracks in the shutters closed against the outside chill.

"Did you get him?" Hettie asked.

Stillman holstered his Colt. His ears rang from the blasts. "Got him."

Hettie's voice teemed with sarcasm. "You have a dead aim—don't ya, Sheriff?"

"Yeah, well, he's dead," Stillman said, heading back toward the open cellblock door. "Now, sew your lip or you won't get supper."

Hettie leaped down off the cot and, drawing the blankets tighter around her shoulders, moved to the door of her cell. Her breath jetted into the corridor, touched by a vagrant ray of sunlight. She wrapped her hands around two bars and bayoneted Stillman with her passionate gaze.

"We have to talk."

"No, I ain't gonna run away to Mexico with you and the money." Stillman glanced at the saddlebags residing on the cot of the cell just down from Hettie's. "My wife ain't the grudgeful type but she might make an exception for that."

"Shut up," the girl whispered, squeezing the bars tighter. "We're in trouble, you and me. Big trouble."

Stillman stopped at the cellblock door.

"Tell me," Hettie said with a desperate air, "have you seen any strangers in town?"

Stillman stared at her.

"If you have," Hettie said, keeping her voice low and pitched with fear, "you and me might be in even bigger trouble than I thought."

CHAPTER 18

"Not just us," Hettie added under her breath. "But your deputy, too. Maybe even your wife and little boy. Big trouble."

"What the hell are you talking about?" Stillman squared his shoulders at the girl and balled his hands into tight fists at his sides, feeling a stab of pain in his right forearm.

He walked over to stand in front of Hettie. She was a good foot shorter than he, and she took a step back from the door, as though a little taken aback by his dark demeanor. She stared up at him from beneath her brows.

"What are you talking about?" he asked again.

Hettie swallowed, shuddering inside the blankets wrapped around her shoulders. "You ain't gonna come in here and beat me, now, are you? You do that, and you won't get one more word out of me."

"Is this some kind of game to you, Miss Styles?"

She shook her head slowly, pursing her lips, her dimpled cheeks touched with shadows. "Bein' slapped around by men twice my size ain't no game at all, Sheriff. Not to me. Been beaten more than a few times, and I don't cotton to it."

Stillman's anger burned a little less hotly. Suddenly, instead of a half-rabid polecat, Hettie resembled a vulnerable young girl standing before him. It occurred to him that she probably hadn't ended up where she was without some help. She reminded him a little of Evelyn Vincent in that way, for the young waitress had come from a hard, previous life though she'd never had as foul a mouth as Miss Styles.

"I'm not going to slap you around, Hettie. Now, go ahead and tell me why my family might be in danger."

He was growing weary of having to worry about Fay and Little Ben. He and Leon could take care of themselves, but Fay and Little Ben were innocent, defenseless prey, and his worry for them was like a cancer inside him.

Hettie said, "I'm afraid I made a mistake, puttin' that bounty on your head."

"You sure as hell did."

"For a reason you ain't considered and wouldn't think to consider it, unless you knew—"

"That there were others involved in the holdup—aside from you and the five owlhoots just now being planted on Boot Hill?" That's what the telegram from the Sulphur sheriff had informed Stillman.

"Okay, so you've done your homework. Good boy, Sheriff. But that's only half of the problem."

Stillman stared at her.

"The plan was for the two groups to split up, ride south around the Crazy Mountains and meet up at a stage relay station in Paradise Valley. There were two pairs of saddlebags, but I put most of the money in one, and held onto the heavier ones. We intended to divide the loot evenly before we split into two gangs, but there was no time. The posse was hot on our heels. My group rode north . . . with most of the money, including some jewelry and gold watches."

"You cut the others out."

Hettie chewed her upper lip. "Me an' Arthur and Johnny decided we didn't need them anymore—especially since I was the woman of the leader of that other group, Otis Natchez, and me an' Otis weren't exactly seein' eye to eye anymore."

"So, you cut Natchez and the others out because you decided

you liked Johnny and Arthur better?" Nothing about outlaw ways surprised Stillman anymore, but he wanted to get his mind around what was happening here.

"Yeah, kinda," Hettie said with a shrug. "They got *some* money." She snickered then put a little salt in her tone as she added, "Men get on my nerves after a while, Sheriff. Just like women get on men's nerves. Ain't much difference. Besides, Natchez's bunch was startin' to get on the nerves of Johnny Vermilion and his brother, and I heard Natchez one night talkin' to his boys about doin' the very same thing to Vermilion."

Stillman sighed. "All right, so Vermilion double-crossed them before they could double-cross Vermilion, and since you and Johnny were getting cozy after you got tired of Natchez, you slipped over to Vermilion's side. All right. I think I follow you. You think they'll track you here?"

"They might not have if I hadn't been so vocal about putting that bounty on your head." Hettie lowered her eyes and pursed her lips in disgust.

Stillman chuckled though he didn't find anything at all humorous about the topic at hand. "Yeah, that'll call them in." He raked a thumb down his left sideburn. "Might already have."

"Strangers in town?" Hettie asked nervously.

Stillman ignored the question. "How many in this other group?"

"Five."

"One wear a black vest and a bowler hat with a rabbit's foot pinned to the brim?"

"Oh, shit!" Hettie intoned. "That's Merle Wainwright!"

"Another one wear a top hat and little round glasses and carry two matched Remingtons on the outside of his duster, on the left side?"

Hettie stared at Stillman. Crestfallen, she sat down on the edge of her cot, leaned forward, rested her elbows on her knees, and ran a hand through her long hair. "That's Four-Eyes Eldon Jones from Calabasas. I knew him in Bannack for a while. Man's a snake. A venomous snake that lives for killin'," Hettie said, snapping her anxious gaze at Stillman, "just like every man of the five, including Natchez himself."

Hettie dropped the blankets and lifted her shirt and chemise to her neck, exposing her breasts. She lifted her left breast to reveal a knotted white scar beneath it. The scar was about two inches long and an inch wide.

"That's an 'E' for Eldon. He gave that to me in Bannack," Hettie said bitterly, letting the shirt and chemise drop back down into place. "I never told any of the other boys who gave that to me. I was savin' Eldon for myself to kill. I was bidin' my time. Besides, he was a good safecracker."

Stillman shucked his Colt from its holster, flicked open the loading gate, and began removing the spent cartridges, replacing them with fresh ones from his shell belt.

"You gotta let me go, Sheriff," Hettie said, staring at the gun. The empty shell casings clinked onto the floor around Stillman's boots. The fresh ones made soft clicks as he slid them into the empty chambers. "They'll get in here any way they can, kill you, kill your deputy . . . kill me. I'm defenseless in here. At least out there I got a chance!"

"Yeah, well, there's no chance you're getting out of here," Stillman said, having filled the Colt's empty chambers, including the one beneath the hammer, which he usually kept empty. He spun the cylinder; it whined shrilly until the lawman slipped the gun back into its holster and snapped the keeper thong over the hammer.

"If they can't get to you in here," Hettie said, her voice pitched with dread. She rose, moved to the cell door, and slowly closed her hands around the bars. "They'll get to you through your wife or your baby."

"Shut up," Stillman said.

"You know it's true. If you let me out, let me haul my outlaw ass out of your town, you and your deputy and your *family*, Stillman, will be safe!"

"I said shut up," Stillman said again as he strode back into his office, drew the cellblock door closed behind him, and locked it with a key from the heavy ring.

"You ain't a well man, Sheriff!" Hettie bellowed behind the door. "That dustup in the cabin done you in. No reason for me to die because you're old and stove up!"

Stillman opened a desk drawer. He pulled out two sets of handcuffs, and shoved a cuff of each behind his cartridge belt, letting the other one dangle outside his trousers. He went to the gun rack on the far wall, pulled down a spare Colt, and filled the empty revolver from a box of .45-caliber shells. He shoved the gun behind his shell belt, tipped his hat down low on his forehead, shrugged into his denim jacket with fleece-lined collar, and left the jailhouse.

His lower jaw jutted, and his eyes were intense as he made his way toward the Drovers Saloon. Several men greeted him in passing. Stillman didn't return the greeting. He'd hardly seen them, and neither did he see them turn to regard him dubiously once he'd passed.

The horses he'd seen the two strangers ride into town on were tied with several others and a mule to one of the two hitchracks fronting the Drovers. Both were sweaty despite the chill in the air; they were mud-splattered and they owned a heavy layer of trail dust. They'd ridden far and hard and had crossed several creeks to get here.

A mud-splattered buckboard sat in front of the saloon, as well. A beefy, sad-eyed mongrel dog stood in the box, staring anxiously toward the saloon doors. As Stillman walked past the dog, he freed the keeper thong from over his holstered Colt's hammer.

He stopped atop the stoop fronting the saloon, and stared over the batwings. His eyes swept the inner shadows webbed with tobacco smoke and tanged with the molasses smells of whiskey, coal oil, and wood polish. There were a dozen or so customers—mostly ranch hands who'd come into town for supplies and had stopped to oil their tonsils before heading back out to their ramrods for further instructions.

The two men Stillman had seen earlier weren't hard to pick out. The top hat and round glasses of one and the rabbit foot dangling from the crown of the other man's bowler hat were distinctive. They stood about a third of the way down the bar, the nearest other customer several feet away.

They were facing each other, one elbow of each atop the zinc-covered bar, and their mouths moved as they conversed. They owned serious expressions—at least, the one facing the front of the saloon did. That was the bespectacled one, Four-Eyes Eldon Jones.

Most likely, Four-Eyes and Wainwright were discussing Stillman himself, how they were going to shoot him through his jailhouse window, or maybe they were considering going up to his house to kidnap his wife and child.

Stillman's heart tattooed a fervid rhythm against his breastbone. He drew a slow breath deep into his lungs, filling up his chest. He had to be steady for what he was about to do. Steady and purposeful, his mind on only the task at hand. Otherwise, he was likely to get himself greased. These were hardened desperados, seasoned killers.

They'd come for their money and they would get it any way they could.

Stillman's body might be failing him, but he had his experience and his confidence and his cool head. Those would have to be enough. He should have McMannigle backing him, but Leon had worked till noon and now was getting some sleep over at Mrs. Lee's place, as he'd be on night duty, guarding the outlaw girl as well as the Sulphur bank loot.

Stillman moved through the batwings. As he did, several heads turned toward him, including that of Four-Eyes Jones, who frowned behind his spectacles. Merle Wainwright turned to see what his partner was looking at, and then Stillman was nearly on top of them, pulling both pistols as he strode along the bar, cocking them. He aimed one Colt at Wainwright and one at Four-Eyes. Both outlaws were turned to face him now, and the other men at the bar were shuttling on out of the way.

"You two are under arrest," Stillman said. "Get those hands up."

Wainwright said, "Like hell we are!"

"Like hell you aren't!" Stillman smashed the barrel of his right-hand Colt across Wainwright's left temple, knocking the man's bowler hat off his head.

"God*damn*!" Wainwright bellowed, crouching and clapping both hands to his head, blood oozing from a gash.

At the same time, Four-Eyes reached for both the matched Remingtons jutting from his hips, their butts angled forward. He stopped when he saw Stillman aiming a Colt at the bridge of his nose, from a foot away, Stillman's icy blue eyes clear and steady beneath his bushy, dark-brown brows.

Wainwright must have seen that Stillman's eyes were on his partner. In the periphery of his right eye, Stillman watched the outlaw now down on one knee reach for one of his own pistols.

Keeping both eyes on Four-Eyes, Stillman rammed his right boot so deep into Wainwright's belly that he thought the toe of that boot nicked the man's backbone.

"*Ahh-ohhh!*" the outlaw loosed on a wave of expelled air, tumbling back onto his butt, and holding one arm down across

157

his belly, as though to ward off another blow. *"Ch-christ!"* Wainwright wheezed, his face brick red and pinched as he tried in vain to suck a breath.

Ramming one of his Colts down behind his cartridge belt, Stillman kept the other one aimed at Four-Eyes. He stooped to relieve Wainwright of both his pistols and a derringer from the pocket of his wash-worn paisley vest. He tossed all three pistols back behind him and threw a set of handcuffs to Four-Eyes.

"Put those bracelets on your partner. *Behind* his back. Be quick about it, and make 'em good an' tight. I'll be checkin', and I'll tattoo your head, too, if I don't like your work."

"Pound sand!"

Stillman lurched forward, raising the barrel of his Colt.

"All right!" Four-Eyes yelled, cowering.

Glowering at Stillman, he stooped to retrieve the cuffs, which had fallen to the floor. As Four-Eyes cuffed Wainwright's wrists behind his back, Stillman relieved Four-Eyes of both of his own pistols as well as a bowie knife jutting from the well of his left boot.

When Four-Eyes had both of Wainwright's wrists cuffed, Stillman tossed him the second pair of cuffs. When both men stood with their wrists cuffed behind their backs, Stillman stepped back and away from the bar, waving his prisoners toward the doors. As he did, he spied movement off his left flank. He'd been hearing very low whispering from that quarter, and now as he turned his head, he saw one of four men who'd been playing cards lurch to his feet, an expression of anxious cunning in his eyes as he brought up a Russian .44 and swung it toward Stillman.

Stillman whipped his Colt across his belly and under his left arm, and sent a slug careening between two of the card players, across the table, and into the belly of the man with the Russian. The Russian-wielder's name was Fielding Bellows, a cork-headed puncher for the Triple J Ranch over by Chinook. Middle-aged and dirty, with a dark-red neckerchief billowing down his calico shirt, he dropped the Russian on the table while his partners threw themselves from their chairs, and then Bellows stumbled back to pile up, screaming, onto another table behind him.

"Anyone else?" Stillman asked, waving his Colt around the room while also keeping his attention on his two handcuffed prisoners.

The other customers, including two soldiers from the fort, regarded Stillman warily. None appeared willing to cash in on Hettie's bounty offer. Not now, anyway, with Bellows writhing in a pool of his own blood on the floor.

Stillman turned to the town handyman, Olaf Weisinger, who stood to the right of the batwings, holding a frothy beer schooner in one fist, a smoking pipe in the other. "Olaf, best ring for the doc." When Evans was needed, it had become the custom for someone to run over to the church at the east end of town and ring the church bell four times. Evans would hear the bell up at his bluff-top house. "Three rings for the Trinity, four for the doc," was how the saying went.

Weisinger drained his glass, knocked the dottle out of his pipe, hurried through the batwings, and mounted his mule.

"Move," Stillman told his two prisoners. "You know the way."

He marched them through the batwings and east along the street. By now, most everyone on First Street had heard the shot he'd fired, and shopkeepers and customers were standing outside shops, staring. Wainwright was dragging his feet, wobbly-kneed, and groaning as he tossed his battered head around.

"You hurt me, Sheriff," Wainwright said. "You hurt me bad. I'm gonna remember that!"

"Shut up," Stillman said as he rammed his pistol into the middle of the man's back, evoking an angry curse.

When he got them inside the jailhouse, he ordered them to lie flat on the floor while he checked them over more thoroughly for weapons, finding another derringer, another Remington, and two more knives. Then he opened the cellblock door and led them down the alley between the cages.

Hettie was standing at the door of her own cell, eyes wide and lower jaw hanging in shock.

"Well, look what the cat dragged in," she said, removing her hands from the bars and taking one step back from the door.

Four-Eyes and Wainwright stopped in front of her cell.

"Bitch!" Four-Eyes ground out at her.

Hettie turned to Stillman. "Sheriff, you can't lock them two in here with me! You can't do it! They'll kill me!"

"Shut up," Stillman said, or "I'll lock them in your cell, and we'll see who's standin' come mornin'."

CHAPTER 19

" 'For medicinal purposes only,' " Doc Evans said in a mocking tone as he popped the cork on the bottle of Spanish brandy that Evelyn Vincent had brought over for him. He was mocking the Widow Kemmett, not Evelyn. Evelyn had sent the bottle over with a delicious lunch but with no admonishment per the manner in which the brandy was consumed.

Evans was mocking Katherine Kemmett, for those had been the widow's words when he'd come down from his afternoon nap the other day and had discovered the basket of food on the table as well as the bottle standing beside it.

Evans was standing on his porch now, staring out over the rooftops of Clantick to the east. He sniffed the cork and then the lip of the bottle, which bore an etching of King Ferdinand. The doctor closed his eyes and smiled at the wonderful aroma—like old leather books and prunes—wafting up from the dark-amber-colored liquid. He supposed he should have felt grateful that Katherine hadn't thrown out the precious liquor, so rare in these parts, and not mentioned a word about it. She'd probably figured she'd have been found out the next time the doc spoke to Evelyn, however, so she'd left it on the table with her harpy's admonition.

"For medicinal purposes only, Clyde," he said, chuckling around the cork he'd stuck between his lips as he poured an inch of the lovely liquid into a snifter.

He supposed he wasn't being fair to the widow. Katherine

was no liar. She was trying to make him into a full-fledged abstainer by the time they were married next month, but she hadn't come right out and forbidden him from having a drink now and then. She knew that forbidding Clyde Evans from doing anything was a surefire way to get him to do just the opposite of what she wanted. She admonished his "weakness" in a joking way, condemning him and his habit while smiling, remarking that "wholesomeness was the path to a whole heart," and other such rot.

She did the same concerning his penchant for cigars.

Evans sank with a grunt into his favorite wicker porch chair, where he whiled away many a temperate afternoon reading, drinking, and smoking. He reached into a shirt pocket for a stogie, and bit off the end. He'd given up the doxies at Mrs. Lee's place but only because the widow was allowing him a premarital poke now and then.

He'd be damned if he'd give up alcohol and tobacco. It just wasn't his way, and he wasn't trying to pull the wool over Katherine's eyes about it. He'd made sure that she understood that she and Evans couldn't be married if she thought a marriage license were a warrant to turn him into the old Reverend Kemmett, her former husband who'd probably never cussed in his life much less smoked or drank or enjoyed a mattress dance with a giggling whore not yet twenty.

Evans doubted that Reverend Kemmett had ever given Katherine much of a thrill in the old mattress sack, either, for when Evans had finally bedded the widow that first time, he'd never heard any woman or girl, including a *dove du pave,* squeal with such abandon, as though she'd never known that the act could actually be pleasant and not just something she were forced to do, like cleaning out the pantry once a month.

After that first, energetic mattress dance, however, she'd grown guarded and apprehensive. The few times they'd love-wrestled since then, she'd been stiff and impassive, as though she were ashamed of how her body had responded to his the first time they'd enjoyed each other's company. All signs pointed to Katherine not growing any more comfortable with the pleasures of the flesh even after they were married, and Evans wasn't sure how he could endure such a relationship.

He looked at the coal on the stogie he'd just lit, and sighed.

After all, pleasures of the flesh were about all we human animals really had. What else was there when you really stopped to think about it? Evans had been alone a long time, however. He wasn't getting any younger. As his closest confidante, Evelyn Vincent, had once counseled him, "Where was the value in a life that wasn't shared with someone you loved?"

"Come on, Doc," she'd added. "Are percentage girls going to be around to comfort you in your old age? The widow loves you and you love her—you know you do. Go ahead and marry the woman and live happily ever after!"

"Happily ever after," Evans grumbled now, blowing out a long plume of cigar smoke into the chill, September air.

His confusion over the marriage matter making him feel desolate, he puffed the cigar and raised the brandy snifter to his lips. Just as he did, the church bell clanged. Evans jerked with a start, as though it were his own death knells rolling up from the west end of Clantick.

The bell tolled once, twice, three, and then four times, the clangs echoing chillingly. The bell was for him, he realized, as the tolls reverberated, fading to silence until he could hear the chill breeze once again ruffling the dead grass around his house, and the piping of the meadowlarks.

They were for him, but not to announce his death, only to call him to work.

"Shit," the doctor said, scowling into the snifter. He hadn't had one sip of the brandy. For a moment, he imagined it was

Katherine down there, jerking on the church bell's rope to keep him from his libation, and he chuckled at the thought—just like her to do something like that—as he poured the brandy back into the bottle.

No point in taking one sip when he couldn't enjoy a full glass. He'd savor it while he went down and tended his chores in the name of ole Hippocrates. Some mule-skinner with a shattered knee, most likely, or some drunk gambler had roughed up a saloon girl and his reward had been a stiletto bristling from his scrotum.

Happened all the time. Snake bites, too. Cowpunchers would ride into the river breaks where diamondbacks were rife, to rescue bogged calves, and come out howling from a snake bite.

Some made it to town in time, some didn't. All Evans could do for those who didn't was quiet their howling with cheap whiskey and a swatch of leather to chomp down on, though some begged for a bullet.

"The pleasures of the flesh," Evans said with another long, raking sigh as he grabbed his heavy wool coat and bowler hat and headed out to the barn to saddle Faustus.

Ten minutes later, his medical kit hanging from his saddle horn, Doc Evans galloped down the bluff from his house and into the outskirts of Clantick. As he passed the Lutheran church on his right, where the widow's husband had preached until he'd died, he looked ahead to see Olaf Weisinger, dressed in a bulky canvas coat and canvas, fur-lined hat with ear flaps, standing in the middle of the street out front of the Drovers Saloon, waving an arm broadly, slowly, above his head.

Evans pulled Faustus up to a hitch rack and, when the chestnut's hoof thuds had died, he could hear howls and curses emanating from over the saloon's batwing doors. The inside cold-weather doors were pulled only half-closed despite the day's unseasonable chill.

"Don't tell me, let me guess," Evans said as Weisinger approached. "One drunk gambler tried to carve a smile onto the poker face of his opponent with a broken beer bottle."

He climbed down from the saddle and pulled his bag down from the horn. "Or were a couple of prospective jakes fighting over the attentions of Miss Versailles?"

"Neither one, Doc," Weisinger said, trudging up the saloon's porch steps in front of the doc. "The sheriff gave that jasper Fielding Bellows a pill he's having a devil of a time digesting."

"Bellows," the doc said. "The drunken lunatic who works for the Triple J?"

Weisinger pushed the left batwing and the left cold-weather door open, and stepped aside to let the medico pass. "One and the same, Doc. One and the same."

The bellowing and cursing continued as Evans paused a few feet inside the doors, letting his eyes adjust to the dim, smoky shadows.

"Down here, Doc," he heard Evelyn Vincent call, and saw the girl wave from a table about halfway down the long, dark room.

Blinking and squinting behind his glasses, Evans saw that Evelyn was crouching over a man with a big, barrel-shaped belly sprawled across two shoved-together tables. The doc made his way between the tables, most of which were unoccupied though many were littered with the remnants of recent customers. There were only three men standing at the bar, staring toward the wounded man. Evans saw that two men, both of whom he recognized from the Triple J, were holding Fielding Bellows's arms down against the table, to keep him from thrashing around and bleeding himself dry.

Evelyn was holding a towel over the wounded man's left side, up high on his belly. She glanced at Evans, several stray locks of blond hair dangling along her flushed cheeks. "I'm tryin' to

165

keep him from pumpin' himself dry, Doc, but it don't seem to be doin' much good."

Evans wasn't surprised to find the waitress here. Sam Wa's would be closed this time of the day. When there was trouble in town, Evelyn was usually one of the first folks to lend a hand. She often assisted the doctor when Katherine Kemmett was tied up with her midwifing or church-boosting chores, and the energetic young woman had learned enough about doctoring from watching Evans work that she could set minor breaks and keep a wounded man from unnecessarily bleeding to death. Once, she'd even saved a boy from drowning in the Milk River when the beaver dam he'd been trying to cross with his fishing pole had broken away beneath his feet, and afterwards she'd cleared his lungs of water.

Evans moved up to the table.

"Let me have a look," he said, avoiding Bellows's spurred boots, which he was kicking and sliding around as he writhed.

Evelyn stepped aside. Evans removed the towel, instantly replaced it, and pushed down on it hard, causing Bellows to tip his head back sharply, scrunch up his eyes, and howl.

Evans looked at the two rough sorts holding his arms. "We gotta get him up to my house. He requires surgery."

"Is it bad, Doc?" asked the buck-toothed man holding Bellows's right arm.

"Bad enough. His liver's shredded." Evans looked down at the pig-eyed, freckled-faced man in disgust. "What in the hell did you do to deserve that bullet, Bellows, you old rat? And I don't doubt that you *did* deserve—not in the least."

His two friends said nothing but merely looked down in chagrin while they continued to hold down Bellows's arms.

"He tried to back-shoot Ben," Evelyn said in the same disgusted tone as Evans. "Ben was arresting two of that Hettie girl's partners, and Mr. Bellows decided to take the opportunity to earn the reward she set on Ben's head!"

"Oh, for Christ sakes," Evans said. "Why can't everyone just stay home and behave themselves." He was thinking about something the late great Plato had said about most of the world's problems vanishing if everyone could just sit quietly in their own rooms.

The doctor turned to Olaf Weisinger standing behind him and wincing down at the miserably writhing and howling Bellows. "Olaf, can you bring a wagon over from Auld's?"

"Sure thing, Doc," the handyman said, and limped on out of the saloon.

Evans turned to the young waitress, whom he vaguely realized had been staring up at him with a peculiar cast to her gaze. "Evelyn, I'm going to need some help with the surgery, and Katherine's out of town visiting a friend in the family way up on the border. Doubt she'll be home till tomor—"

"Absolutely, Doc," Evelyn said, shaking her head. "No problem at all!"

CHAPTER 20

"You did everything you could, Doc," Evelyn said, when later in the early evening she and Evans stood atop his porch, watching Auld and Weisinger haul the dead body of Fielding Bellows away in their buckboard.

The hooves of the horse thudded along the trail that dropped down the side of the bluff, and the wagon rattled loudly over the chuckholes. Evans could see Bellows's pointed-toed boots bouncing in the back of the wagon, and the blanket slide off to reveal half of his slack face.

"Yes, I did," the doc said with a sigh. "And don't tell Katherine I said this, but the world is a better place without Fielding Bellows in it. The man was a drunken lout; never heard or seen him do a lick of good anywhere to anyone. One time he damn near sawed a doxie's head off with a broken beer bottle, down in that old hog pen that Canadian once ran down along the river—until Ben ran him out and burned his rat-infested whorehouse to the ground."

"Why the long face, then, Doc?" Standing to his right, Evelyn rubbed his back.

"A very ridiculous reason," Evans said. "I don't like to get beat. Not at chess, checkers, poker, or healing. Even when it comes to a no-good, bottom-feeding, carp like Fielding Bellows." He shook his head. "But there's no saving a man with a liver that looked as though it had gone through a meat grinder. Could have passed for pâté."

"Doctor Evans!" Evelyn laughed and covered her mouth in mock shame.

Evans turned to her, chuckling. "You know—Katherine would have shaken her finger at me for saying such a crass thing as that."

Evelyn laughed again into her hand. "Don't worry, Doc. You know I come from a far different place than Katherine does."

"That's right—you do, don't you?" Evans knew that she'd once ridden with a small but nasty band of outlaws, though she'd been a far cry from the duplicitous and murderous Hettie Styles. And it hadn't taken Stillman much work to set Evelyn onto the straight and narrow, which is where she'd likely always belonged. She'd mostly just needed a show of respect from others, a kind hand, and a good job. "Sometimes it takes a little darkness for folks to truly appreciate the light—wouldn't you say, Evelyn?"

"I reckon, Doc. Thanks to Ben, you, and Sam, I reckon I'm enjoying the light—if that's what you mean. I do love Clantick and the folks here."

"Speaking of Sam . . ."

"Not to worry, Doc," Evelyn said. "Sam gave me the night off when he heard you needed my help. There's not usually much of a supper crowd on a weeknight. Sam's likely handled it fine himself. I'll go in first thing in the morning and clean up."

"I can't thank you enough for your assistance," the doctor said, fishing out the stogie he'd only half-smoked earlier from his shirt pocket. "There's no way I could have performed such an operation, albeit an unsuccessful one, alone." He gestured to the door as he dug a stove match from a vest pocket. "Let's go in. Chilly out here. I do believe there's a bite of winter in the air. I'll throw another log on the fire and stir us a toddy."

"I shouldn't stay, Doc," Evelyn said when he'd drawn the

door closed and they stood in the big house's gloomy entrance hall.

"Please, stay." Evens wrapped his hand around her right forearm. "There's uh . . . there's something I'd like to discuss with you. Something I need to say if only to hear how it sounds."

Evelyn's eyes brightened. She placed an affectionate hand over his. "In that case, Doc, of course. Why don't I cook supper while I'm here?"

"You must get tired of preparing food. No, I—"

"Don't mind a bit," the girl said, wheeling and heading off into the dark bowels of the house.

Evans couldn't help glancing at the girl's rump just before the shadows consumed her. So young and firm behind the muslin of her blue and white housedress. The uncharacteristic feeling of shame burned through him. Evelyn was fifteen years younger than he—a pretty, wholesome girl and his strongest ally and only real confidant here in Clantick, and here he was, ogling her behind. He supposed he'd been a little aroused by the warmth of her supple hand on the back of his.

He snorted ironically to himself. Katherine was right—he was a child in so many ways, a man in so few. Not only a child, he amended his estimation of himself as, just before entering the kitchen, he swerved off into the parlor, where he had a fire snapping in the stone hearth. He was a devilish boy with a secret, dark world in his head fed in no small part by his eclectic reading of old classics and contemporary trash.

Against his will, as he chunked a couple of pine logs on the grate and arranged them with the poker, he imagined Evelyn's pink, round rump in his hands. He imagined how she would appear, naked and pink and . . .

"You nasty son of a bitch," he muttered as he opened the sitting room door wide so that the heat would penetrate the kitchen.

"What's that, Doc?" Evelyn glanced at him from where she was bent forward, dress drawn taut across her round hips, lighting the range.

"Oh, I was just remarking it's going to be a cold night—I can feel it in my bones," Evans said, rubbing his arms as he entered the kitchen and headed for his customary chair at the far end of the table, near a window that looked out over the river to the north. The brandy was there. "Drink?"

Evelyn looked at the bottle she'd given him, and the corners of her mouth twitched as she turned back to her task at hand. "Sure. Why not?"

Evans lit a Rochester lamp against the growing dark and then retrieved another brandy snifter from a shelf by his chair, splashed a couple of fingers of the leathery-smelling liquor into it, and slid it to the side of the table nearest her as she worked. He half-filled his own glass, retrieved an ashtray from where Katherine had half-hid it on a high shelf, and then he slacked into his rocking chair. The chair, like most of the hodgepodge furniture in his house, had been given to him in payment of services rendered. The chair was stoutly built of woven cottonwood branches, padded with cowhide to which the cream and brown fur was still attached, and decorated with bullhorns on the ends of the back and on the arms.

Evans loved the chair—it both amused him and had come to fit him like a glove. He'd spent many hours reading and smoking and drinking in this chair while staring out over the river.

Tonight, however, he faced the table and the kitchen and the pretty, blond-headed girl toiling for him. He smoked and sipped the brandy while Evelyn hummed softly to herself while she fried a couple of steaks from a side of beef the doc had hanging in his keeper shed and springhouse. It didn't take her long to fry the steak and a couple of large, red potatoes also from the keeper shed, humming happily all the while.

Evans helped her clear the table and scrub the dishes after they'd finished eating, and then he brewed a pot of coffee, added more wood to the range as well as to the fireplace in the sitting room, and replenished their brandy snifters though Evelyn had drunk only half of hers. They sat down again at the table with their drinks.

It was dark outside, and Evans was enjoying how the lantern light played across Evelyn's pale blue eyes. She seemed to be looking at him more than usual tonight, with a curious, speculative radiance, as though she were concealing a secret that was on the tip of her tongue. Evans made only fleeting, sporadic note of this, however, consumed as he was by his misgivings about his proposed marriage and Evelyn's possible reaction to them.

After all, the waitress was the one who'd finally convinced him that he should marry Katherine, and settle down.

"What was it you wanted to talk to me about, Doc?" Evelyn asked, blowing ripples on the surface of her steaming coffee.

Evans dumped some of his brandy into the coffee, sniffed the steam, and then sipped the heady concoction. He wasn't sure how to proceed. Shame again touched his cheeks. He needed to get the weight off his chest, however. He'd always felt so much better after discussing his problems with Evelyn. She'd been a good friend, and he'd found it helpful to have a woman he could talk openly to and who, in return, would furnish him with her female brand of advice, which he'd always found practical and wise.

"I don't think I can go through with it," he blurted out, staring down at the brandy snifter he'd taken in both hands. He held his breath, waiting for his friend's reaction.

She said nothing. He felt her eyes on him. When he couldn't bare the silence any longer, he lifted his eyes to Evelyn's. She was staring at him. Tears glistened in her eyes. A couple of tears were rolling down along the sides of her nose, sparking in the light of the lamp hanging over the table.

Evans felt the burn of her disappointment reach up into his ears. There was a low humming in his head. He hadn't realized how badly Evelyn had wanted him to marry Katherine. Suddenly, he realized that by getting married he was becoming the man that Evelyn had always hoped he would become.

His not marrying her would signify a return to his old, lecherous, hard-drinking ways.

But, then, just as he was silently scrambling for the words with which he could justify his reasons, the girl smiled, showing the tips of her white teeth, a few of which were slightly crooked. Her pale cheeks dimpled. She peeled a hand from her brandy snifter, slid it across the table, and placed it on one of Evans's. She squeezed, sniffed.

"Doc?"

"What is it?"

"I have something to tell *you* now. A secret I've been keeping for months."

Evans waited, confusion rippling through him, complicating the shame still humming in his ears.

Evelyn rose slowly from her chair. She dropped to one knee beside him, again placed her hand on his, and looked up, smiling through the tears continuing to dribble down her cheeks. "God forgive me, but . . . I'm in love with you, Doc."

Evans felt as though he'd been struck with a bung starter. He sagged back in his chair. He was in such shock that he could have been knocked over with a feather duster.

"You . . . are?" he said.

"I didn't want it . . . I wasn't expectin' it to happen. I guess when you're around a man as much as I've been around you the past year, and after we've shared all the things we've shared, the feelings just started to grow. I've never known anyone like you, Doc. You're so smart and handsome. I feel so guilty . . . so bad for the Wid—I mean, Mrs. Kemmett." More tears dribbled down Evelyn's smooth cheeks. "But I just can't help myself. I wasn't gonna say anything. I wasn't! Fay told me it was only a passing fancy and that I probably shouldn't mention it, that I should think of Katherine! But now that you've decided—well, I think you're right not to marry her. She doesn't . . . she can't possibly love you the way I do!"

Gradually, Evelyn had lifted up off her knee, leaning toward Evans. Now she had one hand on a bullhorn bristling from the chair arm, and another hand splayed across Evans's chest. "Do you feel the same way I do, Doc? Do you feel *anything*?" She sobbed as she pressed her hand harder against his chest. "Please, say you do!"

Evans's heart thudded. A sudden desire was a living, breathing beast inside him—wooly and unkempt and ravenous. Evelyn's face was only inches from his. He could feel her breath coming fast and warm against his lips.

"Evelyn," Evans said, placing his left hand on the back of her neck, his right hand on her left arm, and drawing her closer, closing his mouth over hers. Her lips were plump and red and cool as she opened them slightly against his own, and they tasted like apricots. He slid his tongue between them and the tip of hers was there to meet it—warm and wet and gently caressing.

He kissed her, and she returned the kiss, until his desire was hammering away inside him like a locomotive's fully stoked engine. He pushed her away from him slightly while still holding her tightly, and said, "Why don't we go upstairs?"

Evelyn averted her gaze, suddenly shy, her cheeks and her ears under her hair reddening, and she nodded.

Evans rose, took the girl by her hand, and began leading her toward the stairway. He stopped, swung back around, grabbed the brandy bottle and the two snifters, and continued leading her through the house and up the stairs to his spartanly furnished bedroom. He did have a large, canopied bed, however, which he'd had shipped in from Great Falls. It nearly filled the room. Evans spent many cold, winter days when business was slow simply lying in bed like a drunken Lord, drinking, reading, snoozing, and stoking the small wood stove in a corner.

Evans lit a lamp. Breathing hard, he sat the girl down on the edge of the bed, and kissed her. "Are you sure about this?" he asked.

"We shouldn't, but . . . yes. I love you, Doc. Do you love me?"

Evans dropped to a knee in front of her. As much as he wanted to make love to her, he couldn't lie to her. He took both of her hands in his. "Frankly, Evelyn, I don't know. I've been so confused lately about Katherine . . ." He shook his head. "I can't say for sure. All I do know is that I love being with you, and tonight was pure joy. It still would be . . . even if we ended it right here."

Evelyn gazed up at him, her eyes intent. "I'm all yours, Doc. I'm all yours, because I love you, and I want you to have me if you want me."

"I want you."

She began unbuttoning the top of her dress. "All right, then."

"Let me do that," Evans said, and unbuttoned the dress, staring at her pale, heart-shaped face with its small, alluring nose and red lips that were slightly parted. Evelyn's eyes were two smoldering coals in the room's dense shadows. Her breasts rose and fell sharply behind the dress as he unbuttoned it.

He pulled the dress off her pale, delicate body, and then removed her stockings, garters, and pantaloons. Last, he lifted her chemise up over her head, and her small, perfectly shaped breasts jostled slightly as the fabric raked her nipples. Her long hair spilled over her slender shoulders and down her long arms.

She sat naked on the bed before him, hands resting palm up in her lap, one bare foot resting girlishly atop the other.

Evans gasped at the girl's pale, cherubic beauty. She was nearly perfectly formed, but with just the amount of extra flesh that the doctor preferred on a woman. She had full, round hips for easy childbearing.

Evelyn sat looking down while Evans kicked out of his half boots and then shucked out of the rest of his clothes.

He had no idea how long they'd been making love, causing the bed to bark and squawk and the floor to creak beneath it, when he thought he heard something in the hall. He was too enmeshed in his endeavor, Evelyn writhing beneath him as she'd done in his fantasy, running her fingertips up and down his sides, gently tickling him, to give the sound much thought except to think it was probably one of the four or five half-wild cats he fed and provided inside beds for when the weather turned cold.

Just after the bed had fallen quiet, a horse whinnied in the yard below Evans's room. He and Evelyn shared an anxious look. Evans slipped out of bed, moved naked to the window, and looked out into the cold dark night.

Starlight winked off a pair of red buggy wheels as Katherine's chaise rattled out of the yard and into the darkness.

CHAPTER 21

The grinding of buggy wheels and the clattering of a light wagon rose ahead and to Stillman's right in the darkness.

The din grew quickly louder. Someone was rolling into town way too fast for this late at night. Stillman had slowed Sweets to nearly a halt as he was riding back into town after having supper with Fay and Little Ben. But now he touched spurs to the bay's flanks and cantered ahead along the side street that would intersect with First Street another block ahead. It was too dark out here, the trace lit only by lights from the shacks on either side of it, to safely gallop the horse.

Stillman was half a block from First Street when he saw the buggy dash into view ahead of him—a dark murky blur on the better-lit main drag. He saw a flash of red wheel spokes and then the horse and the buggy pulled out of view behind the storefronts on the sheriff's left. A man cursed loudly and then Stillman turned Sweets onto First Street.

The Drovers was ahead—the best-lit building on this end of town. Men were milling behind the horses clumped at the two hitch racks. One man appeared to be down, and he was yelling loudly, cursing angrily, while a couple of others were crouching over him. The buggy then turned off the main street, heading south and disappearing from Stillman's view.

"Good Lord!" one of the men crouching over the fallen man was saying. "What in tarnation is wrong with that woman?"

Stillman checked Sweets near the three men. The man on the

177

ground between the two sets of jittery horses was a tinker from Chinook who pulled through Clantick once a week. Stillman thought the gent probably drank up every penny he made going door to door, mending pots and pans, in the saloons and brothels after business hours.

"You all right, Haley?" Stillman asked the man, who was being helped up by two other men.

Haley Brewer looked at Stillman, grunting and nudging his spectacles up on his long, hooked nose with a gloved right fist. Indignantly, he said, "She like to run me over, Sheriff!"

"Who was it?"

"The widow," said one of the other two men. "The Widow Kemmett. What in the hell is she drivin' so fast for?"

"Seen her leave town in a hurry when a lady was about to deliver a child," said the third man, who had a shotgun ranch a mile east. "But I never seen her return in a whirlwind like that!"

"You need the doc, Haley?" Stillman asked.

"Nah, I'll be all right," the tinker said, bending forward to brush off the knees of his patched, striped trousers. "Just wonder what bee the widow's got in her bonnet's all . . ."

"Me, too," Stillman said, touching spurs to Sweets's flanks again and trotting forward along First Street.

He'd thought he'd recognized the rig despite the darkness, as there weren't many people in Clantick who owned as stylish a black leather, red-wheeled buggy with a folding top as that which the widow drove. Her husband, the Reverend, had driven it around the countryside, preaching to those folks who couldn't make it into town for church on Sundays, and now she drove it around the county, tending pregnant women.

Stillman turned down the side street that led to the widow's small but neat shotgun shack near the Fawcett Boarding House. He saw the leather buggy with its red wheels pull up the short, oval-shaped gravel drive that led to the house, which squatted darkly under the stars, and stop in front of the white buggy shed ensconced in shrubbery and flanked by a large box elder. A covered well hunched near the street. Sweets shook his head and rattled the bit in his teeth as Stillman turned before the well, into the widow's driveway. The widow's horse whinnied; Sweets returned the greeting.

"Hush, Biscuit." The widow climbed down from the buggy and stared toward Stillman. She was a slender figure in the darkness. "Is that you, Sheriff Stillman?"

"It's me, Mrs. Kemmett." Stillman stopped Sweets beside the chaise. "Are you all right, ma'am?"

"I'm fine," she said crisply as she started unhitching the horse from her rig.

"You almost ran over Haley Brewer on First Street."

"I do apologize," she said in a none-too-apologetic tone. "When they're drunk, as they usually are, they shouldn't be on the street after dark, is how I see it."

Stillman watched her, puzzled. He thought he'd heard a tremor in her otherwise cold, toneless voice. "Would you like me to stable your horse for you, ma'am?"

"No, thank you," she said, dropping the shafts away from the horse and leading the animal into the open-fronted shed. From inside she said, "I don't need any man to help me unharness my horse—thank you, Sheriff Stillman, and good night."

He could hear her and the horse moving around in the stable, which the starlight did not penetrate. He could no longer see the widow, but he heard the quick raking of a currycomb.

"All right, ma'am. You need anything, you let me know."

Stillman urged Sweets on around the oval drive and back out to the side street, heading toward First Street and the heart of town. He rode slowly, his mind on the widow. Obviously, she and Evans had had another one of their infamous fights. He hoped the doc hadn't done anything to hinder his and Mrs.

Kemmett's wedding plans. Getting hitched to the woman, despite how persnickety she could be, would be the best thing for the lonely, middle-aged sawbones.

Everyone in town could see that, including Stillman himself. Marrying Fay and starting a family had been the best thing he'd ever done. Besides, if Evans kept relying solely on whores for his satisfaction, sooner or later he was going to come down with a case of clap or syphilis that even he couldn't cure despite the shelf full of concoctions he'd formulated for just that purpose.

Stillman pulled back abruptly on Sweets's reins, and glanced behind him. His lawman's ears had picked up something. A shadow slipped off the street and behind a cottonwood that towered over the old Shelty horse stable. Stillman turned the bay around and slid his Henry repeater from its sheath. One-handed, he racked a round into the chamber.

He stared toward the cottonwood that stood dark and silent in the quiet night. There was no other movement, so Stillman rode over and peered cautiously around behind the tree and toward where an old freighting warehouse had once stood before a fire had consumed it one Christmas eve many years ago. There was only the charred ruin of the brick foundation left.

Something moved along the left side of the foundation, and then the shadow slipped into the dry creek bed that curved along the foundation's left rear corner.

"Hold it!" Stillman shouted. "Stop right there or I'll shoot— it's Sheriff Stillman!"

There was only the crunch of dry grass and the low grind of gravel, and then silence.

Stillman hurried Sweets up along the side of the foundation. Anger chewed at him. Someone had been trying to set up another bushwhack—possibly the same person who'd fired into his house. If he could run him down, he'd have the son of a bitch who'd endangered his family.

Moving with less caution than he should have, as the darkness was relieved only by starlight, he put Sweets through a gap in some spindly willows, and dropped down into the creek bottom. The shadow was moving straight ahead of him, and then it suddenly disappeared.

"Halt!" Stillman fired a shot into the air. The report was a loud hiccup that, after a few seconds, started a dog to barking off to the west.

Ahead, the stony creek bed meandered toward the southwest.

Stillman urged the bay ahead. Sweets's hooves seemed suddenly heavy, and the horse was whickering very softly and twitching his ears. The horse sensed his rider's unease; that, in turn, made the horse nervous. For good reason, Stillman thought. At night, any man who wanted to kill you had the advantage. He could hole up and just wait for you to ride into his rifle sites.

Still, the sheriff pushed the horse forward. Where the creek began to trail off toward the south, he stopped. To his right there was the high-pitched crackle of a boot breaking through the thin, platelike ice of a mud puddle. A man's muffled curse reached Stillman's ears.

"I said stop!" Stillman shouted in exasperation, and neck-reined Sweets sharply right, climbing the low bank, bulling through some willows and heading back in the direction of First Street.

He stopped the horse again, and looked around. His heart was beating in his ears. He had that crawling feeling he got whenever he suspected someone might be drawing a bead on him. Half expecting to see the flash of a rifle at any moment, he probed the layered, sundry-shaped shadows around him. There were several neat frame houses to his far left, all with their windows showing pale lamplight. It was near one of those houses that the dog was barking.

Straight ahead was an alley and on the other side of the alley were the dark backs of the buildings that lined First Street. Nothing moved between him and the buildings.

Between some of the buildings were gaps of various widths, and Stillman gigged Sweets toward the nearest gap. A wooden building on each side closed around him, muffling the dog's angry barking. The clomping of Sweets's hooves echoed. Stillman smelled old lumber and the gamey smell of trash. The horse kicked an empty bottle and a tin can and tramped across an old newspaper, and then Sweets walked out of the break and into the wide, deserted street opening ahead and on both sides, intermittent puddles of lamplight spilling from street-facing windows.

Stillman stopped the horse just beyond the mouth of the gap. He could hear voices emanating dully from up and down the street. Someone was playing a guitar. There was a short bout of raucous male laughter. Ahead, a man was walking along the boardwalk on the other side of First Street. A vaguely familiar figure. The only one around.

Stillman's stalker?

Stillman watched the familiar figure walk into a small gathering of men out front of the Milk River Saloon—one of the oldest of the town's business establishments and a favorite of the old-timers. It was a small, low place built of mud, brick, and stone. The front of the sagging building looked like a mine portal with heavy timbers and a sign over the front door announcing the place's name in badly faded letters that weren't visible now in the darkness.

An oil pot burned on the street in front of the place. Sparks sprayed from the pot, some glowing like fireflies before burning out. It was around the torch that four or five burly men in fur coats and hats were gathered with soapy beer mugs in their fists. A woman was amongst them, and she was speaking in low tones to one of the men, her and the men standing a few intimate feet away from the others.

The familiar figure stepped through this small crowd, opened the Milk River's front door, and slipped inside, allowing a woman's ribald laughter to boil into the street for a second before he drew the door closed behind him, cutting off the voice.

Stillman gigged Sweets ahead and turned the bay toward the hitchrack at which three other saddled horses stood. He swung down from the leather, and, still holding the Henry, threw the bridle reins over the hitchrack. He mounted the rickety front stoop beneath a brush roof through the large gaps in which he could see the stars.

"Hey, Sheriff, was that the widow we seen tear by here a few minutes ago?" asked a man standing nearest the door. His name was Dawkins, a freighter who had a pig farm at the edge of town, just east of Katherine Kemmett's place, and supplied most of the town's pork.

Stillman told him it was.

"What's got her neck in a hump?" Dawkins asked. His eyes were bleary from drink, and his breath smelled like a beer keg.

"Couldn't tell you." Stillman started to open the Milk River's front door.

"Might have somethin' to do with Sam Wa's purty waitress bein' over at the doc's place."

Stillman turned to the man who'd spoken—Alvin Mac-Donald, a part-time telegrapher at the Western Union office. "What's that?"

MacDonald grinned and dipped his chin importantly. His eyes, too, were drink bleary, and the right one was half-closed against the smoke curling upward from the quirley dangling between his teeth. "That's what Olaf Weisinger told me earlier.

Said that purty, li'l waitress went over to help the doc and she was still there when Weisinger and Auld hauled old Bellows's carcass away to be crated up at the livery barn. I'm thinkin' she, that li'l waitress, might just be the bee the wider's got in her bonnet."

He chuckled lewdly, as did the others around him.

"MacDonald," Stillman said, in no mood for idle gossip, "why don't you hobble your lip and mind your own damn business?"

He strode into the saloon and closed the door behind him.

CHAPTER 22

There were only three customers in the small saloon, including a plump, redheaded saloon girl sitting at the piano toward the back, paging through a songbook as though trying to figure out what to play next. She was overdressed for the shabby place. One of the customers was the kid Stillman had seen in the Drovers when Stillman had first encountered Battles. Gandy Miller was sitting at a table near the rough-hewn bar manned by a squat half-breed named Carl Mourning Day, who sat on a stool trimming his nails with a skinning knife, a black cigar smoldering in an ashtray before him. Mourning Day nodded at Stillman and arched his brows. The sheriff waved a hand to indicate he did not want anything to drink.

The sheriff tromped past the other two customers, who were playing checkers at a table near the door, and walked over to where the baby-faced kid in the battered black Stetson and steerhide vest, Miller, was leaning over a fresh beer and a newspaper spread open on the table before him.

Miller glanced up from his paper, looked down, and then jerked his eyes up in surprise. "Well, hello there, Marshal Still . . . I mean *Sheriff* Stillman!" He chuckled. "What can I do for you this fine, crisp September evenin'?"

"Mind if I sit down?"

"Shit, I'd be right honored." Miller kicked the chair out across from him.

Stillman laid his Henry across the corner of the table, to his right, and slacked into the chair. "What you readin' there?"

Miller blushed and turned the paper around so that Stillman could read it. The rag was a *Policeman's Gazette* from a dozen years ago. It was crinkled, yellowed, and coffee-stained, and some of its edges were charred, as though it had been read around campfires. The headline of the illustrated yarn lying face up on the table announced in bold, black letters:

THE LAST RIDE OF JACOB HENRY BATTLES.

To the right was a pen and ink illustration of a narrow-eyed, grimacing, mustached badman shooting out from inside a narrow box canyon at three men firing in at him. It was a dark, murky night. Stillman could almost smell the powder smoke puffing from the maws of the blasting guns, hear the rocketing reports, and see the red-blue lightning-like flashes. Not because the illustration was particularly effective, though it wasn't bad— but because he so well remembered the night itself.

It had looked nothing like the picture, however. The box canyon had been much broader and deeper than the one depicted, and all the players had been widely separated from each other. One of the two South Dakota federals, Mortimer Walker, had been puking sick from drinking tainted water, and he'd held far back but had also been part of the gauntlet that Battles had tried to run. That's why it was hard to know which lawman's bullet had cost Battles his arm.

Below the illustration lay the article's subtitle in rollicking italics feathered by gun smoke trailing away from the illustration's rifles: "The Old Regulator Meets His Match in Crafty Montana Lawman Ben Stillman!"

Stillman turned the paper back around toward Miller, and arched a skeptical brow.

"It's one of my favorites," Miller said, still blushing.

"You been carrying that around all these years?" Stillman asked.

Miller shrugged. "My war bag's plum near full of others just like it. I love readin' these rags. Sorta takes my mind away. Fills it with dreams."

"Makes the world feel bigger, don't it?"

"That's it," Miller said.

"Even though what's in most of them yarns is wrong. At least, that one there has to be mostly gilded lily. No one ever interviewed me for the story, and they couldn't have interviewed Battles because he was laid up for three months afterwards, before they shipped him off to Deer Lodge. They must've taken most of it from the few lines in the Milestown newspaper, and embellished it all from there."

"Oh, I don't know," Miller said, running a dirty thumbnail across the illustration. "They coulda gotten it mostly right. Leastways, it seems like it musta happened the way they have it. If you don't mind, Sheriff, I'd like to think so, anyways."

"Where were you four nights ago, about this time?" Stillman had fired it point blank, and he stared at Miller, gauging his re- action.

The kid frowned. "Four nights ago? Well, let me think." He fingered his chin and pondered the low ceiling from which sooty cobwebs hung. "I'll be hanged if I can remember!"

Stillman looked under the table. "Your boots are muddy."

Miller looked under the table, as well. "Well, hell, Sheriff, the streets are muddy. Look at the boots of them fellas over there. Their boots're muddy, too!"

Stillman looked at the boots of the two men playing checkers near the front door. Miller was right. Their boots were also muddy.

"Yours are freshly muddy," Stillman pointed out.

"Well, I'm freshly in from the mud!"

"You were following me a few minutes ago, weren't you?"

"Followin' you?" Miller looked both perplexed and indignant.

"A few minutes ago? Hell, no. I just came from my job. Got off work not fifteen minutes ago."

"Job?"

"Sure, I'm workin' for Auld now in his livery barn. Ask Mr. Auld himself, if you don't believe me. I was ridin' by his barn the other day when him and Mr. Weisinger was gettin' ready to haul them men you and Mr. Battles killed up to Boot Hill, and he offered me a buck and two bits to help him get them boys in the ground. Since I'm a little light in the pockets, havin' spent the last of my coinage on Kansas Kate and a few beers, I was glad for the offer. Auld offered me a dollar a day to help him out in his barn three days a week. I reckon he was needin' a little younger help than what he was gettin' in Mr. Weisinger, no offense to Mr. Weisinger, of course."

"Of course not."

"Say, what's this about, Sheriff?"

"Someone took a shot at my house the other night."

"And you think I would do a lowdown dirty nasty thing such as that?" Miller looked hurt. Stillman couldn't tell if the expression was genuine. Every emotion the kid expressed was exaggerated to the point of absurdity, and he was as groveling as a snake-oil salesman.

He was either shrewd or soft in his thinker box. Stillman didn't trust him any more than he'd trust a chicken-thieving coyote.

"I don't know," Stillman said. "Maybe."

"Why on God's green earth would I do such a thing?"

"Maybe because you wanted me to think it was Battles who'd fired that shot."

Miller stared across the table at Stillman, appearing pensive, perplexed. "Why would I want you to think that?"

"Maybe because you'd like to see another article like the one you're just now rereadin'. One that was a little fresher—not quite so yellowed and charred."

"Oh," Miller said, nodding slowly. "You think I'd like to pit you two against each other to see how it'd turn out."

"Isn't that why you're still in town, muckin' out Auld's livery stalls?"

Still nodding slowly, the kid shaped a sheepish smile. He lifted his beer to his lips and, staring over the glass at Stillman, took a sip. He licked the foam from his clean-shaven upper lip. "I reckon that is why I'm here, Sheriff. Shoulda known you'd figure it out. Sure, I'd like to see a rematch. One a little more equally sided. One against one instead of three against one. Yeah, that'd be a fight to watch. Two old, cross-grained bulls crawlin' each other's humps. That'd be the pumpkins!"

"Not gonna happen, kid."

"How do you know?" Miller smiled again, shrewdly. "And how do you know it wasn't Battles who fired that shot at your house?"

"Because he wouldn't have missed."

"Maybe he wasn't tryin' to hit anything. Maybe he was just toyin' with you, Sheriff. Maybe hittin' you that first time woulda been too easy. You gotta remember—Battles was in the pen for a long time. A dozen years. You don't think he'd get his revenge so quick-like, now, do you?"

Stillman scowled across the table at the kid smiling with infuriating insouciance. He had to admit that Miller had a point. Maybe a good one. Maybe Battles was just egging Stillman on, worrying him, biding his time, waiting to kill one of the men who'd put the old regulator away for so long until he'd thought he'd worn him down. Until Battles had gotten his money's worth.

What did Battles have to lose? The risk involved in a slow stalk would mean little to a dying man.

Even though Battles had an alibi for that night, Stillman

couldn't exclude him. Battles was cagey. But, then, again, Gandy Miller was cagey, too.

"I don't know, Sheriff," the kid continued, running his hands over the table as though clearing it of dust, "I don't think I'd let my guard down with that old enemy of yours in town. Say, I thought you'd run him *out* of town? What happened, anyways?"

"If I run anybody out of town, kid, it's most likely going to be you. So you keep your nose clean, hear? If I even think you might be playing me and Battles against each other, and if I see you anywhere near my house, I'll run you out of town on a rail. That is, if I'm not plantin' you up on that hill where Auld hired you to plant the others."

He'd have run him out of town now, but he didn't want to leave Auld in the lurch. Besides, he wasn't sure he wasn't seeing things through a cloud of untempered emotion.

"All right," the kid said, poker-faced. "I heard you loud and clear, Sheriff. But can I just assure you, sir, that you're barkin' up the wrong tree here, tonight? It ain't me you got to worry about. No sir—not me. It's the bounty that purty prisoner placed on your head . . . and the Devil's Left-Hand Man."

He smiled and looked dreamily down at the paper.

Stillman glanced at the redheaded saloon girl sitting at the piano at the rear of the room. She was staring toward Stillman and Miller with a nervous expression, absently rifling the pages of the music book in her lap.

Stillman pinched his hat brim to the girl, trying to assure her that no lead would be swapped here tonight. Possibly somewhere else in town later—likely later—but not here and not tonight.

He glanced once more at Miller and then scooped his rifle up off the table and headed for the batwings.

Stillman rode over to the jailhouse to make sure all was well with his deputy, McMannigle.

With possibly three more outlaws lurking around town, waiting for an opportunity to retrieve the money they'd stolen from
the Sulphur Bank, he didn't want Leon to make his usual
rounds. Ambush was too big a risk. He instructed the deputy to
stay with the prisoners. Stillman had ridden down from his
house after supper to make one final round before heading
home to spend the night with his family.

He'd relieve his deputy in the morning.

The sheriff from Sulphur would be here soon, to retrieve the
prisoners and the money, but until that happened, the prisoners
and the loot were Stillman's responsibility. He'd be glad to see
the Sulphur sheriff and say goodbye to Hettie Styles and the
two others from her gang.

Stillman rode up the bluff toward his house feeling anxious.
His right arm was heavy, but it was still working. And for that
he was glad. His left leg was stiff and tight, but he could still
walk and ride. He didn't know for how much longer, or what
he'd do when he could no longer do his job. The thought of it
so horrified him that his mind shrank away from it.

Letting Sweets tromp along the path at the horse's own pace,
his breath and Stillman's breath frosting in the chill air beneath
the crisp stars, the sheriff dropped his left hand into the pocket
of his jacket. He pulled out a small, flat, hide-covered traveling
flask, pulled the cork, and took a sip. He let the whiskey run
down his throat and sooth his nerves, lifting a flush in his
leathery cheeks. Chicken flesh rose across his back.

"Ahh," he said, enjoying what he knew to be a fleeting abate-
ment of his generalized unease.

He took another, larger sip of the whiskey and then returned
the flask to his pocket, shoving it far enough down that Fay
would not see it. If she saw the bulge she would think it only
some papers or maybe a pocket pistol that Stillman carried
from time to time, especially on night rounds, when a bullet

from any quarter was a possibility for a lawman who'd been around as long as Stillman had and had made a corresponding number of enemies.

Especially when an infamous old enemy was loitering around Clantick, as Battles still was.

He shouldn't be drinking the hard stuff, he knew. He'd promised Fay long ago that he would never imbibe in anything stronger than beer again, as the hard stuff had nearly ruined his life. But he needed something with sharper teeth than beer to cut through the nerves knotted at the back of his neck. He was up against too much confusion, too many formidable foes— Battles, the Sulphur robbers, whoever had fired that bullet into his house, the bounty that the outlaw girl had placed on his head—and Fay would not understand that he needed a drink now and then to give him some space in which to think.

His own body, however, was turning out to be his mightiest foe of all. If his plate were less full, he'd ask Evans to make him an appointment with the surgeon in Denver, and he'd have the operation before winter. But there was too much trouble hanging in a large, invisible, fetid cloud over Clantick to even consider the procedure now.

Stillman rode to the top of the hill. His house came into view. He frowned at it growing larger ahead of him as he and Sweets continued toward it.

All the windows were dark. No lamp appeared to be burning anywhere in the house. Stillman's breathing grew shallow.

Not like Fay to not leave a lamp on for him.

Usually, in fact, she waited up for him when she knew he wouldn't be gone all night. She sewed or read in a sitting room chair, or she prepared food for the next day's meals in the kitchen.

Those knots clumped at the back of the sheriff's neck grew tighter.

Something was wrong.

CHAPTER 23

Stillman galloped Sweets around the west side of the house and dismounted at the back door. His right knee buckled, and he fell, cursing and losing his hat.

He rolled onto his knees with another curse, maneuvered both feet beneath him, and rose. His right knee quavered. That arm was tight. He plucked his hat off the ground, swept his hair back from his eyes, and turned to the house as Sweets sidled away from him, whickering nervously.

He stared at the dark house and slid his Colt from its holster. He moved to the door, turned the porcelain knob slowly until the latch clicked, and stepped inside. He stood to the left of the door, staring through the mudroom toward the kitchen, which was all murky, dark shadows before him, a couple of shades lighter than the mudroom, which had no windows.

He said, "Fay?"

No response. Like the darkness, the silence was thick and eerie.

He hefted the Colt in his right hand, sliding his index finger through the trigger guard. He felt as though he were wearing a glove, but he was not. It was the frightening lack of feeling in that hand. He caressed the trigger as he moved forward through the mudroom and into the kitchen, looking around.

He could smell the night's supper, liver and onions, hovering in the air. There was also the smell of coal oil and tea, a pot of which Fay had brewed before Stillman had headed into town to make the night's final rounds. She'd been going to wash out some of Little Ben's underpants and then settle in to work on the afghan she'd been knitting.

Again, quietly, he said his wife's name. His heart shuddered when he was met with nothing but silence.

He scoured the small kitchen with the hulking range and the counter near it with dry sink and the painted wooden shelves to either side of it, pots and pans hanging from hooks in the ceiling over the warm water reservoir. The table sat to his right, covered by an oilcloth and centered with pussy willows in a stone vase.

A brass lantern with a frosted glass shade hung over the table. Stillman leaned over and touched it. Still warm. It hadn't been out for more than a few minutes.

Stillman continued across the kitchen and through the doorway, which opened onto the foot of the stairs that rose to the second story, and the sitting room beyond.

"Ben?" Fay's voice, pitched low, stopped him in his tracks.

He turned his head to look up the stairs on his right. Fay stood on the first landing, a pale, dark-haired figure facing him. Stillman could tell she was holding something in her hands, but he couldn't tell what it was. A gun?

Before he could speak, Fay whispered, "There's someone in the house."

Just then, Stillman smelled it.

The smell of man sweat, leather, and chewing tobacco.

Stillman said softly, "Where's Little Ben?"

"In our room."

Stillman was staring straight ahead, into the sitting room and the large front window, which, since the cream curtains were closed, formed a pale rectangle twenty feet away, flanking the sofa. Between him and the window, and slightly to the left, a shadow moved suddenly.

"Go back to him and lock the door!" Stillman said, bringing his Colt up.

As Fay bolted up the stairs and out of sight, Stillman saw ambient light wink off something the figure before him was holding. The sheriff took one step back behind the kitchen wall as a gun flashed blindingly, wickedly, and the crash of a revolver caused the whole house to jump.

The bullet rang off an iron skillet hanging over the range behind Stillman. The reverberations were drowned out by two more banging reports, the flashes momentarily lighting up the entire parlor and showing the tall, hatted gunman in menacing, dark relief. One bullet clipped the side of the doorframe, the other one bulled through the wall and nipped the nap from Stillman's jacket, over his right shoulder, before spanging off the range and shattering glass.

Upstairs, Little Ben began wailing.

Stillman gritted his teeth as he whipped around the door and cut loose with his Peacemaker.

Standing on the jailhouse's front stoop, Leon McMannigle twisted closed the quirley he'd been building, sealed it by licking it, and then fired a stove match to life on his cartridge belt. A shadow moved to his right, and, jerking with a start, he dropped the match and reached for the Schofield holstered on his right thigh.

The shadow moved again, and there was a soft meow as a fat tabby cat lit upon the two stacked crates that served as a porch table between two hide bottom chairs to the deputy's right. During slack times, McMannigle and Stillman often used the table to support their cribbage board. The cat meowed again and curled its tail up over its back.

"Well, Gustav!" Leon said, chuckling his relief. "You sure know how to make an entrance—you know that? You 'bout scared the devil outta me!"

He could hear the cat trilling deep in its chest as it stood atop the table, rising up on the tips of its paws, jutting its head toward Leon, and working its nose.

"Ridin' the grubline again, are ya?" the deputy asked. "Fat as you are, you catchin' enough mice and rats, and I seen how Auld feeds you, so you ain't gettin' no handouts from this thirty-a-month badge toter. Besides that, I'm fresh out of cream."

He scratched another match to life on his cartridge belt, and touched it to the quirley drooping from between his lips. "Shoulda come by yesterday. I had goose livers for lunch."

He puffed smoke into the darkness beyond the stoop. "Mmmm—mhmmmm! They was good, too!" he teased the cat.

Gustav leaped down off the table to rub against the deputy's right boot.

"You cold, kitty?" Leon asked. "Chilly night for a puss to be out, even one tough as you, Gustav. You oughta go back to the barn and dig you a nice nest in the loft instead of makin' the rounds, cadgin' for cream. Bet it's warm . . ."

Leon let his voice trail off as Gustav gave another, louder, sharper meow, leaped back up onto the table, and from there to the railing at the far end of the stoop. He leaped off the rail and into the darkness, gone as suddenly as he'd appeared.

Just then, Leon heard the hollow pops of a revolver being triggered up in the buttes to the north. In the direction of Stillman's place.

He turned to his left, intending to peer around the jailhouse, and froze as a bulky shadow stepped out from the side of the building. Starlight flickered off the steel barrels of a sawed-off shotgun in the man's hands—a thickset hombre with a long beard with two hide-wrapped braids in it, and a broad-brimmed canvas hat, a leather duster brushing the tops of his boots.

"One move, Blackie, and I'll cut you in two with this greener, understand?" He had a toneless, rasping voice, as though his voice box had been injured.

McMannigle stopped his right hand's instinctive movement toward his revolver, about halfway between his belly button and his right thigh. He opened his lips and the quirley dropped out of his mouth to bounce off the porch rail, sparking. It rolled onto the ground near the boots of the big man holding the barn-blaster on him.

The bearded man stamped it out with his boot, saying, "Don't want no fires, right?"

Another man stepped out from the side of the jailhouse, and, aiming two pistols at Leon, said, "Hold that greener on him, Kilgore. He moves, blast him."

The man with the pistols, who had a black beard and black eyes beneath a bullet-crowned Stetson, and was wearing a short wolf coat, moved to the front of the stoop. He climbed the steps, aiming his pistols at McMannigle, who had stiffly raised his hands shoulder high, and whose heart was skirmishing with his lungs inside his chest as the snaps of those pistols to the north kept recurring inside his head.

The black-eyed man then pulled the deputy's Smithy from his holster and shoved it down behind the waistband of his black denim trousers.

"Got another one on ya?"

"Nope."

The black-eyed man smiled shrewdly. "Come on. If I pat you down and find one, I'm gonna cave your head in." He turned his pistols slightly, showing Leon the brass-plated grips.

McMannigle gave a frustrated grunt and reached behind to pull a Remington Elliot Ring Trigger .32 derringer from a pocket he'd sewn into the back of his black leather vest. The four-shot pocket pistol occasionally came in handy, especially in the tight confines of Mrs. Lee's place.

"Damn," the black-eyed man said in mild amusement at the curious, stubby little pistol, and shoved it into a pocket of his coat.

He waved both Remingtons at the door. "Inside."

"What happened up at Stillman's place?"

The black-eyed man grinned. He appeared to me missing every other tooth. "Oh, we just shot him and his whole family— that's all!" He laughed through the gaps in his teeth.

McMannigle began to lurch forward, nostrils flaring.

"Uh-uh," warned the man holding the sawed-off shotgun at him. Leon held his ground, heart hammering, and glanced at the gent with the braided beard. Light from inside the jailhouse laid a red sheen along the gut-shredder's blue barrels.

McMannigle had few options. What these two were here for was obvious. He couldn't make a move on them now or his head would likely go bouncing off along the stoop in the same direction in which Gustav had fled. He had to wait for a reasonable opportunity.

He turned slowly, opened the jailhouse door, and stepped inside.

"That door locked?" the dark-eyed man asked behind him, meaning the door to the cellblock.

" 'Course it is."

The bearded man with the shotgun moved into the jailhouse behind the black-eyed gent. "Don't get smart. Just open the door or I'll blow you in two, and we'll have two darkies instead of one, floppin' around on the floor."

"Oh, go diddle yourselves," Leon raked out as he grabbed the key ring off the side of the roll-top desk and moved to the cellblock door. Behind him, the two men snickered.

"He's a smart one," said the black-eyed man as Leon shoved the key into the lock.

"Don't get too smart," warned the man with the gut-shredder.

Leon took his time unlocking the door and then opening it. He wasn't in any hurry. He was waiting for one or both of the men behind him to give him an opening of any kind—any opportunity for him to make a play for one of their guns. It was a slender hope but he had to hope for something while dread for what had occurred up at Stillman's place lifted a low whine in his head.

"Move it!" The bearded man rammed the shotgun against McMannigle's back, sending him stumbling into the cellblock. He dropped the ring of keys, and it clattered loudly to the cell-block floor.

"Oh, no!" Hettie Styles said sharply, slowly rising from her cell cot. "Ah, shit—Deputy, you done just killed me, you worthless son of a bitch!"

The other two prisoners were two cells down from Hettie's. The cell containing the stolen Sulphur money lay between them. Merle Wainwright and Four-Eyes Eldon Jones came alive, as well, both men bounding up to the cellblock door, laughing and grinning their pleasure at seeing their partners. "Hey, fellas—I'll be damned if you ain't a sight for my near-sighted eyes!" exclaimed Jones.

Wainwright said, "Come on—get us outta here! The money's right there! Let's pull foot before Stillman gets here."

"I don't think Stillman's getting anywhere no more," said the bearded man. "Bell went up there to take care of Stillman while we let you rats out of your cage."

"Not like you deserve to be let out, seein' as how some stove-up old lawman threw a loop around you not five minutes after you rode into town to *scope things out.*"

"We wasn't expectin' him to get onto us so soon!" Four-Eyes exclaimed, defensively. "Your girl must've put him onto us,

Natchez! How was we to know she was gonna do *that*—turn on her *own*!"

The black-eyed man with the wolf coat and bullet-crowned hat turned to the girl staring through the door of her cell at him. Hettie's face was bleached out and her eyes were liquid with fear.

"You shoulda known because she done turned on us before." The black-eyed man in the wolf coat, who must have been Otis Natchez, said, "You double-crossing bitch."

"Just go ahead and shoot me, Otis," Hettie said, backing away from the cell door and opening her arms. "Go ahead and shoot me and be done with it. Blow my heart out. I know I deserve it!"

Tears were dribbling down her cheeks. She looked miserable, but Leon couldn't tell if she was just putting on a show, hoping to appeal to her former lover's sympathy so he'd spare her life. He now knew the girl well enough to know she was capable of any deception.

She bawled. "Oh, god—I messed up sooo bad. Hurting, deceiving the only man I ever loved!"

Yep, Leon amended his earlier suspicion. She was putting on a show, all right. Not a very good one.

"The only man you ever loved, huh?" Natchez scoffed.

"Come on, Natchez!" urged Four-Eyes. "Just shoot that double-crossing bitch and let us outta here, and let's ride!"

Natchez turned to McMannigle, who stood in front of the cell. The bearded man was aiming his shotgun at the deputy's belly from six feet away, too far away for Leon to try making a move on him.

"Four-Eyes has a point," said Kilgore. "Kill her, Natchez." He moved closer to Leon. "Open the door, Blackie. Quick!"

Hettie squealed and covered her face with her hands. "Go ahead and shoot me, Otis! I don't deserve any better!"

Leon had started turning toward the cell containing the incarcerated outlaws when he saw Kilgore, who was only three feet away from him now, shuttling his gaze to the bawling girl. The shotgun wilted in his arms. McMannigle dropped the keys and lunged toward the shotgun, wrapping both hands around it and jerking it free from the startled Kilgore's grip.

Natchez and the two prisoners gave cries of alarm as Leon stepped back and swung the shotgun toward Natchez.

Before he could get either of the two-bore's hammers drawn back, he saw Natchez raise his two pistols, which blossomed smoke and fire. The reports sounded like near thunder peeling up and down the cellblock as several .44-caliber rounds ripped through Leon's flesh and sent him flying back down the cellblock toward the far end.

He dropped the shotgun, the rear stock barking off his shin before it clattered to the floor.

Waves of agony rippled through the deputy.

He lay supine on the cold wooden floor, hands brushing at his chest covered with what felt like warm oil. He lifted his head, blinked his eyes, and saw Natchez bearing down on him again with his two aimed pistols. The guns again lapped smoke and flames, the explosions again rocketing around the cellblock, making the iron bars ring.

Each bullet struck Leon like lightning, the hot chunks of lead blasting through him on lances of searing pain.

The guns fell silent. Leon lay his head back on the floor and closed his eyes.

"There, that oughta do him," he heard someone say as though from a long ways away.

Someone else laughed.

"Oh," McMannigle heard someone else mutter.

Then he realized that he himself had muttered it . . . before everything went dark and silent.

Chapter 24

Stillman ran out the front door of his house and out onto the front stoop. He dropped to a knee behind a porch post. The intruder had run out the front door after Stillman had returned fire inside the house, and now the sheriff expected the man to stop and turn back and sling more lead. Obviously the shooter's job wasn't finished here tonight.

Stillman counted to three and then he slid his cocked Colt around the side of the porch post, aiming into the dark night. He blinked, trying to rid his retinas of the lingering flare of the gun flashes that had lit up the house like lightning strikes. As far as he could tell, nothing moved in the front yard.

Then he heard the distant clomps of a horse.

He rose stiffly and ran out into the yard and stopped where the wild rye and yucca took over, where the bluff dropped away to the south. Down the grade and to his right, a shadow bounced along the trail that dropped gradually toward Clantick. The town was a dark stain farther to the south, the bowl of darkness relieved here and there by the pale glow of torches or burning oil pots or lamp-lit cabin windows.

Stillman aimed at the bouncing shadow dwindling before him, and fired two quick shots out of sheer frustration. A waste of lead. There was no way he could have hit the invader of his home from this far away in the darkness.

The shadow slipped around the black shoulder of a butte, and was gone. Even the clomps of the horse's galloping hooves faded beneath the barks of several dogs down in Clantick.

Stillman cursed harshly, flicked open his Colt's loading gate, and quickly shook out the spent cartridge casings, replacing them with fresh from his shell belt. He flicked the loading gate closed, spun the cylinder, and tramped back into the dark house.

"Ben?" Fay called tonelessly from the second story.

"It's all right," Stillman said, climbing the stairs, breathing hard, having to drag his right foot a little. "He's gone."

Fay stood silhouetted in the open doorway of their room. She was rocking Little Ben in her arms. The boy was crying hysterically. Stillman went to her, ushered her back into the room, and fumbled around until he'd gotten the wick on an oil lamp turned up, shunting the darkness deep into the room's corners.

Fay stood near the door. She was crying while she rocked the bawling Little Ben in her arms. The sight of them both in so much misery was like a knife to the lawman's heart.

"What on earth is going on, Ben?" Fay wanted to know. "How did he get in our *house*? Who *was* he?"

"I don't know," Stillman said, taking Little Ben from her, drawing the boy close, pressing the child's head against his chest, squeezing him gently. "I don't know, Fay." He drew her to him, as well, kissing her forehead. She was quivering. "I don't know, but I'm going to find out. I'll find out, and I'll put a stop to it."

Suddenly, a discordant thought leeched through the swarming concerns for his family. The rider had been galloping toward Clantick. Stillman lurched back, causing Little Ben to cry harder and for Fay to gasp with a start.

"What is it?" she cried, placing a soothing hand on the boy's head.

Leon . . .

"I have to get down to the office," he said, dread prickling along his spine.

He handed Little Ben over to Fay and said, "You stay here in the room until I tell you it's safe to come out."

"Ben, what is it?"

"I don't know, but I think there's a good chance whoever was in the house might be in cahoots with the prisoners Leon and I have locked up." Stillman turned back to his wife and crying child, one hand on the doorknob. "Whatever you do, do not leave this house until I either come for you or send someone you can trust. Lock the bedroom door, and keep that pistol handy."

Fay stared at him wide-eyed, nodding, rocking their child in her arms.

"I love you," Stillman said.

"I love you, too, Ben," Fay said, more tears dribbling down her cheeks.

He turned, drew the door closed behind him, and made his way down the stairs as quickly as he could. He closed and locked the front door and then went out the back door, locking it, too, behind him. Sweets had retreated from the gunfire. Stillman found the horse grazing the long grass growing up along the base of the closed chicken coop, inside of which he could hear his chickens nervously clucking from their roosts.

He heaved himself into the saddle, turned the horse around, and, throwing caution to the wind, galloped through the yard and onto the trail that jogged down the south side of the butte. He was on the outskirts of Clantick inside of a minute, but he held the horse to a gallop as he made his way along a narrow avenue between squat cabins and small houses that cast trapezoids of lamplight onto the rutted street.

By the time he gained First Street, a chill having nothing to do with the cold night swept through him. More people than usual for this time of the night were out on the street, and they were gravitating toward the jailhouse.

What he'd feared had come to pass.

Three or four men and a saloon girl from the Drovers were milling around outside of the jailhouse as Stillman put Sweets up to the hitchrack. He swung down from the saddle, dropped the reins, and mounted the stoop.

No one said anything but only stood around whispering and looking worried.

Stillman's boots were heavy as he hurried through the open jailhouse door, but this time it had only a little to do with the bullet in his back. Dread was like a hot, wet blanket hanging heavy on his shoulders. Footsteps and voices sounded in the cellblock, and a portly gent wearing an open overcoat over a green suit and fawn vest stepped through the half-open door. The mayor's eyes were drink bleary beneath the narrow brim of his bowler, and his cheeks above his salt-and-pepper beard were mottled red from shock and exertion. He was breathing hard.

He stopped with a start when he saw Stillman, and then he said, "Oh, Ben! I was just about to fetch a buckboard sitting in front of the Drovers. Figure we might as well take him right up to the doc's place as ring for him."

"You do that," Stillman said absently, stepping around Crandall, through the cellblock door, and hurrying down the cellblock toward where three men were hunkered down over a body on the floor. The three cells that had once housed prisoners and the stolen Sulphur money were empty. The rotten egg smell of gun smoke hung heavy in the air, as did the coppery smell of blood.

The kid, Gandy Miller, was on one knee, staring down at Leon, as were the liveryman, Auld, and Olaf Weisinger. As Stillman approached, the kid stood and turned toward Stillman, shaking his head, his eyes wide and bright as he said, "Never seen the like. They shot him up good, but he's still breathin'. The mayor went to fetch a wagon, Sheriff."

As young Miller stepped aside, Stillman took his place beside Leon. Blood matted the deputy's chest and belly. More oozed from a hole in his right thigh. Stillman pressed a hand over the thigh wound, trying to stem the blood, and Leon convulsed and opened his eyes, groaning. His dark-eyed gaze, bright with misery, found Stillman though it appeared his eyes were slow to focus.

"Ah, hell . . . sorry, Ben. I mucked it up bad."

"Shhh."

"Two jumped me. Sprung 'em all . . . and the money."

"Rest easy. We're gonna get you up to the doc's."

Stillman looked around and then rose and stepped into the cell in which Four-Eyes and Wainwright had been housed. He grabbed a blanket off one of the two cots.

As he returned to the cellblock alley, Weisinger said, "There was five of 'em and the girl—six, all told, Sheriff. I was standin' over on the porch at the Drovers, havin' a smoke. They all rode past me, headin' west, like bats outta hell!"

Auld said, "One of 'em had them saddlebags draped over his shoulder. They got their money back, all right. Left Leon in here bleedin' out, them devils!"

"Musta shot him six, seven times," speculated Miller tonelessly, standing and pressing his back up to one of the jail cells. "Never seen the like. Leastways, him still livin', an' all."

"Make a helluva story, wouldn't it, kid?" Stillman snapped at the young man.

Gandy Miller turned his mouth corners down, and hiked a sheepish shoulder.

Footsteps rose in the office, and the mayor poked his head through the cellblock door. "Wagon's here, Sheriff!"

Stillman had wrapped the blanket over Leon, who appeared to meander in and out of consciousness. He was groaning, sporadically coughing.

"Let's get him up."

Stillman ignored the pain in his right arm and leg, and lifted his deputy's head and shoulders off the floor. Auld and Weisinger each took a leg. As they moved into the office, the mayor, who was obvious rattled by the sight of a wounded man as well as by so much blood leaching through the blanket, said, "Jody . . . uh . . . Jody Harmon is here. He . . . he was over at the mercantile and he was . . . he and Crystal were already bringing their wagon over when I started for the Drov—"

The mayor cut himself off when Jody and Crystal Harmon rushed into the office, one after the other.

"My god!" Crystal intoned. "What happened, Ben?"

"A breakout," Stillman grunted as he and the other two men pushed past Jody and Crystal as they carried Leon out the door and onto the stoop. "What the hell are you two doing in town this late?" Ben asked the youngsters.

"Supply run," Jody said, leaping down the porch steps ahead of Stillman and releasing the latches on his and Crystal's box wagon parked in front of the jailhouse. "We got to town late. Got stuck in the mud down along Beaver Creek. Creek's runnin' high after all that rain."

Young Harmon leaped up into the back of the wagon and started throwing feed and flour sacks around, forming a soft bed of sorts. Leaping down, he said, "I got him, Ben."

Jody took the groaning deputy under the arms and muscled him into the wagon. At the same time, Crystal leaped up over the off rear wheel, and helped Jody ease Leon onto the burlap bags.

By now, a small crowd, mostly men and working girls from the Drovers and one of the brothels in town, had gathered around the front of the jailhouse. A couple of the girls from Mrs. Lee's place must have gotten word about the shooting, because they came running from up the street, gossamer nightgowns, night ribbons, and housecoats flapping about them, crowding in close to the wagon.

"Leon!" one of the doves screeched. "Oh, Leon—what *happened* to you, baby?"

The other girl tried to climb into the wagon, but Stillman pulled her off the tailgate. He assured both girls that the deputy would be in good hands soon, and that he'd send word of his condition as soon as he knew anything. The sheriff climbed up into the buckboard's box with Crystal and McMannigle. Jody released the wagon break, shook the reins over the horse's back, and they were off, rattling on out of town and then up the bluff trail toward the doc's house, which stood, darkly somber, atop it.

It was all a bit awkward at first, waking up Evans and then finding that young Evelyn Vincent was there, as well, obviously spending the night, her long hair mussed, the girl clad in little more than one of the doctor's shirts and a blanket. Of course, Jody and Crystal and Evelyn all knew each other, and Jody and Crystal were both as surprised and confused by the situation as Stillman was, and as chagrined as the doctor and Evelyn appeared.

Everyone in the county knew that Evans had promised to marry Katherine Kemmett the following month.

The inelegant circumstances were quickly overlooked as all parties rushed to get Leon into the small room off the first floor parlor, where Evans performed his surgeries.

When they'd gotten McMannigle onto the doctor's leather-upholstered operation table, and Evelyn had ushered Stillman, Jody, and Crystal out of the office, assuring them that she and the doc would take good care of Leon, Stillman sagged onto the porch's top step. He needed some fresh air to clear his head, which was swimming, a knife of anxiousness and rage embedded in his gut.

Jody came outside and sat down beside the sheriff. "You all right, Ben?"

"I won't be all right until I've run those owlhoots to ground," Stillman said through gritted teeth.

"I mean *physically*," young Harmon said, looking at him with concern. "You all right?" He shrugged. "Seen you favorin' that right side again."

Stillman ignored the topic of his health. He stared out into the night, organizing his thoughts. Then he turned to Jody.

"I'm glad you and Crystal are here."

"We'll stay as long as you need us, Ben. Crystal's sister is stayin' out at the ranch, takin' care of Billy-Ben."

"Will you do me another favor tonight?"

"Sure, anything."

"Ride over and fetch Fay and Little Ben, bring 'em both over here. I'd just as soon they weren't alone right now. Trouble up there earlier, when that gang was bustin' their pards out of jail."

"You bet," Jody said, nodding.

Sweets had followed the wagon up the bluff and was standing near where the wagon was parked in the darkness beyond the porch. Stillman rose creakily and walked over to the mount, gathering up the dangling reins. "Tell her I'll be gone for a while, but I'll be back as soon as I can."

"Ben, you're not going after them tonight, are you?"

Stillman swung up into the leather. "Sure as hell am."

"Ben, you—"

Stillman cut young Harmon off with: "You can do me another favor. Hang around town for a while, act as my deputy, keep an eye on things. Don't want the place goin' to hell in a handbasket while I'm gone. Can you do that, Jody, or am I asking too much?"

"Hell, no," Jody said, rising. "I'll send Crystal home with the wagon in the morning, and I'll stay on. I'd like to help, Ben.

You know that. But I don't think—"

Stillman cut young Harmon off again with a raise of his hand as he turned Sweets around and started off down the bluff toward town. "You'll find a deputy sheriff's badge in the office. Don't take any chances, kid. Just man the office, for me, all right?"

He touched spurs to Sweets's flanks and galloped off down the bluff.

CHAPTER 25

The activity on First Street had died down considerably. It was close to midnight, and most of the businesses were dark.

Only the Drovers was still open, two horses standing at the hitchracks. Elmer Burk didn't hold to a regular schedule. If and when the place emptied out at night, he shut down. If men were still drinking and playing cards or enjoying his doves, he'd keep it open. If he needed to lie down in his backroom for a time, Burk would have one of the girls tend the cashbox. He trusted the girls who worked for him.

Stillman rode on past the saloon and pulled up at the jailhouse. The door was closed, but a lamp was still burning in the window. Gray wood smoke was issuing from the tin chimney to unfurl against the stars. Stillman swung wearily down from the leather, mounted the porch, and walked over to peer into the window over his desk. He cursed as he turned away from the window and pushed the door open.

"What the hell are you doin' here?" he growled.

"Coffee, Sheriff?" Jacob Henry Battles, kicked back in Stillman's chair, boots crossed on the roll-top desk, held up the smoking tin cup he held in his lone hand, the hook resting on his thigh. "Fresh pot on the stove. I figured you might need a cup before you headed out after that crazy bunch."

Stillman looked at the coffee pot gurgling atop the potbelly stove, smoke puffing from the spout. Annoyance rippled through the lawman. He went over and swept Battles's feet off his desk.

"Get the hell out of my chair, Battles. What in the hell you think you're doin', makin' yourself to home?"

"Don't worry," the regulator said, heaving up from the chair. "I intend to pay you back for the coffee." He stepped aside and, giving a smug half-smile, lifted the cup to his lips.

"Oh? How?"

"By givin' you a hand, if you'll pardon the very bad pun, which was completely unintentional, I assure you."

"By givin' me a hand," Stillman said, opening a desk drawer and pulling out his spare Colt. "How in the hell do you think you're going to give me a hand?"

"By riding out with you, of course. You're obviously not a posse man or you'd be forming one right now."

"Sometimes one lawman is more effective than two dozen citizen riders. Especially against this bunch." Stillman extracted two boxes of .44 shells from the drawer in the gun rack, and shoved the cartridges into a pair of saddlebags hanging from a peg in the wall. "I don't need your help, Battles. Wouldn't accept it even if I did."

"Come on, Ben—you're not as young as you used to be. Besides, you're damn near as stove-up as I am. Look at the way you move."

Stillman was shoving some foodstuffs from a shelf into the saddlebags, which he'd draped over his shoulder. He hadn't realized that the stiffness on his right side had been apparent, though of course it would have been. He was moving like a man twenty years older than he actually was—an old man with the chilblains or rheumatism gumming up his joints like cement.

When he'd filled the saddlebag pouches with enough coffee, jerky, flour, and canned peaches for a couple of days' ride, he fished his bottle out of the desk drawer and stuffed that down in the bags, as well. His bedroll hung from another peg by a leather lanyard; he draped the lanyard over his left shoulder.

He brushed past the regulator as he headed for the door, pausing to say, "Go to hell, Battles."

Battles sighed and wagged his head. He coughed softly, raspily, and ran a handkerchief across his mouth. Stillman went out and draped his saddlebags over Sweets's back. He tied his bedroll behind the saddle cantle, over the bags. Knowing that Battles was watching from the open jailhouse door, he tried to appear fleeter than he felt as he swung into the leather.

He pulled Sweets back away from the hitching post, pinched his hat brim ironically to Battles. "Close up when you're done enjoying my coffee, will you?"

He touched spurs to the bay's flanks and cantered on up the street to the west.

Battles stared after him, steam from the regulator's coffee curling tendrils up around the pencil-thin mustache mantling his smiling mouth. He sipped the coffee, coughed, and wiped a fleck of blood from his lips, which continued to smile.

Hettie took a deep breath and jerked her horse off to the right side of the trail and, the mount's hooves slashing at the ground as it swung off away from the gang, lowered her head and gritted her teeth. She batted her heels against the horse's flanks, urging more speed.

"There she goes!" shouted one of the men in the galloping pack, which was a dark, jostling blob slipping away behind her.

Natchez gave a shrill curse. Hettie glanced back over her shoulder to see one of the horse-and-rider silhouettes pull away from the rest of the pack. Natchez whipped his rein ends against his horse's hip and hunkered low in the saddle, giving chase.

Hettie gasped. He'd kill her if he caught her. He'd been going to kill her, anyway—she knew that for certain—so she had nothing to lose trying to escape. He'd only taken her out of her cell so he could do it in his own good time, maybe use her a couple of times first. She didn't like the way he galloped toward her without yelling and cussing her. She knew from experience that when Natchez didn't say a word, that was when he was supremely, murderously angry.

Hettie lowered her head and whipped her reins against her own mount's right wither, gritting her teeth. She was about forty yards ahead of Natchez, and the gap between them was neither widening nor narrowing. Could her horse outrun his? She'd find out. Ahead, there was a black, fuzzy line denoting brush. Probably a creek. Maybe she could shake him from her trail in there. The darkness would work to her advantage.

Hettie kept whipping her reins against her mount's withers, urging more and more speed. There was a good possibility the horse would trip over a rock or step in a gopher hole, and that she'd get a broken neck for her trouble. But better a broken neck than being whipped to death, which is what she knew she had coming if she stayed with Natchez. Brutal whippings were the punishment he doled out to those who crossed him. At least they were to *men* who crossed him.

Why would a woman who crossed him get any better treatment?

Suddenly, she started to hear the fierce clatter of hooves and the bellows-like pumping of Natchez's horse's straining lungs. She glanced over her left shoulder to see the pursuing horse and rider now thirty feet away and closing fast.

An icy chill oozed down Hettie's spine.

The bastard had gotten a good angle on her!

She jerked her own horse to the right, away from the man, but the horse faltered slightly beneath her. And then Natchez was right up beside her so close that she could hear him breathing, now, too, and hear his horse's bridle chains rattling.

"No, you son of a bitch!" Hettie screamed.

She didn't quite get "bitch" all the way out before Natchez

lashed out with his right arm and slammed the back of that gloved hand against Hettie's head. It was a savage blow, causing her ears to ring. It threw her way out to the side. She instinctively pulled her boots free of her stirrups. She knew she was leaving her saddle, and she didn't want to get hung up in the saddle and dragged.

The ground came up to smack her right hip and shoulder hard. A scream was pummeled out of her, and she found herself rolling wildly down a hill that had been concealed by the darkness. She rolled and rolled, punched and gouged by rocks and scratched by brush.

She went airborne for about a half a second, and then—*wham!*—she landed in what was probably a creek bottom. It was relatively sandy, and that had cushioned that last fall, though she lay writhing, trying in vain to suck a breath into her battered lungs. There seemed to be a constriction in both her throat and her chest. Her hips, shoulder, and legs ached miserably.

Her head felt as though someone were beating her with a sledgehammer.

When she'd finally gotten a couple of complete breaths into her lungs, she rolled onto her belly, and pushed up onto her hands and knees. She sucked more raw breaths, and it sounded like the wind howling through a narrow pipe. A shadow slid across the sand and rocks to her left. She looked up to see Natchez standing over her.

He was a menacing silhouetted figure in his bullet-crowned hat and wolf coat, shimmering in the starlight.

"If you an' me is gonna grow old together, Miss Hettie, we're gonna have to come to an understandin'."

She didn't like the sound of that. Instinctively, panic screaming inside her, she began to crawl wildly away. She hadn't gotten four feet before he grabbed the back of her denims, jerked her back toward him, and then kicked her over onto her back.

"Yep," he said. "An understandin'." His hands dropped to his fly.

"Bastard!" Hettie wailed.

Again, she tried to crawl away. He grabbed her again, kicked her onto her back, backhanded her viciously, and then ripped her shirt open. She cursed him again, flailed her fists at his face. He punched her this time, hard, and she slumped back against the ground, half-conscious.

Ten minutes later, he half-dragged her back up the slope toward where the rest of the gang waited, standing with their horses, which were calmly foraging.

"Everything all right?" asked Four-Eyes, who was smoking a quirley.

Natchez was breathing hard from the climb up from the creek. "We had us a misunderstandin' there for a while," he said. "But now we're back to seein' eye to eye on things. Ain't we, honey?"

Hettie was holding the tatters of her torn blouse to her breasts. She dropped to her knees in misery and weariness.

"I said, 'ain't we, honey?' " Natchez repeated.

Hettie rubbed blood from her cut upper lip. "Yeah—that's right," she said without passion, and spat to one side. "We came to an understandin'."

The girl was genuinely cowed. She'd never been treated so savagely.

"Best get a move on," said one of the other men in the bunch, Mason Bell.

"Why's that?" asked Natchez, tucking his shirt into his pants. "No posse'll be comin' tonight."

"I don't mean a posse," said Bell. "I mean Stillman. That's what I been meanin' to tell ya. I went up to his house to wait for him an' kill him, only I didn't kill him. I distracted him a bunch, but he's still kickin'."

All the others stared at Bell, who was a second cousin of Four-Eyes. Bell stared back silently, sheepishly, his red scarf blowing around his neck in the breeze. He was a big man, a little soft in his thinker box, but he was a good, cold-blooded killer, and no one—not even Natchez—enjoyed seeing him riled.

Bell shrugged and filled the silence with, "If any of you thought you could do better, you shoulda done better. He's slippery, that bastard. I was gonna bring his wife along, once I killed him, but I reckon I fouled that up, too. I'm sorry. That's all I can say. She's a looker, too!"

Natchez sighed. "Yeah, well—maybe some other time." He looked back in the direction of Clantick, which sat low amongst the pale river buttes to the north. "For now, I reckon we'd best assume Stillman's behind us, and get him scoured from our trail."

CHAPTER 26

Midmorning of the next day, Stillman caught a whiff of wood smoke on the wind.

He reined Sweets to a stop and looked around. He was following a deep valley between two high, forested ridges spotted with the yellows of turning aspens. Blowing leaves were stitching the wind under a cobalt Montana sky clean-scoured by the storm and the ensuing cold front.

The wind was out of the southwest. It was blowing the smoke toward Stillman through a notch in the southern ridge. Louis Shambeau, an old Métis hider and trapper who once lived in these mountains, had had one of several cabins in this neck of the Two-Bears.

Stillman had a feeling the gang had either known about Shambeau's cabin or they'd come upon it accidentally. Stillman had never heard of anyone moving in after Shambeau had died—killed by Stillman himself, in fact, at the tail end of a long hunt that the sheriff would just as soon forget about.

The wood smoke told Stillman that, one way or another, the gang had found the cabin. He gave a wry smile beneath his thick mustache, which the wind was grooming. They'd found the cabin, and now they were calling him in. The gang had been at their game too long to not know how far smoke would carry on a day as windy as this one.

Well, he had a pretty good idea where they were. No use rushing.

Stillman turned Sweets into a notch in the side of the valley, dismounted, unsaddled the horse to give him a blow, and gathered wood for a fire. He brewed a pot of coffee over low flames inside a small rock ring, and then sank back against a deadfall to lace the coffee with whiskey from his bottle.

He built a cigarette from his makings sack, and leisurely smoked and sipped the spicy, hot brew, as he recalled the high mountain plateau on which Shambeau had built his cabin. Or had retooled and tightened an old one. A couple of German prospectors had built the original shack, and had worked a mine in the ridge above it.

Stillman called forth that whole area, scrutinizing it through the eye in his lawman's mind. He'd overnighted in the shack a time or two while out hunting outlaws of one stripe or another, mostly rustlers, a couple of claim jumpers. Now he went over the details in his memory. When he had done so to his satisfaction, worry over Leon's condition crept into his mind. Knowing there was nothing he could do but hope and pray for his friend and deputy in his own inept way, he drank the last of his coffee, kicked dirt on his fire, and saddled up.

Late in the afternoon, he lay belly down on a flat-topped ridge well to the southeast of the valley in which Shambeau's cabin sat. He scrutinized the area around that valley and the cabin, which he couldn't see from this distance and vantage, with his field glasses. After he'd stared through the glasses a long time, and then took a break before resuming, to let his vision clear, he saw him—a man standing on a bald ridge crest on the other side of that valley.

Stillman wouldn't have noticed him if he hadn't moved from shade to a ray of golden-umber, late-afternoon light, but now the lawman was relatively certain he was staring at a man just now moving on the crest of that ridge, raising his hand and lowering it, as though smoking a cigarette, and then turning and disappearing into the timber behind him. If there was a man on that ridge, there were likely more men on the other ridges around the cabin.

Waiting for Stillman.

As the lawman had figured they would, they'd set a trap for him, intending to wipe him from their trail. Then they could likely hole up in this neck of the territory indefinitely, until their trails had cooled. Before the winter snows fell in earnest, they'd probably start making their gradual way down to the Southwest and find a town suitable for enjoying the fruits of their labor. Denver, maybe, or Santa Fe.

Casually, in no hurry, Stillman made his way down the backside of the ridge, returned the field glasses to his saddlebags, tightened Sweets's saddle straps, and stepped into the leather. He followed valleys and coulees and creek bottoms around to the south of the valley in which the Shambeau cabin lay. The sun was pivoting on the sawtooth-like mountains of the Great Divide farther to the west, when he came upon the rear entrance to the mineshaft.

It was surrounded by slag, boulders, and lodge pole pines, with a little creek trickling at its base. No one could know it was here unless they'd either carved it out of the mountain themselves, or stumbled on it by sheer happenstance, as Stillman had done a little over a year ago, when he'd been chasing a couple of Basque cattle rustlers. Curiosity had compelled Stillman to explore the man-made cavern, which was about fifty feet long. It gave out just behind the Shambeau cabin, on the other side of the ridge it was cut into.

Since the outlaws likely didn't know that the mine had a back door, it was doubtful they'd be watching the front one. They'd be concentrating on the timbered ridges surrounding the cabin, and the small gap that led into the valley, which was the only entrance to the valley that they probably knew of.

Stillman dismounted Sweets in front of the mine portal. He ground-reined the bay near the stream, so it would have plenty of water. He slid his Henry from the saddle boot, wedged his spare Colt behind his cartridge belt, and stepped up to the mine portal, which had not been sealed. There wasn't even a door. There were only cobwebs hanging from the support timbers.

Stillman tore the cobwebs with his hand, ducked into the opening that was about six inches shorter than he was, and began tramping into the shaft. As he did, the purple shadows grew denser; daylight slipped behind him. Wings fluttered insanely ahead, and he dropped to one knee and lowered his head as several mud swallows cut through the air above him, like winged bullets, and exited the mine, screeching.

He continued walking, cobwebs raking him and clinging. The moldy air smelled like bird shit, bat guano, damp earth, and rotting support timbers. He stepped over rocks and around fallen beams.

When he moved around a dogleg in the shaft, nearly complete darkness engulfed him. It was relieved slightly by purple shadows cast by faint daylight at the far end of the shaft. He struck a match and held it aloft, to get him around the dogleg without tripping and falling over debris. When the match stung him through his glove, he dropped it, and continued striding, crouching beneath the low ceiling, toward the lightening shadows ahead.

Occasionally, he heard the warbling of roosting bats. Water made soft tinkling sounds as it dribbled down the stone walls.

The opening grew ahead of him—a ragged oval of salmon-green light. It grew wider, and when it loomed only twenty feet ahead, Stillman racked a cartridge into his Henry's breech, sidled up against the left wall, and slowed his pace. When he gained the entrance, he dropped to one knee beside it, and stared out.

Maybe forty yards straight out from the opening lay the cabin—a low, gray log affair with a brush roof. Like the mine, it had a back door, and Stillman was staring at it. There was a window to the left of the door, and he had to hope that no one would be looking out when he made his approach. He also had to hope that the eyes of the pickets who were likely posted atop the ridges would not be on the rear of the cabin.

If anyone saw him before he gained the cabin, he'd have a hell of a fight on his hands. He probably would, anyway, but if he could get into the cabin he'd at least own the element of surprise. No telling how many were on the ridges or in the cabin.

He was about to find out.

He looked around the cabin, which sat in the valley that sloped off toward evergreen timber another hundred yards beyond the shack. Five-hundred- to thousand-foot ridges ringed the valley. Rotten slash littered the valley floor, as fifty or sixty years ago a leapfrogging forest fire had burned some of the timber.

Stillman could see no movement amidst any of the upright or scarred, fallen trees. All he could hear was the happy patter of birds and the breeze humming through treetops and brushing past the mine opening. The only sign of life was thin, gray smoke unfurling from the cabin's stone chimney, which lay up near the front and against the right wall.

The light was that brilliant golden-salmon just before sunset, casting long, gauzy shadows as the sun tumbled in the west. Nice time of the day to take down some badmen . . . and women.

Stillman hefted his rifle and stepped out away from the mine-shaft. He strode quickly down the grade, glancing around him, hoping like hell he wasn't spotted. He could see no one around, but he knew there were men around the cabin. When he passed the dilapidated privy, several old, steel-banded barrels, and the ruins of a long tom grown up with weeds, he crouched down against the back door. The remains of moldering firewood stacked on both sides of the door somewhat concealed him from the ridges.

There was a metal-and-wire latch on the door. Very gently, using only one finger, Stillman tripped it. It grated rustily. He gritted his teeth when the latch bolt clanked free of its moorings. The door sagged on its ancient leather hinges, the front dropping to the worn ground in front of it.

Stillman opened the door halfway, stepping quickly inside. He remembered that the cabin, little larger than his own sitting parlor at home, consisted of one room. Instantly, he raised the Henry, pressed the brass butt plate to his shoulder, and clicked the hammer back, waving the barrel to and fro, trying to pick out a target.

He eased the tension on his trigger finger.

There were only two people in the cabin. They occupied a crude timber bed to his right. As when Stillman had first encountered her, Hettie Styles was coital. Only, this time she didn't seem to be enjoying it. She lay on her back, wrists and ankles tied to the bed's woven cottonwood-sapling frame. Her hair was flopping on her face, obscuring her bleeding lips, as a black-haired man in red balbriggans was throwing the wood to her.

The man was propped on outstretched arms, his long hair hanging down over both sides of his face as he toiled, grunting savagely. His hair screened the lawman from his view. The squawking of the bed had covered Stillman's entrance into the cabin. Hettie, however, had seen the interloper.

She stared at Stillman, dull-eyed, through the thin screen of her hair.

She said nothing as Stillman walked slowly over to the bed, moving on the balls of his boots. When he stopped beside the bed, the man stopped hammering away at Hettie. For a moment, there was only silence. Hettie slid her gaze to the man on top of her, and her cracked and bleeding lips quirked an ironic half-smile.

Suddenly, the man jerked his head up, turning his wide-eyed face to Stillman, who swung his Henry club-like, smashing the edge of the butt against the dead center of the man's forehead.

The outlaw gave a clipped grunt and flew off the side of the bed to pile up against the wall. Stillman walked around the bed. The outlaw stared up at him, his dark eyes wide and owning a silver sheen of fear.

Just as he opened his mouth to call out to the others, Stillman smashed the Henry against his forehead once more, before the dazed outlaw could raise his hands to shield himself. The back of the man's head bounced off the wall. It wobbled on his shoulders, but he continued sitting upright, blinking as blood trickled down from the deep, four-inch gash above his nose.

"He's the one who shot your deputy," Hettie said.

The outlaw looked at her. "You . . . bitch," he muttered.

"Sheriff Stillman, Otis Natchez," Hettie said. "Otis, Sheriff Stillman."

Natchez turned his unfocused gaze back to Stillman. His eyes narrowed and sharpened in rage.

He took a deep breath. Again, he opened his mouth to scream, but the butt of Stillman's Henry sent the garbled cry hurling back down the man's throat.

Otis Natchez sagged unconscious to the cabin's dirt floor and lay twitching one pale, bare foot as he died.

CHAPTER 27

When he was sure that Otis Natchez was dead, Stillman leaned his rifle against the wall, fished his Barlow knife out of his pocket, and cut the ropes tying the girl to the bed. He threw a blanket over Hettie's naked body, and said, "Do I need to gag you?"

She lay on the bed, staring up at him with the same dullness he'd seen in her eyes before. She shook her head. Stillman believed her. She was in pretty bad shape. She had no reason to alert the others who, in light of her having double-crossed them, would likely treat her as shabbily as Natchez had.

Stillman looked around, and saw the saddlebags with the stolen Sulphur money sitting against the wall by the front door. He snorted. The money had become one hell of a prickly bur under his saddle blanket, so to speak. He'd be glad to be rid of it. The sheriff of Sulphur was probably on his way to retrieve it, but it was a good week's journey cross-country from Sulphur.

Stillman sat down at the cabin's scarred table, in front of a small, rust-spotted, grease-coated range. He cleared a patch of dust and mouse droppings from the table with his jacket sleeve, and dropped his makings sack onto it. He fished his flask out of his jacket, took a deep swallow, returned the flask to the pocket, and then reached into the makings sack for his rolling papers.

"What now?" Hettie asked, still lying on the bed, her voice forlorn.

As he sprinkled tobacco on a wheat paper, Stillman looked

through the two unshuttered windows on either side of the door. The light was changing hues and the shadows were deepening across the burned slash fronting the cabin.

"Now, we wait."

"For what?"

"For your friends. They'll likely return to the cabin when it's too dark to see anything out there."

"They're no friends of mine."

Hettie sat up and twisted around on the bed, dropping her feet to the floor. She sat there naked for a moment, and then she wrapped a blanket around her shoulders and moved slowly over to the table, and sat down on the edge of it, to Stillman's right. She stretched her arms out on the table and rested her head on them. "A girl really oughta pick her friends more wisely." She groaned, moved her head. "I ain't feelin' so good, Mister Sheriff, sir."

"You're right—you should have picked your friends more wisely."

"There an echo in here?"

Stillman lit the quirley and smoked it as he shuttled his gaze from one front window to the other. Hettie kept her head down, sound asleep. The sun dropped beyond the western ridges and the light began to dwindle more dramatically in the canyon. Stillman took another pull from his flask, slid his Colt from its holster, made sure all chambers showed brass, and returned it to the holster. He checked his belly gun, as well, and then he rose stiffly from the table, ignoring the heaviness in his right arm and leg.

For the past few minutes, he'd heard voices. Now as he peered out the windows on the other side of the table, he saw four silhouetted figures moving toward him from the timber at the bottom of the grade. They were a hundred yards away, walking abreast, all holding rifles, their heavy coats billowing, breath

227

rising in the darkening air around them as the temperature dropped.

Stillman picked up the Henry and moved to the front of the cabin. He opened the door and stood staring out over the slash that resembled black jackstraws strewn about a table bathed in the soft tans and dark yellows of the dwindling daylight. Beyond the men moving toward him, the timber was a dark, smoky green.

"Hey, Natchez," one of the men shouted as they continued moving toward the cabin, "we seen neither hide nor hair of Stillman. Maybe he ain't comin', after all."

One of the others spat to the side and yelled, "With that looker of a wife he's got, maybe it's a little harder for him to leave home these days!" He laughed at his own joke.

Stillman remained standing in the open doorway, concealed by the shadows of the porch roof.

"Hey, what's for supper?" asked the first man who'd spoken. "I'm hog-hungry!"

When Stillman did not respond but only watched the four men approach the cabin, one of the others said, "Hope you got the girl cookin' instead of just satisfyin' your goatish desires, Natchez. I mean, not that I blame you none for partakin' so to speak, but, shit, us boys done spent all day up on them ridges waitin' on a man who never showed, and we're hungry!"

They were within forty yards now, stepping over the slash, grunting, spitting, breathing hard with the walk up the slope. The last rays were slanting over their right shoulders, bathing that side of their faces. All they could see of Stillman was a tall man's silhouette. Still, though they could not see him, they must have started to sense that things weren't right.

At least the one on the far left of the small pack did, for he stepped over another fallen aspen, took two more slow steps, and then stopped. Then the man next to him stopped. The other two on the right kept coming. They were within twenty feet of the cabin's narrow stoop when one stopped and glanced at the two others behind him, chuckled, and said, "Hey, what you two stoppin' for?"

Then the fourth man, farthest right of the pack, stopped, as well.

He was about ten feet from the bottom porch step, staring tensely up at Stillman still standing in the open doorway. The outlaw was holding his carbine on his right shoulder. Stillman could tell by his build that he'd been the man in his house the other night. He was big, and the sheriff recognized the shape of his hat.

The man stared toward the open front door. His chest neither rose nor fell, as though he'd stopped breathing.

The man to his right, who'd stopped to ask the other two why they themselves had stopped, must have realized the situation, because he turned his head slowly, dreadfully, back toward the cabin. He said softly, "Well, I'll be ding-dong-damned."

"Nope. You'll be in irons, or you'll be dead."

Stillman stepped out onto the porch where a weak ray of light found the badge pinned to his leather vest, inside his open denim jacket. His heart beat slowly, heavily, as he shuttled his gaze from right to left and back again, across the quartet of laws. The man closest to Stillman moved first, which his eyes had foretold he would, and Stillman pressed his Henry's butt against his shoulder and dispatched the big man in short order.

The next nearest man, to his left, was raising and cocking his Winchester, cursing shrilly, when Stillman's second bullet took him through his left shoulder and spun him around and caused him to fire his rifle back toward the timber.

The other two men each leaped slash at the same time, the one to the right ducking down behind a stump while the other tripped over a fallen tree and fell forward just in time for Stillman's next bullet to career through the air where his head had been a quarter-second before. The wounded man howled and thrashed on the ground about twenty feet from Stillman, and raised his Winchester, awkwardly working the cocking mechanism.

At the same time, one of the other two opened up on Stillman, bullets slamming the porch posts and rail and barking into the front of the cabin. The lawman ran across the stoop and to the right as slivers flew over and around him, and ducked behind a rain barrel.

A slug hammered the rain barrel with a loud, reverberating *thunk!*

Stillman snaked his Henry around the barrel's right side and fired three quick rounds, gritting his teeth and squinting against blowing wood and screeching lead and powder smoke. His first bullet clipped an ear of one of the two rear shooters, evoking a screech. His third barked off the barrel of the wounded shooter nearest him, and the fact that the man's gritted teeth suddenly disappeared and his head slammed wickedly back on his shoulders told Stillman the ricochet had bored into his mouth and out the back of his head, instantly killing him.

A renewed onslaught of lead being thrown by the two shooters farthest away from him drove Stillman back behind the barrel, which thundered with the impact of the bullets hammering its far side. He pressed his back to the barrel, gritting his teeth, the barrel lurching against him, lead singing over and around him and hammering the cabin.

He waited until he could tell that only one man was shooting, and then he took the Henry in his left hand, snugged the butt up against the shoulder, and aimed around the barrel's left side. The shooter to the left was reloading, the top of his hatless head showing above a fallen, charred tree. Stillman squeezed the Henry's trigger and sent a bullet slamming into the crown of the man's skull, causing his sandy hair to buffet as blood sprayed out behind him.

A bullet fired by the other shooter carved a shallow, burning notch across Stillman's forehead. The sheriff raked out a low curse, drew his head back behind the barrel, twisted around, and aimed around the barrel's right side. The last surviving shooter's Winchester was aimed at Stillman, but a ping rose as the hammer dropped benignly onto the firing pin.

Empty.

The man cursed, rose, filled his hands with two .45's, fired each gun once, and then turned and ran toward a boulder to Stillman's right. Stillman aimed hastily and fired, as he watched the shooter's left knee buckle. The shooter screamed and dropped. Through the slash, Stillman tracked the man crawling, clutching the back of his left thigh, toward the boulder. The sheriff fired once, twice, three times, all slugs either hammering slash and causing gobbets of charred wood to spew, or puffing dust and green moss from the boulder.

Stillman held fire, staring down the smoking barrel of his rifle. He could see no movement behind the boulder. He aimed at the boulder's left edge. And then he heard a branch snap.

A barrel of a rifle slid slowly out from the side of the boulder. The top of a brown-haired, hatless head appeared. A bloody right ear. One eye, then two eyes, both bright with anxiety, and a broad nose. The man was gritting his teeth.

Stillman held his breath, slowly squeezing the Henry's trigger.

The man's left eye disappeared, red vapor spewing behind him. He gave a grunt and fell straight back with a crunching thud.

Stillman heaved a ragged sigh. He heaved himself to his feet. His right knee was stiff. It felt like cork. He took his rifle in his left hand to give the right one a rest, letting it hang heavily at his side. He stared out over the yard fronting the cabin. Darkening shadows concealed the dead men. A coyote was howling somewhere to the east.

"There . . . that oughta do it," Stillman said, spitting the peppery taste of cordite from his mouth.

He turned to the cabin's open doorway. Hettie was sitting as he'd left her, head resting on her arms on the table. Stillman frowned, walked to her, and placed a hand on her shoulder. She did not lift her head. At first, he thought she'd taken a bullet, but there wasn't a mark anywhere on her. He lay his rifle on the table and lifted her head from her arms. She flopped back in her chair, lifeless eyes regarding Stillman glassily. Her bruised face was drawn and pale, the blood dried on her lips.

Her chin dropped toward her right shoulder. She sat there, still, her hair hanging down to partly conceal her face. She'd been right. Natchez had hurt her bad.

Stillman set his spare pistol on the table beside his rifle and started to sink back into the nearest chair, when a floorboard squawked behind him. He started to drag his heavy, shaking right hand across his belly, toward his holstered Colt, but before he could even unsnap the keeper thong from over the hammer, he saw a tall, dark-clad figure step into the cabin.

"Hold it, Stillman."

Battles was aiming a pepperbox revolver in his right hand, his hook hanging straight down at his left side. He wore a long, black wool coat, and black gloves. He stood silhouetted against the doorway, but his eyes seemed to glow with a soft yellow light beneath the flat brim of his hat.

The pepperbox flashed, the report hammering Stillman's ears. The slug tore into Stillman's left arm, punching him up and back onto the table, which quivered beneath his weight. His arm throbbed; a low humming rose in his ears.

"You son of a bitch!" he grated out, awkwardly clutching his left arm with his right hand.

He rolled off the end of the table, fell to the hard-packed earthen floor hard with a dull thud. He'd landed on his right side, and now that side was numbing up fast. Foolish move, but he'd wanted to avoid another round from Battles's pepperbox while making another try for his pistol.

As he rolled onto his back, he realized the move had been pointless. His right arm lay flaccid beside him, heavy as a pine log. Battles came around the table, pulled both pistols off of Stillman, and flung them across the cabin. He reached behind Stillman for one of the two pairs of handcuffs hooked over the sheriff's cartridge belt.

Stillman cursed and kicked at the regulator, but his sap was dry. He felt foolish and helpless as Battles quickly closed one end of a handcuff around Stillman's right wrist. Battles used the other end of the cuff to pull Stillman around slightly, and then the regulator closed the other cuff around a short leg of the cast-iron monkey stove.

"You son of a *bitch*!" Stillman bellowed, his voice raspy and taut with pain. "What in the hell is the point of that, you bastard?"

"Congratulations, Sheriff," Battles said, lifting one of his polished black boots onto a chair seat and grinning down at Stillman in the near-dark cabin. "You didn't need my help, after all. Have to admit I'm not really all that surprised. Even gimped up like both of us are, we can still each take on a relatively small army to modest success. Too bad about the girl. She had spunk."

"Let me go!"

"That's not going to happen. I'm going to leave you cuffed there to that stove, wounded and bleeding and as helpless as a fish on a line . . . and with the knowledge that I'm riding back to Clantick with the full intention of killing your wife and son."

Stillman stopped thrashing. His heart turned a painful

somersault in his chest. He stared up in horror at the old regulator still grinning down at him. Blood flecked Battles's lower lip.

"So, you did come for revenge."

"Of course, I did," Battles laughed and then coughed.

"For the arm."

"For the arm," Battle said, "for the twelve years in prison, and, well . . . because it's the kind of man I am."

"Why my family? Christ, hack off my arm, if it'll make you feel better. Shoot me. Hang me! But leave my family out of it. They had nothing to do with shooting your arm off and throwing you in Deer Lodge, which is right where you belonged, Battles. Where you still belong!"

Stillman jerked hard against the cuff locked around the stove leg. The stove jerked but the leg and the wood plank supporting it were ground deep into the earthen floor. Neither the stove nor Stillman's wrist was going anywhere. All Stillman did by jerking on it was cause the fire in his right arm to blaze brighter behind the grinding numbness.

"Here, let me help you," Battles said, pulling a red handkerchief from a back pocket. He holstered the pepperbox under his coat and crouched over Stillman to wrap the handkerchief tightly around the sheriff's bullet-torn right arm. "Don't want you to die too fast," he said, grunting as he drew the knot tight. "Want you to lie here a good, long time, pondering all the ways your family might be dying."

Stillman's arms were useless. All he had were his legs, and, despite the agony the violent move aggravated in both his arms, he kicked out with both feet, hoping to trip Battles, possibly drive the man to the floor where he might then kick him to death.

But it wasn't happening. As soon as Battles had bandaged Stillman's arm, he jerked back as though from a trapped mountain lion, laughing.

Battles adjusted his hat on his head. "Have a good night, Stillman. You can bet around . . . oh . . . say . . . noon tomorrow, the deeds will have been done."

He laughed again and walked out of the shack, leaving the door standing wide behind him.

"No!" Stillman bellowed. "Come back here, Battles, you chicken-livered son of a bitch!"

The only response from outside the shack was Battles's dwindling laughter punctuated by ragged coughs.

Stillman screamed the man's name, shouted incoherently, cursed.

Out in the dark, quiet night, hooves drummed into the distance before they faded and there was only the sporadic yammering of the coyote and the breeze.

CHAPTER 28

"Am I dyin', Doc?" Leon McMannigle asked around eleven o'clock the next morning.

Evans had been listening to the sluggish beating of the wounded man's heart through his stethoscope. McMannigle was in the bed in the room that Evans used for overnight patients, though the deputy would likely be here for much longer than one night. He'd already been here for two.

Evans looped the stethoscope's earpieces around his neck, dropped the chest piece into a breast pocket of his shirt. "Don't know yet," he said, staring down at the man who'd been drifting in and out of consciousness since the ether had worn off. "I dug three chunks of lead out of you night before last. Only three because the other four went all the way through. None of your organs was damaged beyond repair, but a couple were nicked. You have several fractured ribs, a nicked sternum from a ricochet, a fractured femur, and a fractured left humerus."

"Humerus," the deputy said, his lips spreading a grin while his eyes remained closed, his head buried deep in a goose-down pillow.

"Think that's funny, do you?" Evans placed a finger on the man's left arm, which was in a plaster of paris cast and was suspended in a sling across the deputy's chest. "Well, that's the humerus. Upper arm. It was shattered."

"I feel like pretty much all of me is shattered."

"And you've lost a lot of blood. Which is why you have to eat and drink to keep your strength up." Evans glanced at the breakfast that Fay Stillman had fed Leon earlier and which was sitting on the low table on the other side of the bed. "You left a good bit of eggs and sausage."

"Wasn't hungry."

"Well, you'd best be hungry for lunch, because if you don't eat it willingly, I'll be force-feeding it to you on a long, wooden spoon. That's what I use on my most troublesome patients." Evans took a sponge from a porcelain bowl and used it to swab fever sweat from Leon's brows and forehead.

"What's that stench?" Leon asked.

"Arnica. You'll be smelling it for quite some time, I'm afraid. Cleans the wounds, cuts down on the risk of infection."

"Stinks worse than Apache balm, Doc." Leon chuckled, winced at the battering that even a chuckle gave his broken ribs. Years ago, he'd fought the Chiricahua Apaches as a buffalo soldier in the Tenth Cavalry down in Arizona. "Oh, Lordy—I'm hangin' by a whisker here, ain't I?"

"You're gonna make it, Leon," Evans said, his mock-angry tone leaching from his voice. "I've never seen anyone survive this many bullet wounds, but you're going to make it." His former humor returned. "You have a very good sawbones looking after you, if I may say so myself, and I have a reputation to uphold. Besides, I doubt you've saved enough money for a proper funeral, having spent it all on the girls over at Mrs. Lee's. You have no choice but to remain on this side of the sod."

Again, McMannigle smiled. "I get it for free over there, Doc."

"Oh, that's right. I forgot, you cheap bastard. How does one get a job like that?"

"You don't need a job like that. You're gonna be married soon."

Evans didn't respond to that. Leon's eyelids fluttered open, and he gazed up curiously at Evans and then turned his head slightly to look around the room. "Where is she, anyways—the widow?"

Evans dropped the sponge back into the basin of cool water. He hesitated, rolled his right shirtsleeve down, and buttoned it. "She's in the country, delivering another child or forcing castor oil down some poor shaver's throat." In addition to midwifing, Katherine often tended cases of minor illness. "You hurting pretty bad? Do you need more laudanum?"

"How 'bout some whiskey?"

"Sure." Evans opened a dresser drawer, pulled out a bottle without a label on it. "Pretty much the same thing and a hell of a lot cheaper." He half-filled a water glass and brought it over to Leon. "Not exactly from the top shelf but just as effective."

He helped the deputy drink a few swallows of the barbed wire, then set the glass on the table by the bed. "It'll be right here. Whenever you want a drink, help yourself if you can manage, or give a yell. Either Fay or I will check on you again in a few minutes."

"Fay?" Leon frowned. His eyes were closed again. "What's she doin' here?"

"Never mind," Evans said. He doubted that the deputy remembered much of what had happened or the circumstances surrounding it. There was no point in stirring him up with the information that Stillman had headed out after the outlaws alone. "You just sleep, my good fellow."

The whiskey was doing its job, taking the patient down into the healing soup of sleep. McMannigle only grumbled. Evans rolled down his other shirtsleeve, and left the room. He moved through the house and found Fay down on her hands and knees in the kitchen, scrubbing a patch of blood that had spilled out of Leon when he'd been carried into the house.

"Good Lord, woman—you don't have to do that!" Evans said.

"I want to, Doc. Little Ben's upstairs taking a nap, and I need to stay busy." Fay looked up at the doctor, her cheeks flushed from exertion as well as worry, the doctor knew. Worry over Ben—his situation and his compromised physical condition.

Evans nodded and continued to the range. He filled a stone mug from a pot of coffee on the warming rack, and sagged into a chair at the table. The bottle of brandy that Evelyn had given him was nearly empty. He poured the last of the brandy into his coffee, added a spoonful of brown sugar from a small bowl on the table, and stirred the concoction with a spoon.

He sighed. He was tired but he didn't know if the fatigue was from having to tend to Leon almost constantly since he'd been brought in from the jailhouse, or from personal matters, as well. Still scrubbing at the stain on the wooden floor, Fay looked up at him, a curl of her chocolate hair sliding back and forth across her forehead.

Evans met her gaze. Neither said anything until Fay dropped the brush into the bucket, wiped her hands on a towel, and sat in a chair across from Evans, leaning forward on her crossed arms. She looked at him levelly, concern showing in her lustrous brown eyes. Her beauty was always a little startling. Today, it was a little annoying. He could not help reacting to such beauty as Fay Stillman's, feel a shard of jealousy toward the man lucky enough to be her husband. But Evans was tired of skirmishing with his own baser desires and weaknesses. He'd grown weary of his own company.

He was glad she was wearing a high-necked dress, at least.

"Doc," Fay began, haltingly, looking down at the table and clearing her throat.

"No need to continue," Evans said, taking a sip of his coffee. "I know what you're going to say." Fay had made no mention of Evelyn's having been here late the other night, when Jody Harmon had fetched Fay and Little Ben over from the Stillman house, but the subject had been hanging heavy in the air for the past two days.

Fay looked at Evans searchingly for a time, before she said softly, "Do you love her?"

"Hell, I don't know. I'm not sure I even know what the word means." Evans raised his voice in frustration, and glanced at the books stacked against two walls around him. A couple of stacks were teetering precariously, appearing as though they would fall with the slightest nudge. "I read the word all the time in my books here . . . in all these damn books I always have my nose buried in. You'd think I'd know what it meant by now, wouldn't you? *Love.* I'm a learned man, for chrissakes!"

He waved an arm at the stacks. "Hell, I've read *Romeo and Juliette, Midsummer Night's Dream.* 'Love looks not with the eyes, but with the mind, And therefore is winged Cupid painted blind.' There's Ivanhoe over there—that's essentially a love story. Jane Eyre by that Brontë woman. There's a love story, for you. A sad one. Hell, most of 'em are sad. End badly."

He laughed without mirth. "Yeah, you'd think from all my 'book-learnin',' as they say, I'd have gotten at least an inkling about love. Fleshed it out, deciphered it, filed it away, be able to recognize it when I felt it, or was shown it. You'd think I'd have some *appreciation* for it. But, no—I don't know the first thing about it. I don't know if I'm even capable of feeling it. I seriously doubt I ever have felt it, and I doubt that I feel it now for anyone, including Evelyn."

He took another couple of deep sips of his coffee and brandy, and smacked his lips. He regarded Fay sitting back in her chair, regarding him almost sympathetically, her hands held flat against the table before her.

Fay said, "If thou remember'st not the slightest folly That ever love did make thee run into, Thou hast not loved."

Evans gave a weak smile. "*As You Like It.*"

"I was a schoolteacher once—remember?"

Evans blew on his coffee but did not sip. "I laid with the poor girl, because she seemed willing. I think she was only willing because she, the poor wretch, has for some unthinkable reason fallen in love with me! So I spent the night with her . . . I made love with her. But, no, I seriously doubt that I love her. I was in love with her body two nights ago, but about all I can really say I feel for her now is lust and . . . and . . . sadness, because we were friends before that night, and, now—all that is gone. Only my lust is left. And my sadness."

"What about Katherine?" Fay asked. "She hasn't been by here since Leon . . ." She let her voice trail off.

"That's because she was here the night Evelyn was here. I heard her in the hall when . . . during . . . and then I looked out the window and saw her buggy rolling away toward town." Evans was surprised to find himself staring through a wavering veil of tears in his eyes. Those tears were dribbling down his cheeks, one after another spilling down like raindrops over a window. He sucked a deep breath, stifled a sob, wiped the tears from his cheeks with his shirt cuffs, and stared down at the table, trying hard not to break down in girlish bawling.

He hadn't realized quite how wretched he was feeling. Now it frightened him almost as much as what he'd allowed himself to do with Evelyn Vincent the other night, here in this house he'd intended on sharing with Katherine after they were married. He hadn't realized until now how sad he felt for the loss.

Suddenly, Fay was beside him, her arm around his shoulders, squeezing him.

He found profound comfort in that squeeze, and he was almost surprised that, despite the allure of her warm flesh against his, he wasn't feeling the slightest bit of lust.

"You need to have a visit with Katherine," Fay said softly.

"You two have come too far together to turn back now. She loves you, Doc, and whether you believe it or even understand it, or not, you love her. Your love has caused you to run into much folly. But you *have* loved. You make it too complicated. Take it from me, a woman who is very thoroughly in love, it's really very simple."

Evans sobbed at that. He bit down on his fist so he wouldn't sob again, embarrass himself again. When he got himself somewhat under control, he slid his chair back and awkwardly gained his feet.

"I think I'd best go up and lay down for a while."

"Go ahead. I'll keep an eye on Leon."

"Thank you," Evans said, drawing a deep, phlegmy breath.

Fay gave him a tender smile, kissed his bearded cheek. That almost caused him to sob again, so he turned quickly away, strode out of the kitchen, and climbed the stairs.

Fay stood there in the kitchen, hearing the doctor's plaintive steps in the second story, and the latching of his bedroom door. She listened to hear if Little Ben awakened. When she did not hear her son's cries, Fay strolled aimlessly into the sitting room and stared out the large window that looked out over the front porch toward the rooftops of town.

Her breath grew shallow when a tall, dark-clad rider cantered up the trail from Clantick, heading for the house. He appeared to have only one hand. Autumn sunlight flashed off of what appeared to be a hook where the other hand should have been.

The previous night, around ten-thirty, Stillman lay breathing like a landed fish on the earthen floor of the Shambeau cabin.

He was exhausted, his wrist bloody from desperately trying to pull his hand free of the cuff securing him to the stove leg. His left arm felt like a lead bar stretched above his head. His right arm was on fire from the bullet wound. He lay on his side, trying once again to summon enough strength to try jerking the handcuff over his hand.

There was enough blood now from torn skin to make it slide easier, he hoped.

He was about to try again when he heard a horse whinny in the distance. Another horse, probably one of the outlaws' horses nearer the cabin, whinnied in response. Hooves thudded.

Stillman frowned, glancing toward the open door through which, beyond the porch roof, he could see stars twinkling wanly beyond the pale, blue light of a rising moon. The hoof clomps continued. Was Battles returning?

Stillman waited. The horse drew up to the cabin. There was a squawk of leather as the rider dismounted. A boot thumped on the porch.

"Sheriff Stillman?"

Stillman recognized the voice of Gandy Miller.

Stillman had never thought he'd be happy to see the peculiar, wheedling youth. "Christ, kid, get over here and free me from these cuffs!"

"What're you doin' down there, Sheriff?"

"Get over here!"

"I'm comin'!" Miller said, stumbling over a chair in the darkness.

He crouched over Stillman and said, "Jesus jump—what in the hell . . . ?"

"Give me your pistol."

Miller handed Stillman his Colt. Stillman groaned against the pain in his right arm as he took the revolver in his right hand, cocking back the hammer. He missed the chain between the cuffs with his first shot so he had to fire again. The second bullet tore through the chain, and Stillman pulled his left hand up off the floor, the chain dangling from the cuff still encircling his wrist.

"Rode out here to see the showdown firsthand, eh?" Stillman said as he heaved himself to his feet, groaning and grunting in agony. He leaned against the table to steady himself and to try to regain his depleted strength. He had a good idea that it was Miller who'd fired that shot into his and Fay's bedroom window. It had likely also been Miller who'd shadowed him around Clantick the other night—all in an effort to keep Stillman's edge up and to keep the tension between the sheriff and Battles drawn as taut as possible.

For the kid's own amusement.

Of course, Stillman couldn't prove it. Even if he could, at the moment he needed the kid's help.

"I reckon you could say that," Miller said, twirling his pistol on his finger. "Didn't play out the way I figured, but I was mightily impressed by the way you single-handedly dispatched them outlaws. I was watching from that big butte yonder. Ouch! Glad I didn't wager no money on you an' Battles, though. I bet you'd like to know about somethin' I heard from the telegrapher. He was lookin' for you in town the other night, but you'd just ridden out after them outlaws."

"Kid, go out and saddle me two of the best horses you can find in the gang's remuda. *Hurry!*"

"Don't you wanna heard what I heard the telegrapher yellin' about?"

"Saddle the horses!" Stillman staggered around the cabin, looking for his pistols. His Henry was still on the table, where he'd left it. "I gotta haul my ass to town before Battles kills my wife and baby, and I'm too damn weak to throw the leather on 'em myself!"

Miller hurried to the door but stopped to say, "The telegrapher said he just got a telegram from the territorial governor of South Dakota. Them two lawmen you rode with when you brought down Battles a dozen years ago? They were both found dead—just days after Battles was released from Deer Lodge."

Then Miller ran out to where the outlaws had rope-corraled their horses.

Stillman set his pistols on the table and sagged into a chair to gather his strength for the all-night ride back to Clantick. He raked a hand across his face and muttered under his ragged breath, "Fay, just hold on, honey. You and Little Ben hold on. I'm comin'."

Chapter 29

Fay walked to the front door.

Through the window in the door's upper half, she saw Battles tying his horse to the rod-iron hitchrack off the corner of the doctor's house. It was sunny and a breeze was shuttling cloud shadows across Evans's overgrown yard, and it was snatching at the tails of the tall man's black wool overcoat.

Battles unbuttoned the coat partway down, and reached in as though to adjust something behind it. He stood staring at the house. The man's ghoulish countenance made Fay's skin crawl. Everything about him—from the cold, gray-blue eyes set deep in leathery sockets to the carefully trimmed mustache mantling his lip, to the hook he wore in place of an arm, bespoke a killer.

He stood tall and rigid by his horse, his features grim. But when he lowered his gaze from the second story in which Little Ben lay sleeping, and saw Fay in the window, his lips quickly fashioned a chilling grin. His eyes were like doll's eyes beneath the broad brim of his black hat.

Fay opened the door and stepped out onto the porch, the breeze catching loose strands of her hair, the bulk of which she wore clipped behind her head. It whipped them around her cheeks and forehead. She drew the door closed behind her.

She shuddered at the man's frigid stare despite his smiling mouth, and she shuddered again when he said her name: "Ah, Mrs. Stillman."

"How can I help you, Mister Battles?" Fay said from the porch.

Battles lost the smile and removed his hat. Holding it in both hands in front of his chest, he said, "I learned from Mr. Auld you were here. I'm afraid I have some bad news, Fay."

Fay's heart hiccupped. Her knees grew weak. She did not say anything.

"Perhaps we should go inside," Battles said.

Fay swallowed an obstruction in her throat and said, "You can tell me here." She did not want him in the doctor's house. She imagined that she could smell death on him, see the faces of the men he'd killed reflected in his pale, glassy eyes.

"I'm sorry to be the one to have to tell you this," Battles said, casting his gaze toward the ground between him and the porch, "but your husband is dead, Fay."

Her knees buckled, and she dropped straight down to the porch floor. She could feel all the blood in her body careening toward her feet. Suddenly, she couldn't breathe. Invisible hands were wrapped around her neck, strangling her. She fell forward onto her hands and knees, gasping.

Through a dark haze, she could see Battles moving toward her, his coat blowing in the wind. Cloud shadows swept over him. Beneath the screeching in Fay's ears, she heard the crunch of his boots in the weeds and gravel. And then she could smell the slop bucket smell of the man. Real or imagined, it was the smell of death. It grew heavier as he approached her.

"A tragedy." Battles climbed the porch steps. "Rest assured, he died valiantly, Mrs. Stillman. Dispatched five men himself, up in the Two-Bears. You would have been proud."

Fay sobbed uncontrollably, hanging her head. Her tears made dark spots on the worn, gray floorboards.

"How?" she asked through her sobs. "How do you know?"

"I saw it all. I would have lent a hand, but I didn't feel able."

Battles showed her his hook. "Only one hand and all."

Fay took her head in her hands, and bawled, sorrow ripping through her like shockwaves. Vaguely, as though through a mirage, she saw in the upper periphery of her vision Battles slide his hand into his coat. At the same time, above the shrill racking of her own sobs, she heard something on the wind.

Hooves thudded. She could feel them through the porch floor.

Battles's gloved hand slid out of his coat. A stubby, multi-bored pistol was clamped in it. Battles turned to look away toward Clantick, as though he too had heard something from that direction. When he turned his face back toward Fay, his eyes snapped wide. He tightened his jaws as he snapped up the pepperbox.

The derringer in Fay's hand bucked and popped.

Battles jerked back, his lower jaw falling. His gun hand dropped straight down to his side.

He looked down at the small, round hole showing in the vest behind his coat. Dark-red blood welled up in it. Battles looked at Fay and blinked slowly, as though she'd just told him something he could not for the life of him work his mind around.

"You might be a good killer, Battles," Fay said, rising from her knees, holding the pearl-gripped derringer, which she'd plucked from her dress pocket when she'd heard the familiar voice calling to her, tightly in her right fist. "But you're a terrible liar."

Battles started to raise his revolver again. It shook in his shaking hand.

Again, Fay's derringer jerked and popped, flames lapping from the barrel.

★ ★ ★ ★ ★

Stillman heeled his mount up the butte toward Evans's place. The horse was sweat-lathered from the long ride, and it didn't have much left in it. The sheriff had dropped the reins of his second horse just before reaching Clantick. Tired as it was, the horse beneath him stretched its stride into one last, loose-legged gallop.

Gandy Miller galloped his own blown mount behind Stillman.

The sheriff whipped his rein ends against the tired beast's hindquarters, urging more speed as they gained the top of the bluff and followed the curve of the trail toward the sprawling, gray house in dire need of paint. Soot-colored smoke rose from one of the house's three chimneys and was ripped away on the breeze. A horse stood at the hitchrack off the house's right front corner.

Battles's grulla.

Stillman reined his own horse to a halt in front of the stoop.

He'd raised his rifle, but now he slowly lowered it. He stared down at the old regulator sitting on the second porch step up from the ground.

Battles's hat and pepperbox revolver lay on the ground near his boots. He sat back against a square porch post, head tipped back at an angle, as though he were bathing his face in the warm autumn sunshine. His eyes were open, staring in what appeared amazement at the sky. His thin, gray-brown hair swirled around the nearly bald crown of his skull.

Blood oozed from two small holes in his chest, side by side and about four inches apart.

"Jesus jump," said Gandy Miller in shock.

The front door opened. Fay stepped out. She was holding Little Ben in her arms, jostling him up and down. The boy smiled and pointed a little, wet finger at his father.

Fay stared at Stillman. Stillman stared back at her.

Fay's hair blew around her face in the wind.

"Look, Little Ben," she said, pressing her lips to the boy's forehead. "Daddy's home."

ABOUT THE AUTHOR

Western novelist **Peter Brandvold** has penned over 70 fast-action westerns under his own name and his pen name, **Frank Leslie.** He is the author of the ever-popular .45-Caliber books featuring Cuno Massey as well as the Lou Prophet and Yakima Henry novels. The Ben Stillman books are a long-running series with previous volumes available as ebooks. Recently, Brandvold published two horror westerns—*Canyon of a Thousand Eyes* and *Dust of the Damned.* Head honcho at "Mean Pete Publishing," publisher of lightning-fast western ebooks, he writes and travels in the Four Corners area of the American Southwest with his dog in a 35-foot motorhome. Visit his website at www.peter brandvold.com. Follow his blog at: www.peterbrandvold.blog spot.com.